DOWNFALL AND FREEDOM

DOWNFALL AND FREEDOM

A Novel about the Arms Trade, South Africa, and the KwaZulu

BY

CHARLES E. WEBB

iUniverse, Inc.
Bloomington

DOWNFALL AND FREEDOM
A Novel about the Arms Trade, South Africa, and the KwaZulu

Copyright © 2009, 2011 by Charles E. Webb.

All rights reserved. No part of this book may be used or reproduced by any means, graphic, electronic, or mechanical, including photocopying, recording, taping or by any information storage retrieval system without the written permission of the publisher except in the case of brief quotations embodied in critical articles and reviews.

This is a work of fiction. All of the characters, names, incidents, organizations, and dialogue in this novel are either the products of the author's imagination or are used fictitiously.

iUniverse books may be ordered through booksellers or by contacting:

iUniverse
1663 Liberty Drive
Bloomington, IN 47403
www.iuniverse.com
1-800-Authors (1-800-288-4677)

Because of the dynamic nature of the Internet, any web addresses or links contained in this book may have changed since publication and may no longer be valid. The views expressed in this work are solely those of the author and do not necessarily reflect the views of the publisher, and the publisher hereby disclaims any responsibility for them.

Any people depicted in stock imagery provided by Thinkstock are models, and such images are being used for illustrative purposes only.
Certain stock imagery © Thinkstock.

ISBN: 978-1-4620-6817-3 (sc)
ISBN: 978-1-4620-6816-6 (hc)
ISBN: 978-1-4620-6815-9 (ebk)

Library of Congress Control Number: 2011960853

Printed in the United States of America

iUniverse rev. date: 12/07/2011

For my friend, Michael, for the inspiration; for my wife and daughters, for their love, critiques, and constant support; for my friends for their constant support . . . and they all know who they are; for my mother, who believed in this and died the year I started writing *Downfall*; and especially to the people of South Africa and KwaZulu Natal, black, white, colored, and of all national heritages, whose hopes, dreams, and prayers have been partially answered. The future is theirs. May it come in peace.

Charles E. Webb
Allen, Texas
28 November 2009

CHAPTER 1
13 August 1975

He was born to Jane Broosler Zooma in a small hospital in a village in central Natal, South Africa, on April 30, 1965. His father was Matthew Wesley Zooma. Although his father actually had a different tribal name, he used the one given him by the foreign missionaries that came to his village in 1923. When his son was born, he named him after the founder of the Methodist religion that he and his wife practiced as a result of the work and sacrifice of all those missionaries. John Wesley Zooma was a full member of the Zulu tribe. His village was taken over in the 1960s by a cult segment named the Zulu Warrior Society when violence in the townships began. He saw many strange things happen in his village as he grew up, but one incident on August 13, 1975, changed his life.

John Wesley Zooma was on his way home from grade school with three of his friends on this mild, mid-winter day in Natal. The rains had come in July and early August, but now the ground was dry and dusty, and the grass was turning a yellow brown. Each day they stopped by Bulewessi's, a small, local food shop in the township, and bought a cold soda or candy before they continued on. Walking up to the store on this fateful day, they noticed a police township truck, called a Kaspir, coming from the other direction in a hurry, beeping its horn to get people out of its way as it pulled up to the store. The township police truck was very imposing; painted a medium green, it sat on very large, treaded tires almost ten feet high, and it was made of high strength, armored, bulletproof steel—it was more like an armored personnel carrier than a truck, with a .50-caliber machine gun mounted in the front on the top. Ten soldiers—two white, the others black—jumped out from the cab and the back and rushed into the shop.

The four boys ran to the other side of the street, and a small crowd gathered to see what was going on. Zooma and his friends moved to the front of the crowd but were no closer to the shop.

From inside came the ear-piercing screams of women and much shouting. Six of the black soldiers appeared from the store carrying the owner, Mr. Bulewessi—a friend to all the many children in the village—to the middle of the intersection. They tied his feet together and his hands behind him and sat him down. Two more black soldiers followed the others out of the store and went to the huge army truck. The two white lieutenants next came out of the store, pistols drawn. The women inside poured out like a flood, shrieking and crying at the top of their lungs. The noise could be heard throughout the small village, and the crowd swelled around the intersection from all directions.

Two soldiers went to the Kaspir and came back with a tire and a gasoline can. The six soldiers that had brought out Mr. Bulewessi were facing the crowd with rifles ready and Mr. Bulewessi in the center of their circle.

It happened so fast. John Wesley Zooma had heard about these things, but it was spoken about only in whispers. The soldier with the tire placed it around the neck of Mr. Bulewessi, who was pleading for his life—but to no avail. The soldier with the can poured the gasoline on the tire and Mr. Bulewessi, soaking him thoroughly. The soldier dropped the can in the road and moved to the truck while the first soldier lit a match and threw it at the tire. Immediately, the flames shot upward, and Mr. Bulewessi was totally engulfed and screaming. The crowd gave a collective gasp of horror. Almost everyone was screaming or crying, including many men. The leader of the soldiers, a young lieutenant, pointed his pistol in the air and fired two shots as the crowd moved forward. But it was already too late for Mr. Bulewessi. The flames had finally gotten to his brain. His pain and life were ended.

The lieutenant waited for the crowd to stop screaming. Now there was just the sound of soft sobbing. He said to them, "This man was subversive and dealing in contraband. This is a lesson to all of you not to engage in actions against the government!" With that said, the group of soldiers retreated to their truck, climbed in, and drove off, their rifles still pointed at the crowd.

Several men ran and got blankets to smother the remaining flames and cover the charred body of Mr. Bulewessi. Zooma and his friends were crying; they were in front and had witnessed the entire scene. They wondered, what was this subversive activity? What did that mean? Why was there no trial for Mr. Bulewessi? Zooma felt tremendous rage burning immediately within him, and he wanted revenge for seeing a friend of his literally destroyed before his eyes. He and his three friends turned and ran up the dirt street to their houses, which were three blocks away.

John Wesley Zooma ran into the house and into his mother's arms. She had heard the screams, the gunshots, and the wailing of the crowd. She suspected what had happened, but she didn't know yet to whom. She had feared most for her son, for he was not yet home from school and his usual stop at Mr. Bulewessi's. When she heard him come in, she felt so relieved, knowing he was safe. She cried with him as he related his story about what had happened and held him close for a very long time, until he went to his small bedroom to rest until dinner.

John Wesley Zooma lay down on his bed and continued to cry for a while. The emotions of the afternoon event had totally drained him. There were so many questions: Why had they done this? What had Mr. Bulewessi really done? Why did they torture and kill him like that in front of the whole village? Zooma wanted to kill the white lieutenant. And the black soldiers too! How could they do that to one of their own? Finally, sleep came over him.

About two hours later, his mother woke him up with a hug and kiss on the cheek. John Wesley Zooma could hear his father in the other small bedroom. He got up from his small wooden bed, which was only a thin feather mattress, and walked into the one room that served as kitchen, dining area, and living room. His mother smiled at him, and he sat down at the table. His father appeared in a few minutes, walked up to his son, and knelt by him.

"John, today you saw a terrible thing. This is what we call a 'necklacing.'" He pulled his son to him and held him tightly in a hug.

"Daddy, why did that happen? Why did the black soldiers do that to one of us? What did Mr. Bulewessi do to be killed like that? I don't understand."

"Son, there are some things that just can't be explained. Mr. Bulewessi was a good man, and this was unjust. This was our government trying to keep us down and scared. But, someday, we will show them the power and strength of the mighty Zulu, as we have done before. We must wait for our time. Now we must be quiet, pray for the soul of Mr. Bulewessi, and pray for ourselves. I want you to be very careful. Today you saw the power of the government that tries to keep us in fear, but we must be patient. Do not speak of this to anyone. Do you understand me clearly?"

"Yes, Daddy. But I still want to know why."

"John, we may never know why. Accept what has happened and take care of yourself. I love you," his father said quietly.

Matthew Wesley Zooma released his son slowly from his loving grip on his shoulders. He knew the reasons for the killing, but he couldn't fully explain it to his son now. Maybe someday. *Be patient*, he thought.

That night after dinner, John Wesley Zooma went out to visit his three friends. They talked for an hour about all that had happened and how they felt. Each one was ready to fight and die for their homeland. Then and there, they made a pact with each other for life, as friends do when something like this happens. They would get revenge for this and all the many government oppressions and killings. They would gain control of their country. Natal had always been Zulu; someday it would be again.

CHAPTER 2

15 January 2001

Arriving in Sao Paulo, Brazil, late that afternoon was a rather short, bearded, spectacled man carrying only a small briefcase and an under-seat bag. He was dressed in a polo shirt and nice slacks and was indistinguishable from many of the other business class passengers on the flight from Mexico City. He had traveled there the previous day from New Orleans to Chicago to Los Angeles, meeting casually in each location with a business associate in the Admiral's Club of American Airlines. It was a lot of traveling, but the face-to-face encounters were necessary.

An associate met him at the airport in Sao Paulo. Without much talking, they walked the short distance to the parking lot and left for the journey to Santa Rita and another yearly meeting with his longtime partner in several ventures, none of which were legal.

Clarence van Dyke Jackson, an African American, was almost fifty-five now, very rich, and he was thinking that it may be time to quit this dual life he had been living for the last twenty years. Jackson was about 5' 8", medium dark completed, and had deep, brown, eyes that looked intense all the time. He was very fit and tried to continue the exercise routine every other day that he had become accomstomed to in the army. He was the owner of a legitimate, large electrical-contracting business in New Orleans. He'd been very successful over the years, especially since it was a minority business and had gained many local contracts because of that fact. His other business was in supplying arms as needed to the Special Forces, armies of "liberation," and foreign nationals in selected lands. His contacts from the US Army and National Guard knew how to obtain extra weapons from the "surplus" that always seemed to be available and ready for disposal at just the time Jackson needed it.

Jackson was born in Wiggins, a small town in south-central Mississippi whose economy was fueled by the local lumber industry. His father, Jimmy, a large black man, over six feet one inch tall, and weighed just over two-hundred pounds, drove a logging truck for the big, local lumber company that supplied logs to the plywood mill. His mother, Cynthia, was slight in stature, just five feet three inches tall, and her skin was a velvet light brown. She worked at the local hospital and was friends to many in the small town, white and black, because of her caring spirit and always warm smile.

As Jackson grew up in this small town during the forties and fifties, he saw the Klu Klux Klan, he knew well the art of keeping out of trouble with white folks, and he learned the art of the street and survival.

He had not started his life with hatred. It had only come to him once—very personally. In late November, 1953, he was just clearing the dishes for his mother after dinner when he heard a noise behind the back barn where his dad kept the '47 Ford. He looked around the kitchen for his mother, but he didn't see her; he thought she must have gone to the front bedroom. His dad was in the living room, reading the paper and listening to the radio. He decided to go outside and see if the noise was a raccoon looking for something to eat from the garbage.

Clarence went outside and closed the screen door behind him. He walked quietly through the backyard, past the large oak tree with the branches that reminded him of a large octopus, and toward the side of the garage. He walked even slower as he neared the garage, for his worst fears were upon him now.

As he rounded the garage, he was grabbed from behind by strong arms and held very tightly. A big hand was over his mouth, and the voice from it said, "Keep quiet, boy, we have no quarrel with you anyhow." It was useless to yell now, and Clarence couldn't break free of the arms holding him or the hand over his mouth to keep him from crying out.

Several others in white KKK robes and masks came out of the timber stand behind the barn. There were ten in all. They walked quickly to the backyard and yelled for Clarence's dad and mom to come out back and not make any trouble, because they had their son,. James van Dyke Jackson and his very beautiful wife, Cynthia, came to the kitchen door and looked out on the backyard scene where eleven,white, strong, armed men in KKK robes stood, one of them holding their son. The apparent leader of the group now came forward.

"Y'all come on out here now. We jus' want to talk some."

James replied, "Why y'all here? We ain't done nothin', and my son always shows his respect."

"We ain't got no quarrel with your son, Jimmy. We jus' needed to talk a while with you and the missus. You see, we been hearin' that you tryin' to get yourself moved up at the mill, and you better learn now that those foreman jobs are for us whites. Do you understand me?"

"Yes, I understand. I haven't asked for one. I heard talk, you know, but if someone goin' to give me another job managin' the rest of the drivers, I ain't heard it yet. I jus' tryin' to do my job, like I told. I lived here all my life and ain't bothered no one. Y'all know that."

"Well, some of that's right. But we got to show you we mean business. Grab her, boys!"

Three of the KKK took hold of Cynthia while four others each took hold of Jimmy's arms and legs. He struggled to get free, but they were too many, and they were too strong. From out of nowhere a fist came forward and knocked him in the stomach and the face. Meanwhile, Cynthia screamed as the men dragged her to the big oak tree. They put her up against it, face first, and held her arms around the sides. The trunk cut into her arms and face. The leader now came forward again and ripped her dress, baring her back.

"Jimmy, we do this so that each time you see your wife's back, you goin' to know we always behind your back as well."

The leader pulled a whip from under his robe and let go with ten lashes on Cynthia. The cuts were deep, and blood ran down and stained her dress. Jimmy yelled, but was hit again in the stomach, and the wind was knocked from him. Clarence screamed as he tried to break free, tears streaming from his face for the pain of his mother. He would give anything to be in her place and not have her hurt.

Almost as soon as it began, it was over. The men holding Cynthia let her fall to the ground, and they began running to the trees. At the same time, the men holding Jimmy and Clarence let them go and also began to run. The leader now walked backward with one final word: "We know you goin' to remember well this little talk we had, Jimmy. You keep up the good work, but you remember, you only good enough to drive that truck. Don't go talkin' about this little talk now, and we all goin' to get along jus' fine from now on. You hear?" He then disappeared into the darkness.

Clarence was first to his mother, and he held her tightly in his arms. Jimmy crawled and then stumbled to her and held them both. He stood up, keeping his arms around them, took them in the house, and set them both in the kitchen. Jimmy went into the bathroom, brought out a wet cloth and basin, and washed the lash cuts on his wife's back while Clarence watched in silence. After the cuts were cleaned, Jimmy told his son to go to his bedroom and wait for him while he took Cynthia and put her to bed.

Clarence went to his room, filled with a rage and a memory he would never forget. He sat on his bed and cried until he went to sleep.

He awoke with a start to see his dad standing over him. He sat down on the bed and held Clarence tightly.

"They is right, son. Don't you go tellin' anyone about this, now. This is for us to keep to us."

"Daddy, did you really know anything about a foreman's job at the plant?"

"No, but like I said, you know, some of the guys were talkin' that, maybe since the plant is expandin' and needs some more drivers, that one of us might get a job bossin' some drivers. Nothin' much, really, jus' keepin' the time cards, the haul numbers, and each driver's timber stand position each day, while drivin' his own loads in the mornin'."

"Do you know any of the men that were here? Did you recognize anyone? I didn't."

"Well, son, yes and no. I think I know one of them who held me, but I didn' recognize no one else, includin' the son of a bitch that hit your mama. It don' matter none. No one goin' to do anything for us except ourselves. So you jus' keep quiet, you hear?"

"Yes, Daddy."

Jimmy left his son and went outside. He went inside the barn and cried for a while. He was so ashamed that he didn't want his son or wife to hear him.

Clarence pulled off his jeans and went to the bathroom to wash up. When he came back, he looked out his window and saw his dad just standing in the backyard, looking at the big old oak tree. After a few minutes, he pulled the covers back and slipped into bed and immediately went to sleep.

The next day, Clarence awoke to his mother's voice calling him to get up and get ready for school, just like every day. He got dressed, went to the bathroom, and came around the corner into the kitchen. His mama was wearing a sweater and skirt and cooking his eggs and toast, just like always.

"Son, you look real good this mornin'. I want you to go to school, learn real hard, like I always said, and you get yourself out of here someday. I know you never goin' to forget what happened, but you do like your daddy said. Ain't nothin' goin' to change last night, but you can work hard, get them good grades, and your daddy will make sure you go to college so you can get yourself a real good job away from here and not have to deal with them folk. You hear me, son? Your mama loves you so much and wants so much for you."

"Yes, Mama. I understand."

His mother brought over his plate with the steaming eggs just liked he liked them and the toast already buttered. She gave him a big kiss on the cheek.

"You eat up now. You got to get to that school and you show them all what a Van Dyke Jackson is made of."

Clarence finished, picked up his books and the sack lunch, and was out the door. He had to walk about a quarter of a mile to get the bus down a dirt road that was dry now from the lack of rain. He walked along and noticed the dust sitting on the leaves and the honeysuckle like a brown blanket, waiting for the rain to deepen the color and turn the road into a muddy track.

When he got to the junction, he saw his best friend, Bobby Jeff Littleton, coming toward him. As Bobby Jeff got to the bus stop, he dropped his books and gave Clarence a big hug. They looked at each other, and Bobby Jeff started to cry. He knew. Clarence hugged him back. He picked up the books and gave them to Bobby Jeff as he wiped the tears on his sleeve.

"Thanks. Now stop it. I don't want no one to see you cryin'," Clarence whispered to his best friend.

The bus arrived in a couple of minutes and pulled away. After several more stops, they were at the small school where the blacks went to junior high in Wiggins. Clarence could tell they all knew what had happened, but no one said anything. He went inside and to his homeroom first. He put his books away in the cloak area, except for those he needed for the first three classes in the morning, and took his seat.

The teacher, Mr. Williamson, waited until the bell rang and looked up at all the children in his classroom. He got up from the small, battered desk, and told them to rise for the Pledge of Allegiance and a prayer.

Everyone looked at the flag, but somehow the words stuck in Clarence's throat that day: "I pledge allegiance to the flag of the United States of America, and to the republic for which it stands, one nation under God, indivisible, with liberty and justice for all."

"Children, will you bow your heads for our daily prayer? Lord, give us strength and courage to accept what we must, change what we can, the wisdom to know the difference, and faith in You. May we put our hearts and minds to work, to learn, and to take pride in ourselves, our friends, and our families. Our Father, who art in heaven, hallowed be thy name. Thy Kingdom come, Thy will be done, on earth as it is in heaven. Give us this day our daily bread, and forgive us our trespasses as we forgive those who trespass against us. And lead us not into temptation, but deliver us from evil, for Thine is the kingdom, the power, and the glory, forever and ever. Amen."

At the end, as they all finished and looked up. Mr. Williamson and the entire class looked at Clarence for just an instant with smiles of understanding.

From that day on, no one made any trouble for Clarence, and he worked even harder and longer into the nights on his studies. It paid off, and he graduated third in his class of 243 and went on to college in Hattiesburg. After graduation with a degree in electrical engineering, he went into the army as part of his ROTC program, rising quickly to captain before he decided to leave and make his way in the world outside of the military. He never forgot the day that changed his life nor the anger burned deep within. He knew someday he would get his revenge many times over.

CHAPTER 3

15 January 2001

The tall, gray-haired man was the first one out of his seat in business class as the Lufthansa flight from Frankfurt arrived at the gate in Sao Paulo. It had been a very long flight—over twelve hours—and he had slept only a little. He always took business class now, as first class had become too conspicuous. He pulled the hanging bag from the overhead compartment and his briefcase from under the seat in front and moved quickly to the exit door.

The walk to customs was not long, and, since he had nothing checked with the airline, he was close to the front of the line behind the first-class passengers. He had completed the landing document and was fully prepared for any questions, but he really didn't expect any. He had shaved his beard before boarding to coincide with this particular passport and photo—one of four that he used, none of which were really valid. The customs officer took the passport, checked for a valid visa, checked the landing document, made quick chops with the stamping machine, and waved the passenger through.

He walked quickly to the nothing-to-declare line and punched the button that determined at random which passengers with supposedly nothing to declare would be searched. The light went green, and he continued down the corridor to the exit.

The crush of waiting families and business associates was like all South American and European countries. He moved in a straight line through them and found his own driver exactly where they had planned to meet—under the large stairway. The driver took his bag, and both went outside into the early morning fog to the small, but very powerful, BMW sitting in the parking lot. As both got inside and secured their seatbelts, he could finally relax for a few minutes.

* * *

He was born Carl Durnbacher in 1942, in a small town in Bavaria to a father who was in the Luftwaffe and a smallish, but very loving, mother. As the war progressed, his mother moved his sister and Carl to Berlin to stay with her own mother. Carl's father was killed two months before the war ended as he led a final raid on some Allied ships in the English Channel. His body was never recovered. Carl remembered only some vague feelings about his father, but was bitter that he had to grow up without one, even though many of his school friends also did not have fathers either because of the war.

Carl studied hard but in grade school, he was small in stature and not as good in athletics as the other boys until he entered the secondary school. Puberty made all the difference in the world. He grew almost a foot in just a year and, by his third year in high school, he was six feet, two inches tall, and very athletic. He also discovered girls during this year—or rather, many of them discovered him. He was a good dancer and very popular at parties with good jokes and stories for all. He seemed to make everyone around him feel special.

And then the wall was built. He idolized Kennedy and stood with the very closest crowd when Kennedy came to Berlin to speak. When Kennedy was killed shortly after, Carl was destroyed. He vowed to not ever become involved in politics again, but instead to work only for his own gain.

After Durnbacher finished his university studies in mechanical engineering, he took a job with a company that manufactured machine parts for other companies internationally. After two years in sales in the Dusseldorf headquarters office, he was given a position of selling parts to companies that had offices in the Middle East and Africa. He took on this difficult assignment with gusto, traveled extensively and at great length, and made many, many, contacts and friends. He did very well for the company too.

It was a trip to Iraq in 1972 that changed his life. His representative agent there, who was also a friend, offered him a very private deal: if Carl could get some special parts manufactured and sent to a forwarding broker in Marseilles, the agent would pay Carl a fee of 50 percent of the commission separately to any account that Carl wanted, wherever he wanted. Carl knew the risk he was taking and examined the parts request for almost a week while staying in his room in Baghdad. As he studied the drawings, he realized what would be the end use of the parts. He made drawings on his own, and finally decided he would take on the project. The payoff to him would be over two million dollars for just this one project. He envisioned a way to separate the parts into several different pieces that would be manufactured by separate firms he knew, and then they could be taken apart and reconfigured for shipment.

Since the manufacturers would not start making these parts without funds assured, he drew up a contract with the Iraqi agent. He flew back to Zurich and set up a corporation in a few days. Carl opened a bank account with the Zee Bank of Switzerland and wired the account information to the agent. The next day, he checked the account balance, and it was now $26 million!

Carl proceeded to have purchase orders printed and set up a small office, and then he flew back to his office in Dusseldorf. The next day, he quit his job and left to go back to Zurich. He redrew the parts by himself over the next month, working almost nineteen hours each day. He barely ate or slept. Finally, the drawings were done.

Since he knew which companies would be best to produce the variety of parts, he made his appointments for the next three weeks in France, Germany, Belgium, and Italy. All the companies he contacted were very pleased to have the business, especially with half the money upfront and the rest at shipment. Before he went to them, though, he went to Marseilles and spent a long evening at the forwarder's favorite bordello, getting him drunk and laid in order to win his friendship and trust.

The deal went through as planned. The parts all arrived at the forwarder within two weeks, and three shipments were made to a location in Bahrain. From there, the parts were re-crated with other items and sent on a small boat to Basra. Carl's client was very pleased with this work and promised him much more. Carl paid all the invoices and put half the remaining $4 million in Swiss account for the Iraq agent. After expenses, Carl profited a very nice $1.78 million dollars, and his new business was born.

Over the next several years, he made much more. In the 1980s, during the Iraq-Iran war, Carl and his agent helped their client to their own profit of over $100 million for each. Carl made many more contacts and friends. He also became well noted by Interpol, the CIA, MI5, Mossad, and several other organizations that wanted to stop him from his chosen line of work. But the greed of many manufacturers, as well as Carl's expertise in engineering, kept him from being discovered.

Now that the wall had come down, Carl thought about quitting the business. He really didn't need the money anymore. He had a nice apartment in Buenos Aires, a farm in Kentucky, and a townhouse in Paris—all paid for in cash, all owned under one of his four aliases. He became a real taxpayer for several of his enterprises that were clean. He took pains to avoid the limelight now.

In 1976, a group approached Carl from the National African Coalition through two intermediaries during one of his visits to Nairobi. He found their proposition interesting and helped them. The money came from a bank in Nigeria, but he really no longer asked questions about those things. Carl kept track of the balance and, when it was what it was supposed to be, he proceeded. His clients and agents all had to trust him, as Carl never did a deal without full payment in advance. He never trusted others, but always forced the negotiations to his side, since, in the end, the clients knew Carl would either deliver as promised, or he would give back the money with interest.

And Carl always delivered.

CHAPTER 4
February, 1993

In a speech to the Republic of South Africa Parliament on 2 February 1993, Mr. Roelf Meyer, Constitutional Development Minister, said: "Either we negotiate for a new South Africa or . . . prepare for a civil war that will destroy everything."

In 1993, the elections were over. A transition had begun—not totally peacefully, but it had begun. Not everyone was satisfied with the results, and the promised changes were not happening fast enough. Some wanted now what they did not get before the elections, and they did not want to wait any longer.

* * *

The beginning of the beginning of the end of apartheid in South Africa was triggered by the Soweto riots in 1975. Each year in succession brought more killings, riots, and violence. Finally, emergency-protection laws were invoked with the further reduction of civil rights.

As the world began to fall in line behind the theme of "down with apartheid" and "one man, one vote," many countries declared economic boycotts against South Africa, a country rich in natural minerals and resources. Finally, the government of P.T. Botha ended, and the government of DeKlerk began. He immediately sought peace within the country. He freed Nelson Mandela, the president of the African National Congress, who had been imprisoned for over twenty-four years. This was the end of the beginning.

Negotiations began to seek a peaceful transition of power, a new constitution, and the freedoms the black majority wanted. Economic boycotts ended. There was still violence. The power struggles between the African National Congress and the many various factions fought internally for power, and struggles that had gone on between the African tribes of the Xhosa and Zulu for centuries resurfaced. The talks broke down in May, 1992, and violence began to rear its head again with killings and riots, especially in Natal—and even in Johannesburg.

Mandela's wife, Winnie, had been free during his imprisonment and had led the ANC to continue the struggle for freedom, but once he was released, their marriage failed quickly due to her alleged affairs and many lovers. Most importantly, Winnie, now used to power, did not want to give it back to her husband. She wanted change, but she wanted it quickly and with violence.

As the year 1993 started, the winds blew in many directions, sometimes with a violent nature, sometimes with peace and negotiation. The march to the elections in April, 1994, was blackened with violence. The whites of South Africa became more concerned. What to do? Leave? Stay? Hope for the best? Prepare for the worst? What will be the warning signs, and how much time will one have? Even if there is more violence and rioting, are peace and transition possible? Maybe, but what will life for a white minority be like after the blacks gain control politically? Will the new parliament pass laws restricting the whites? Will South Africa become another of the African states deteriorating from strong economies to poor ones, with dictatorships and constant battles, both real and political, between historically warring tribes? Is the election and the passing of the new constitution the beginning of the end? Will it bring the downfall of the country?

The elections were successful. Mandela was voted into power, and a new cabinet was installed. However, two major factions in the country, one black and still very powerful, the KwaZulu of Natal, and the whites of the Orange Free State—both still wanted their own land and power. Both were armed. Both had money for more arms, and both had strong motivation for getting what they wanted with fighting, bloodshed, and death, if necessary. The whites kept arming themselves, but they were the most visible. Much more secretly, the black Zulus of Natal continued to receive arms and set their plans. They would not wait for Mandela to deliver on his promises. They had fought before and had lost. This time they would fight and win. The Zulu would rise again, and the downfall of South Africa would bring them their own republic, world recognition, and power! They were ready.

CHAPTER 5

20 May 2000

Michael and Carter Stephens would try. They had known for over eight years that the days of South Africa were numbered. Fortunately, they had planned an escape. Now, with only months, days, or hours left for them, perhaps they would implement their plan—one they had thoughtfully and carefully worked out in every detail, providing for every eventuality.

For them, the downfall of South Africa meant a new beginning instead of an end.

Michael had made several trips to Rio the past five years, ostensibly to review technical specifications with a consultant and an associate from America. Every time he left South Africa, he took the maximum amount of money allowed by the government, which he promptly exchanged into dollars upon arrival. He knew the trip itself was costly, but for every dollar spent on the plane fare, three would wind up in a week in his bank account in New York. His trusted friend, Craig Thompson, would take care of making wire transfers of the money from the Brazilian bank to the US bank. Now, after five long years, he and Carter knew that the account in New York contained over three hundred thousand dollars, enough to begin again.

Michael Stephens was of average height—five feet, nine inches—and build—a hundred and seventy-five pounds, with a small scar over his left eyebrow from a bicycle fall when he was young. His brown hair was cut in a typical business style, and he was beginning to lose some in the back of his head. Michael was a business manager in charge of power distribution within the large African Anglo Steel Company mill, east of Johannesburg, near Witbank. His brown eyes were warm and friendly to most people, but they could become filled with anger when he thought of his own Jewish parents' past and their need to run away. Michael was also Jewish. His parents had escaped Germany in late 1932 and immigrated to South Africa. He had heard of the narrow escape many times. It was a part of his family ritual at Passover. He was tired of his family running, and this would be the last time.

He had married Carter Parker six years ago. For him it was love at first sight. Carter was five feet, eight inches tall, not slender, but very well-shaped, with terrific legs. She had a confidence about her that immediately took everyone into her grasp. Her black and brown hair was cut to her shoulders, and every so often, she would flip her head to give it a shake and a natural fall. People noticed this movement because she did it so frequently that it seemed like a tic—but it only made her seem sexier. Carter was very smart and had a degree in accounting and an MBA from University of Whitwatersrand. All her life she had been interested in finance, and now she was vice president of finance for a large South African mining equipment manufacturer located in Kempton Park.

They would need all the money they had saved and sacrificed to get away and start over. It would provide a life of new freedom they wanted so badly. They hoped and prayed they might escape the rumored horrors of the civil war to come in South Africa. They had done the planning, but they needed some luck. Religious people might even say God's grace must be with them. Yes, perhaps, but why wasn't God's grace with all the thousands who were to die?

Michael and Carter Stephen's plan depended upon quick action. Michael had made good friends at work with a black who lived in Alexandra, one of the townships from which the attack on Johannesburg might be directed. After a lifesaving incident about a year ago, the black man gave Michael the radio frequency and special radio that would be used by the African Zulu Freedom Party when they would make a move toward the violent overthrow of the new government and power takeover. The day after getting the frequency, Michael installed a base monitor and relay station in their apartment in Johannesburg to provide them the needed warning whenever it might come. They were ready.

CHAPTER 6
28 May 1965

In late May, 1965, Clarence van Dyke Jackson left the army and went to New Orleans. He met with a friend who had started a small electrical-contracting construction company. The friend needed some extra money to keep going and offered part of the company to Clarence. He had saved over five thousand dollars and now decided to risk it all. He bought 51 percent—and control.

His timing was great. In September of that year, Hurricane Betsy hit New Orleans with full force. Clarence had several friends from the army in the area, whites and blacks, whose businesses were hurt by the storm. They needed electrical power at almost any cost to keep the food from spoiling and the air conditioning working. Clarence made three phone calls to some other friends from the army, now working in Tennessee, and asked them to come to New Orleans immediately to work for him and make some big bucks. They came, and the contracting business thrived.

Luckily too, the Civil Rights Acts were being passed, and one of them made it a law for companies, especially public entities such as city governments, the army, navy, etc., to give set-asides to minority-owned businesses. What a boon! Clarence could now get work by bidding to the government locations, and larger, white-owned or larger corporate-owned firms would not get the order.

With business growing, Clarence now was free to spend some time on repaying the whites who had hurt his mother so many years before.

He had made many friends while in the army. He knew how to use his influence to get the pass, the promotion, or the special job—not only for the blacks in his units he commanded, but for whites as well. He only told them that one day he might ask a favor in return. No one ever turned down a favor from Clarence van Dyke Jackson.

CHAPTER 7

January, 1991-May, 1992

Over the next fifteen years, John Wesley Zooma and his friends heard about other necklacing killings. In the 1980s, it became almost a standard practice—and now it was not only coming from the police, but also from death squads of the Zulus and the Xhosas, the age-old tribes that hated each other. The killings and terror escalated. Luckily, John Wesley Zooma and his three friends saw no others like this. They finished school and got jobs in the local ironworks, but one went to work at the local power-generating station. They trained and served their two years of mandatory time in the army and developed into men, always remembering that day when Mr. Bulewessi was killed by the necklacing.

In January, 1991, John Wesley Zooma was invited to visit a small gathering one evening at a friend's house. He went and found out that a paramilitary force was being formed for the future. All wanted patience for now, but they must be trained and ready for the time when they could order the whites to leave or go kill them. Would he join? He answered immediately. The leader was pleased and told him to join them on the soccer field Saturday morning at 6:00 a.m. for work and training. Now he was excited; there was hope and a future.

Over the next three years, he worked and trained hard with his unit—a small band of eight men his own age. The leader was two years older and had been a sergeant in the army for five years. He knew what he was doing, but the greatest fear was that they would be exposed by the spies in the township. Other units were formed and trained in the same period, but the command structure was limited, just in case a commander might be caught and tortured to tell who was in the group. Plus, they had to contend with the Xhosa death squads. They had no rifles or ammo, but those were promised from the regional commander . . . someday.

May of 1992, saw the talks collapse between Mandela and DeKlerk. The fractions of the various parties all wanted part of the power that would come with a transition government. The killings and terror increased.

CHAPTER 8
3 June 1999

On June 3, John Wesley Zooma was working on his normal maintenance job, inspecting various areas of the electrical switchgear for possible problems. His supervisor was a white, Michael Stephens, and he had become somewhat friendly with him. They worked well together, and a mutual respect was developing. This day was to be somewhat different from normal duties as they needed to switch the power from one feeder of the plant to another. It was not necessarily dangerous, but still one had to be careful.

After lunch, they met outside by the ladder to the roof and looked at the sketch of the switching job that had to be done. Michael would go to one substation, and John Wesley Zooma to the other. They would look at the switch positions, record them in the log, and meet again in the center of the roof over the plant. They climbed up the ladder and went in the different directions. Each substation contained electrical switches and transformers to reduce the high-voltage power to a lower voltage for use in the plant for the lights and the machinery.

All appeared in order to Michael at his location. He completed his log record and went out toward the other substation. He saw John Wesley Zooma coming toward him.

"Is everything okay, John?" Michael asked as they neared each other.

"Yes, Mr. Stephens. Everything looks okay at Station A. The contractor that was there yesterday left some tools in the back, that's all."

"Okay, let's do the switching at Station B first and then go to Station A for the final transfer."

They walked back to the substation Michael had just inspected, went inside, and took out the long, iron bar used to trip the switch. John Wesley Zooma put it in the special slot to crank up the spring that operated the switch, gave three cranks downward, and the switch closed. No problem.

The bar was replaced, and they left. They walked back across the roof to Station A, talking about the soccer team scores and the games scheduled for the weekend. John Wesley Zooma entered Station B first and went immediately to the switch in front of him. Michael entered and saw the tools at the end of the aisle between the two lineups of switchgear. He stood by the doorway and watched as he had done just minutes before. John Wesley Zooma took out the iron bar and put it in the slot. With his back to Michael, he gave the three big cranks downward to set the spring and activate the switch. When he came downward on the bar for the third time, the spring was fully tightened and released.

A tremendous fireball exploded four feet away, on the other side of the transformer. John Wesley Zooma was thrown backward against the other switch, and Michael was blown out the door onto the roof by the blast. A second later, another blast went off. Fire began to cover the back part of the substation, and smoke quickly filled the small room.

Michael was stunned. He picked himself up off the roof and saw the flames. He moved up the short ladder into the station and could barely see John Wesley Zooma five feet in front of him, as the smoke and heat were now intense. He crawled on the floor and grabbed the young, black maintenance man and pulled him toward the door. He could hardly breathe now, but with one final effort, he pulled them both back outside, and they fell to the roof. He could hear the sirens of the fire trucks coming quickly. He pulled John Wesley Zooma further away and saw that he was bleeding from the back of his head. Concussion? He was afraid to move him further, but he was afraid to stay even this close to the burning Station A for fear of more explosions. He saw the firemen coming over the edge of the roof and running toward them.

One group went to the station and began pouring a special liquid on the equipment through the doorways and the windows. Two others attended to Michael and Zooma. They put Zooma on a stretcher, took him to the edge of the building and lowered him to the ground personnel and waiting ambulance. Michael was able to climb down himself, but when he reached the bottom, he collapsed. The firemen and rescue squad picked him up and put him in the ambulance with Zooma.

The next day, Michael awoke and realized what had happened. Carter was with him, holding his hand.

"How is John?" Michael asked softly.

"He is okay. He has a concussion, but that is about all. He is in the other wing, of course," Carter replied.

"I want to go see him now."

"I don't think that is such a hot idea. I think you should rest. You have been out for almost eighteen hours. Wait. Maybe later today or tomorrow."

"When can I leave?" Michael asked.

"If you get rest tonight, the doctor says you can leave tomorrow. He wants you to stay here tonight though for observation. Okay, honey?"

"All right. May I have some water?"

"Sure!" She gave him some water and watched him drift off to sleep again.

John Wesley Zooma awoke about the same time as Michael. His mother was by his side, her head bowed in prayer. He opened his eyes, and looked around to see he was in a ward of ten patients. The curtains were pulled around his bed. He could only remember the roar of the blast.

"Mama, what happened?"

"Son, there was an explosion, and you hit your head. You have a concussion. Mr. Stephens pulled you from the burning station and saved your life. I have prayed all night for you both, and thank God, He has spared you both."

"How is Mr. Stephens?"

"He has not awakened yet from what I heard from the nurses about an hour ago. But he is apparently okay. Just exhaustion, they say, from the shock."

"Can I go see him? I want to go see him."

"No. You just rest."

And he drifted off again, wondering about Mr. Stephens and how his life had been saved by a white man. Strange . . .

CHAPTER 9

5 June 1999

That next afternoon after lunch, Michael was seen by the doctor. He said it would be okay to go over to the black ward and see Zooma. Carter helped him into a wheelchair and took him for the trip through the maze of hallways until they arrived. They asked the nurse how John Wesley Zooma was doing and found out he had woken up that morning and was resting. Carter pushed Michael down the hallway to the bed and saw his mother sitting by him.

"Mrs. Zooma, I am Carter Stephens, and this is my husband, Michael. We have come to see how John is."

"Oh, Mrs. Stephens, thank you so very much. And Mr. Stephens, how can I thank you for saving my son's life? Bless you!"

"Mrs. Zooma, it was nothing really," Michael replied.

Michael felt embarrassed while Mrs. Zooma shook his hand so warmly. He knew she wanted to give him a hug, but that just wasn't done in this country.

He moved forward to the bedside of John Wesley Zooma and looked at him closely. Zooma was sleeping. Michael reached out and touched his arm, and Zooma awoke. He looked over at Michael and smiled. "Hi, boss, we made it. Thanks for whatever you did. Someday we will have to talk about that day. I owe you one."

"No, you don't owe me anything. Just rest. I'll stay for a few minutes, and then I'm going to go back and get some more rest too. Take care."

Zooma closed his eyes again and drifted off.

After a couple of minutes, Carter moved back, and pulled the wheelchair away, and said, "Let's go. You need some rest. Goodbye, Mrs. Zooma. I know your son will be okay."

"Yes, I think he will. He is very strong and determined."

Carter and Michael left the ward, and they found their way back to their room. After Michael had fallen asleep she noticed the differences in their beds. *I wonder what will happen now*, she thought. *Will Zooma be fired? Does he feel like he owes Michael something? There is nothing we want. Michael saved his life, but he would have done that for anyone, black or white—or whatever.* As she considered this, the quiet of the room began to give her peace and she too, fell asleep in the big leather chair in Michael's room.

A couple of weeks later, there was a board of inquiry held in the managing director's office of the plant. Someone would have to answer for the costs of the accident.

After some preliminaries, the managing director, Nigel McGregor, spoke directly to Michael, "Mr. Stephens, you have described the accident and what happened. In your opinion, where does the fault lie in this instance? Please be specific."

"Sir, the fault lies with the contractor. He left a steel plate across the transformer's low-voltage bus bars. When we applied the switch and the power to energize the transformer, a massive short circuit was initiated."

"But shouldn't you or your helper, Mr. Zooma, have seen the plate before you energized the transformer?"

"Yes, sir, you are correct. I take responsibility for not making a more thorough inspection with Mr. Zooma."

"Yes, this board of inquiry does find you and Mr. Zooma at fault for that oversight. We are glad that you are both are alive, but nevertheless, we will come to some conclusions regarding this and let you know. This board of inquiry stands adjourned. You are excused, Mr. Stephens."

Michael got up and left the building. He was scared now for his job. It appeared that he was going to be the major person blamed for the incident, and perhaps rightly so. As he walked to his car, he thought, *I should have looked around and made a thorough inspection of the substation. And I was lucky. I was nearest the door and was blown out on the roof.* Zooma felt the full impact of the blast as the short-circuit started. *I wonder how he feels?* He wondered if this was a sign of some sort. He had never really taken death seriously before for himself, even though he had lost both his mother and father a few years ago. But for himself, well, he was not old enough to die. Now he was married to Carter, and they had much to live for. His mind began to go from subject to subject quickly. Finally, as he reached his car, he wondered for several long minutes about his country. Would it survive all the changes and terror? Would he and Carter survive the changes that were sure to occur soon? Would Mandela be able to keep all his promises? He had to make some plans, but how and when and where?

He started the car and drove home to tell Carter about the board of inquiry. He would try to let her know his true feelings about their future in South Africa.

CHAPTER 10
8 July 1999

Four weeks after the accident, Michael was in the office when his boss called for him. He got up from his desk, walked in, and sat down. His boss, Ian Booksporte, closed the door, walked behind his desk, and sat down.

"Michael, I have some bad news. The results of the board of inquiry are in. You are being removed from your management position and reduced to staff engineer with an appropriate cut in salary. Here is a letter explaining your new salary. The board felt that you did not exercise enough management control to have kept the accident from happening."

Michael felt stunned. He had expected a reprimand, or perhaps a letter for the file, but not this! He was put back to the level he started as a young engineer.

"Ian, how long will I be at this level? I think I have been unfairly blamed for this. How can I face the rest of my friends and workers here once they know this? The board has put me in an impossible situation."

"Michael, I'm sorry. This was not my decision or recommendation, but this is the decision. Actually, you are still lucky. Mr. Zooma was let go."

"What! What are you talking about? How could he be fired over this? He was working for me. If anyone should have been fired, it should have been me and not him. This is totally unfair."

Booksporte continued, "Michael, I understand your feelings. I would like you to take the rest of the day off to sort all this out, and come back tomorrow to get on with things here and the new situation. I cannot tell you how long you will be at the staff level again. My boss wants to see you put this behind you and rededicate yourself to the company and its goals. I'm sure that, as you do that, you will be noticed, and your chances for promotion will improve again."

"What you really mean is I'm being punished for an oversight that caused an accident, and now I must serve my purgatory, with everyone watching me to see if I can do better somehow than what I was doing before. I don't see how that is possible. And rededicate myself? I have been dedicated to this company since I started here six years ago. I just don't know what you and they expect of me."

"Michael, go and think about things. I'll see you tomorrow."

Michael left the office, walked back to his desk, and put a few papers in his briefcase. He could feel the stares of people trying hard not to look at him. This was all so unfair. *How could I come back tomorrow? I have got to figure this out now,* he thought and left.

In the parking lot, he found a note on the driver's seat. It was from Zooma. He wanted to meet outside of the city. The note gave directions and time. Michael was not sure he wanted to see him again, but at least he had a job and Zooma didn't. No, he owed it to Zooma to see him again at least once. He would go—tonight at 8:00 p.m.

CHAPTER 11

8 July 1999

John Wesley Zooma knew the spot well. He had chosen it for its secrecy. He needed to have a very private conversation with his friend, Michael. It might be the last time they would be able to talk the way he needed to talk. He had discussed his plan with only one other person, his mother, and she approved heartily. No matter what happened in the future, she said, he would have done the right thing for the person that had saved his life. It was honor, and Zooma very much had honor.

The location of the meeting was off a dirt road southeast of Johannesburg. It was on a high rise on the veldt, and one could see in all directions. There was a group of trees from the top of the hill down the north side, and a small stream flowed at the base. Zooma had been here many times to think and plan—especially since that day when he was a boy and saw the man burned. His hatred had taken form at this very spot.

Zooma saw the car lights come up the road and stop. The lights flashed three times, and then once, and the car door opened. Michael got out of the car and walked toward the base of the hill. As he climbed the slope, Zooma thought for a quick moment how easy it would be to kill him, but that was definitely not his intention tonight.

Michael reached the top and moved to the trees, where he saw Zooma standing in the moonlight.

"John Wesley, how are you tonight?"

"Michael, I am fine."

"Really? I heard the news that you were let go. I'm sorry."

"Man, you do not need to be sorry for me. I'll be okay. I expected this with this company and its damn need to find someone to blame. I only feel like shit because you have been hurt, and you don't deserve what they did to you. You save my life."

"That is okay. I know that, had we been reversed that day, you would have pulled me out."

"Perhaps. I was never sure until that happened. You know, there has been a lot of pain in my life, and I'm very angry at what is going on, and I will do something to make a difference someday. But I can't tell you what that will be. What I do need to tell you is this: you and Carter must prepare to leave this country someday, and you may need to leave quickly. If the election goes okay, the changes people want here will not all work for everyone. There is too much anger and hurt from all these years. There are already too many promises for even most to come true. My Zulu brothers will want their freedom eventually, no matter what happens—and the whites will get it, but I owe you."

"No, you don't, John."

"Yes, I do."

Zooma produced a small package from the ground next to the tree and gave it to him.

"Michael, this is a radio receiver with a specially tuned frequency. It will only receive one station, and that will be a tone signal. When you hear it, and I can't tell you when that will be—it could be tomorrow, maybe next week, maybe a year from now, maybe three years from now, I just don't know for sure. But when you do hear the tone, you must leave immediately. Get out of the country, or you and Carter may be killed. Violence is coming. Many don't want it, and many do. Both sides. But I'm doing this because I owe you. Now take it. Hide it. And prepare for the day that tone goes off. It is the call for people like me to form up in our units for the action. And that action will be against all the whites that have not left and against the Xhosa. Now take it and go."

"John, are you really serious?"

"Never more in my life. This is your chance to save your life. It is up to you. I hope you do something with it. And more than anything, I wish you good luck. You will need it. You have no idea how well organized and well armed we are becoming. Now go."

Michael felt a rush of warmth for his friend, and he also felt scared. What was going to happen? And when? He took the package and put it under his arm. He put out his hand. Zooma took it, and they stood there for another minute, looking at each other for the last time. Michael could see a trace of the anger now in Zooma's eyes. He had never noticed it before, but it was there—but not for him personally; that he could sense. He turned and walked down the hill back to the car with the package of life for Carter and himself. He got into the car and drove home.

Zooma watched Michael go just as he had watched him arrive. He then left and walked the four miles home. He knew he had done the right thing, and maybe he still might have to help further.

The new day came, and Michael went to work. He decided to stay for a while and prove to the company that he was worth it. Actually, he wanted to prove it to himself.

After he arrived home last night, he had plugged the new radio in the wall next to the bed. But that was not going to work for long, so he would have to find someplace else. More importantly, he and Carter needed to develop an escape plan.

He went to work that day and moved the things from his old office to a cubicle in the main staff area. His boss gave him some new projects, and he set his mind to get busy. His co-workers started coming over to him later that morning, and, by lunch, almost everyone was talking and joking with him.

That evening, he went home and, after dinner talked with Carter until 2:00 a.m. about what they might have to do and how to do it. They decided the basics of the plan and decided they must include Carter's father in it. In fact, he would play a large part in actually getting all of them away from their homeland. They agreed to visit him in Durban over the weekend to tell him what they knew, talk about what they didn't know, and come to decisions on a plan that would hopefully save their lives. Their plan needed a lot of luck, and they knew it.

CHAPTER 12

15 January 2001

The BMW moved out of the parking lot at Sao Paulo Garulahos International Airport and onto the expressway. The driver headed west toward the hills while Carl Durnbacher fell asleep in the back seat. The drive was about three hours up into the hills of Minas Gerais, through pastures full of cattle and corn and some very winding roads that would have reminded one of Kentucky, West Virginia, or northern Alabama. Finally, they arrived at their destination, a small city named Santa Rita, and the driver woke Carl.

The car moved through the town and stopped on a side street at the base of the hills in front of a small hotel. It was white stucco, with a long stairway up to the front entrance. The hotel only had three guest rooms, but it was very comfortable, and most certainly private. It had been the residence of a wealthy local manufacturer who still owned the property and used it as a tax deduction.

The hotel was all on one floor, with a large sitting room to the left of the front entrance and a hallway to the right that led to the three bedrooms and baths in a wing of the house. A courtyard separated the bedroom wing from the kitchen and living areas, but, in the back of the house, behind the kitchen and very small dining room, was a sitting area with comfortable sofas, a stereo, and TV. Behind the house was a small backyard, perhaps only ten feet in width, before the hill continued upward at a steep incline. Steps were laid in the hill alongside coffee bean trees, up to two terraces—one with an oval pool. All of this looked over Santa Rita and the hills on the other side of town.

Carl went to the first room, and the driver went down the hall with his own bags to bedroom number three. Carl decided to make a quick security check with the driver before taking a shower. They met at the rear of the house and went to all the rooms individually. They then both climbed the hill to the top past the pool terrace and surveyed the area. When they had completed the review, Carl and the driver made their way back down the hill for a lunch of homemade lasagna and salad.

The woman cook was a cousin of the hotel owner and had lived in Santa Rita all her life. Carl knew all about her—maybe more than she knew about herself, but she knew very little about Carl, his driver, or the person he met here once each year, although not always at the same time. She just did the cooking and the cleaning, kept visitors and other potential guests away, and minded her own business. And so, for good reason, Carl and the other special guest each year always gave her a nice bonus of three month's salary. For that amount in Brazil, she could definitely keep things in the order they wanted for the usual three days they always stayed.

CHAPTER 13
15 January 2001

The two women kept close to the buildings as they walked along the street toward the hill. The sidewalks were narrow, with many cracks and upheavals. It was fully dark now, nearing nine p.m., and the street lights cast an orange and white glow on the buildings and people. Some children were playing hide and seek, reminding the two women of their now once-innocent youth. Neither was young—although they were not in middle age, but rather in their late thirties.

The smaller woman was named Maria Theresa Bounaventure. She had lived in Santa Rita all her life. She had married very early, at seventeen, but her husband had died of pneumonia one winter some six years later. She had decided not to remarry, even though her mother was always trying to get her to see some of the more eligible bachelors in the area. She appeased her mother and did go out with them, and on more than one occasion, she had made these dates into "regulars." For now, she had taken a profession that kept her and her two growing children in a very comfortable lifestyle for Santa Rita. She did not practice this work all the time, since she was an accountant for a local law firm. But when she did receive a call for her practiced art, she was usually available and expensive. She saved the money so that her children could leave Santa Rita if they wished; in any event, she wanted to retire soon on her own.

Maria was somewhat dark of skin, her great grandfather being a partial Indian from northern Brazil. She didn't mind her coloring—in fact no one in Santa Rita paid much mind to anyone's color, as there was such a mix. Her skin was very smooth with no blemishes, and the texture was soft velvet. Her eyes were a medium brown, and her facial features were those of an international beauty. She had an intensity in the eyes that never seemed to stop, certainly attracting one's attention with its directness. She could see through someone to their very soul.

When she had decided to begin a more professional life as an aside to her regular job, she did so because she didn't think she would find anyone to match her husband's warmth, caress, and tenderness. With all the men she had been with over the years, one and only one came close to meeting her standards of perfection in lovemaking. Tonight she would be with that man again as she was last year. She very much looked forward to this night's encounter with the man she knew only as Van.

This evening was arranged with one phone call to her office five days ago. The mistress of the hotel called and told her only to come on this particular night, along with who the man would be. Payment would be as usual for this one night—in cash in a sealed envelope waiting the next morning after breakfast in the desk drawer in the front room, which also doubled as the office. The amount was large, two thousand in US dollars, all in hundred-dollar bills. Actually, as she walked along, she considered the previous six times she had been with Van, and she thought that she really could be with this man without payment for her love.

The woman walking next to Maria was Dorothea Consuelo Grecanao. She was fully white of skin, but with the ever-present tan of many Brazilian women. Her eyes changed with the sky. If it was raining or cloudy, they had a gray cast. But when the weather was clear, they were brilliant blue, with a clarity that astounded those who came near her. She had smaller breasts than Maria, with a figure though that looked like a poster for Brazil, especially when she wore a tenga on the beach or backyard sunning herself.

Dorothea was not a professional, but rather an unspoken amateur. She did this only a few times each year, and she had to know the man—or at least Maria had to know the man and vouch for him. Dorothea was interested in the extra money; it helped provide the trips to the US for shopping and visiting friends.

Grecanao was a medical assistant in a medical office in Santa Rita. She had gone to school in Sao Paulo for two years and returned to Santa Rita, because the pay was better there, she could live quite well with the cost of living lower than Sao Paulo, and her interests did not lie in the big city. She had not married, but had several boyfriends over the years. She valued her independence and felt that marriage was not a commitment she could make yet, even though she was now almost thirty-seven. She enjoyed her life—the freedom she had without other things to keep her tied down.

This would be her third time with the gentleman from Europe that she knew only as Carlos. She knew it wasn't his real name, because she looked at his passport on the second visit last year while he was heavily snoring after their long night of sex. She liked being with him; the money was great, two thousand dollars for one night, and he was not kinky at all. He was "straight," at least according to her experience, and she enjoyed the pleasure he gave to her as well as giving to him. Her friend Maria asked her to come with her three years ago, but only after they had talked about the proposed encounter several times. There were definite rules for this one: no one must know the names or the descriptions of the men. If asked by police or the Brazil secret service, they were to give descriptions that matched only in height, but no other features. Also, after breakfast, they were to leave by the gate that opened on the side street. There, a car with one of the bodyguards would be waiting to take them home. They were not to discuss the nights with each other, but, of course, this was impossible between these two women who were very close friends.

She had received the call just four days ago. She was actually afraid she couldn't make this evening, since her period was just finishing. By now, however, that was over, and she had douched twice before leaving her apartment tonight to meet Maria.

The street that went to the hotel seemed as if there should be a tunnel at the end. It was lined with trees on one side and ran directly to the hill where it stopped abruptly. She noticed the kids playing and thought too of the times when she would stay out with her friends. For some reason, she had never had the desire for children of her own. She had several nieces and nephews from her sisters, but marriage was just not right for her, at least not now, and she hadn't met a man she could totally trust yet.

A car passed them—an old Volkswagen Beetle that spewed noxious fumes. Unfortunately, it was one of many thousands in Brazil. The driver noticed the two women walking together, but he was on his way to his own private meeting and really didn't care about them. The two women watched the car turn left at the corner at the hill, and by the time they got there, its lights were two small red dots almost a mile away. Since leaving Dorothea's apartment where they met and had coffee, they had seen only two other cars, some people they knew in the street, and the children playing. It was good.

With some anticipation of the evening, they crossed the street and made their way up the steps to the hotel. They noticed two cars further up the street, both with Sao Paulo license plates, and they knew their visitors had arrived and were waiting for them. At the front door, Maria knocked softly once, and then three times in the pre-arranged code for this evening. There were only some lights on in the bedrooms and a small glow from the kitchen. The housekeeper opened the door and invited them into the living area to the left of the main hallway. Maria and Dorothea sat down in the soft sofas and were asked by the housekeeper if they wanted a drink. Both said yes, and both had Campari and soda.

Maria was dressed in a light linen dress, a cream color that set off her darker coloring. Dorothea was wearing a light blue-and-white-striped blouse with a mid-length, dark-blue skirt. Their makeup was not heavy, but rather it added to their native coloring and features.

After only a few minutes, the housekeeper beckoned Maria to follow her to the backyard where Van was sitting in the wrought-iron love seat by the garden pool. After she left the living room, Carlos appeared from a room behind the office and in front of the kitchen to greet Dorothea. He walked toward her and sat down close, carrying his own gin and tonic. He was wearing a blue, linen shirt and tan slacks. She thought he looked great and could feel herself becoming warm and moist between her legs with anticipation.

"Good evening, Dorothea. Are you well this day?"

"Yes, Carlos, quite well. I am glad to see you again. I always wonder if you will return."

"Do you ever talk about me to your friends?"

"No, only with Maria sometimes, and then only when we are very private and not at our homes."

"Good. I enjoy coming to Santa Rita, and especially seeing you each time. You are very special, you know."

"Thank you, señor. It also pleases me to receive the call of your coming and that you wish to see me again. I hope I have shown you my loyalty and trust—and, besides that, I truly enjoy our special moments together."

"And me also."

Carefully, he took her hand and squeezed it in a most tender and loving way. He moved closer to her face, and they kissed, briefly at first, and then with the hunger that made them know they really needed each other badly. After this kiss, he held her for a moment on the sofa and stood up, pulling her slowly by the hand. They walked with arms around each other to the bedroom.

When they entered, he closed the door and locked it, but it was almost an afterthought, because he was fixed in a trance, looking at her in the soft light. The doors to the front garden were open, and the moon now shone brightly on the hills of Santa Rita. The lights of the city below were flickering through the trees and plants of the garden as the gentle breeze moved them.

Carlos moved toward Dorothea and held her close. He could smell the perfume on her neck and hair. She put her arms around him and moved her left hand down to the small of his back, feeling the muscles of his shoulders. He pulled her closer with his hands now stroking her buttocks. As their passion built into a long, lingering kiss in which they tasted each other fully, he reached down, moved his right hand up her right thigh under her skirt, and felt her very being. She kissed him with even more hunger as she felt herself burning. His touch was magical! She never felt like this, even with her boyfriends, and not before with him. But now was different.

Carlos moved his arms, placing one under her back and the other under her knees, and carried her to the large bed waiting for them in the soft breeze of the evening. Gently, he set her down, moved her skirt up to her waist, and pulled down her panties. He then moved slowly up her legs, kissing each place carefully and longingly until he reached her. With a tenderness and eroticism she had never known, he placed his lips on her and delved deep. His hands moved upward, and she unbuttoned the blouse for him to ease his way. As she became more aroused, she arched her back upward. He pushed up her bra and gently felt her swollen breasts. The passion in her increased to the breaking point, and she cried out. But even as she did so, he eased away and continued to carefully play with her womanhood and her lower lips. She never came down, but remained high with the erotic feelings, and she continued her upward climb again and again to climax.

Finally, after the fourth time, she could no longer stand not having him. She pulled him up to the bed with a strong tug of her hands on his upper arms. He released his oral grip and allowed himself to move up to the bed beside her.

Dorothea moved upward and over Carlos. She deftly unbuttoned his shirt and pulled it off while admonishing him to remain quiet and let her do her work. Next, her hands moved to the belt and zipper of his trousers, and, with one move, she pulled off his slacks and shorts, fully exposing him. The sight of it sent her soaring again. She moved over him, took him in her hands, and, with slow swirls, moved it slowly into her. Finally joined, they laid there, not moving, in that peace that comes the moments before the fullness of lovemaking happens with a man and a woman who desire each other and truly want only to give the completeness of what God has given them.

She moved slowly at first, and then with a quickness as he moved under her. They tasted each others lips, his on her breasts and neck and mouth and ears, and her on his eyes, and neck and mouth. They moved in a union that was meant to be. She could feel herself coming now and moved even more vigorously. She wanted for them both to be together, and now she could feel the tenseness in his shoulders and arms. They cried out to each other.

And then they laid there in the moonlight with him still erect in her, and they kissed longingly, but slowly. She was everything he had never had in a woman, and he told her so. To her, Carlos was much more now than just a once-a-year john who was fun for a night and three thousand dollars. This moment she realized that she might finally be falling in love with someone, and she really didn't even know his real name. But did that matter?

They rolled together now, and he moved above her with long, slow strokes that began to bring her up. She held him and moved her arms over his back, feeling his behind and the small of his back, all down to his very balls behind him. She played with them as he moved inside her. Carlos moved closer to kiss her neck now and could feel her breasts in his chest. Dorothea loved the weight on her, and, as they moved together, their breathing became as one as well. He pushed himself up on his hands, and she stroked his chest and lower abdomen as he worked to bring them to the point they had shared together before. Now he felt the building of the pressure and the tenseness in his body. She felt it too and, with the movements in her, she knew that the wonderfulness of what was to come was building with a force. Her breasts became harder, and her stomach tightened as she felt the warmth within. Dorothea focused her entire mind and feelings on the love from him.

"Venca! Venca! Venca!"

He responded with the final, deep movements that sent them both into the netherworld of bliss for many long moments. With their mingled sweat and bodies, the wind blessed them with its coolness as they held each other close and looked into each other's face. They found what each had never had to that moment: the most true love between a man and a woman. He knew he could not live without her and, although he was some years older than she, Dorothea vowed to herself at that very instant not to let him go. Finally, their passions spent, he moved over and laid there by her side, their arms stroking each other in the most tender areas. Finally, Carlos fell asleep, but Dorothea leaned up on her elbow and looked at this man who had, in two hours, brought her to more wonderfulness than she had ever known in her life. She kissed him tenderly on his cheek and fell asleep herself, tightly pressed to his body.

CHAPTER 14

15 January 2001

Maria walked out into the small backyard of the hotel, in which coffee plants grew. The walk led to steps straight ahead that went up to the next terrace, where the pool languished on the hillside. At this lowest level, the yard was small, with a garden pool filled with goldfish and a black, wrought-iron love seat facing the pool, with a view away from the hill toward the city of Santa Rita.

Clarence van Dyke Jackson sat and watched Maria move from the house into the clear, moonlit night. He had admired this woman from his first night with her six years ago. She had a presence, a self-confidence, and an assuredness that almost intimidated him with its power. He wasn't sure if Maria even knew she had it, but he had decided not to ask. He only thought, *This woman could hold power over many if she was taught the ways of power and attitude, and that would make others literally beg to be near her.* As she moved closer to him in those few short steps, he arose and greeted her with a quick, tender kiss on the cheek and one on the inviting mouth. Their arms enveloped each other, much as two lovers might greet one another after having been apart for months or years, ready to pick up exactly where they left off, as if they had only been away for a moment.

"Maria, you look beautiful as always. I think you look more beautiful to my eyes each year. I have missed you."

"And I too, Van. I have begun to treasure these moments together. I think of you and us together at these times all year long. You must know you are special to me."

"I have always hoped so—and hoped so because it was me and not the money."

"No. You truly are dear to me. How have you been these months?"

"Very busy. My businesses prospers, and I seem to find new ventures each day that interest me. But . . ." There was a long pause before he continued. ". . . I find that other things in my life don't matter as much, and perhaps I should leave them behind."

She wondered what he meant by this. Maria knew that Van and Carlos were close friends and partners in several ventures, but she had never asked why they came to Santa Rita each year. She only wanted the annual visits to continue or become more frequent—and not for the money. She had plenty saved, and her other clients provided the lifestyle she wanted. No, with Van it had been different.

"Van, have you had problems this year in your personal life, or is there something else that you might be able to tell me and ease your mind?"

"Maria, I don't know how much to tell you of my life outside of here. There are many facets to it that, if you knew, might put you in danger."

She had suspected this. Two men don't come to Santa Rita for three days approximately once each year for their health. She knew this town was quiet and the police very circumspect. No one bothered anyone here unless they went out of their way to make trouble.

They sat down, and Maria put her arm around him and stroked the back of his head and neck. They sat like this for many quiet moments and looked out at the city. For a second, she thought she saw a tear come out of the corner of his eye, and she moved closer to hold him and kiss it away. The salty taste, his more openness of emotions, and the look of need began to bring strong feelings of wanting for him. She felt a tremble in his body and one in her own. The evening breeze and the night brought them closer to a true intimacy—more than sexual, because that part had not even begun. She felt the weight of his cares, but dared not asked him what was making him feel so badly.

Van looked away at the distant hills, covered now with some dew from the evening coolness. The moon made the hills appear to be of fine sugar with the reflections. He thought for several long minutes about telling this woman he had come to love in many ways of the deep concerns now on his mind. He wanted to tell her of how he now thought that what his business arrangements with Durnbacher had done would injure many and cost many lives. He even thought about canceling the deal, but if he did that, he guessed he would die. The persons who wanted these weapons so badly would come after him if he backed out now.

The woman was near, and he felt her warmth next to him in many places. Her legs were next to his, and the pressure of her thighs against his made him want her. But should he or could he tell her? No, he must keep the secret to himself. If he told her in this intimacy now, he would expose her to possible pain and death, and he couldn't bear that. He knew she might someday be questioned, and those doing the questioning would probably not be civilized and might torture her. She must remain to him only his lover in this town of Santa Rita, unless he could find a way to take her away from here.

Van turned now to her, put his arms around her, and held her tight. He could feel the hardness of her breasts against his chest and the heat of her neck. They kissed in a long, passionate kiss that quickly increased their desire and feelings of wanting for each other. He placed his hand on her leg and moved it up to her inner thigh, pushing up her dress to her waist. She moved to feel him and began to unbuckle his belt and pull down his zipper. With one movement together, they stood up from the iron sofa in the garden and moved to the grass by the shimmering pond. As he pulled down the zipper on the back of her dress, she responded in kind with a quick and deft move that sent his trousers and pants to the ground. He lifted off her dress and removed his shirt. The wind caught the hairs on both their bodies and heightened their sensations. Now that they were totally naked with each other in the garden, the moonlight caused the moisture on their bodies to glisten and glow, like the dew on the leaves and grass. He pulled her down, and she immediately wanted him. She could wait no longer for his touch inside and on her. They moved as one as they had done before, and finally felt the supreme sense of giving to each as they went into the final rush of heat.

Van lay there silently after many sweet moments of love and passion. Maria, with her arms around him, kissed the hairs in the center of his chest and looked up to him with the love she knew was in her heart for this man she rarely saw. She asked now, "Why don't you stay in Santa Rita for some days with me? I know you can be safe with me. I want you to stay. Please?"

"I can't."

"Why not."

"It is so difficult. The situation is so very difficult."

"Can you tell me anything? I need you, and I need to know."

"There is so much in my life now," Van said.

"But if you stay here with me, perhaps your life will become easier and less stressful. I can see there is so much on your mind from before."

"Yes, I have many concerns. And now I am beginning to feel guilt for perhaps the first time in my life. I may be an instrument in the deaths of many people."

Maria let a gasp from her mouth escape and said, "Oh, my God, I pray for your soul. Can you do anything to stop what will happen?"

"No. It is too late, I think."

Maria got up from the ground, walked over and picked up her dress, and put it back on. She looked at him still on the ground and realized that, whatever he had done, there was nothing she could do to change that or him; but perhaps with her love and caring, he might give up his guilt.

"Come with me to the bedroom. Let's take a bath and rest. You have your meeting tomorrow with Carl, and, after the meeting, perhaps we can be together again, if you want me?"

"Okay," he said. He got up, put on his slacks, and they walked to the bedroom together.

After the bath when they had gotten in bed, she cradled him in her arms and held him very tight until he went to sleep. In the night, he awoke and walked around the house, making a security check of his own.

He met up with his guard, Jason, in the outer hall. Jason was six feet, four inches, two hundred and twenty pounds, and very quick with a knife and pistol and martial arts. He was paid very well and did not ask questions, and was always alert. He had learned when to sleep and when to leave his boss alone. Jason had been married when he was very young, but the marriage failed. There was a son, now living with Jason's mother in Hattiesburg, but he saw him very little. Jason enjoyed his life now in Brazil, but he was worried about the concern on Van's face. It showed. This deal was like all the others in many ways, and yet it wasn't. He didn't know the details, but he did know the goods were going to Africa.

Van asked, "Have you seen Roberto?"

"Yes, we had a cigarette together about an hour ago in the hallway."

"Did you take the usual precautions?"

"Yes, of course."

"Have you checked the satellite flyovers for tomorrow?"

"Yes, our friend in CIA gave me all the printouts. The best time is from 0822 to 1047, and then from 1136 to 1313. The afternoon is not good. Please stay inside then."

"Good. Carl and I will breakfast without the women and have our discussion in the upper garden by the pool about nine. Come and get us no later than 1030. We will move to the sofa in the hallway by the inner courtyard for the rest of the morning if we are not finished. If the women are up, you and Roberto keep them away from us, they will probably do so anyhow since they have been through this before, and make sure there is some light cover noise in the living room and kitchen. I think we will be finished by lunch."

"When do you want to leave, boss?"

"I think we will stay one more night and leave tomorrow."

"Is this woman getting to you?" Jason asked.

"I don't know."

Jason knew she was as soon as Van said it. It was only a concern of his if his boss was in danger or security might be breached. Jason knew he was not responsible for Van's bed discussions with her or any one of the other women in his life.

"Boss, be careful."

"I will. She does not know anything yet to endanger her or us. I will see you later. When will you sleep?"

"I will get some rest while you are at breakfast and talking with Carl. Roberto and I will split the watch, and I will sleep in the front bedroom, where I'll be close after the women leave. Roberto can sleep this afternoon. Do you know when Carl will return?"

"No. He may stay tomorrow night too, and perhaps longer. See you in a few hours."

Van returned to the bedroom and moved into the warm bed with Maria. She was asleep but stirred softly and moved next to him as he slipped under the sheets. He thought for a few moments of the discussion tomorrow, put his ideas in order—much like his life had been from the army on—slept soundly.

* * *

Van awoke about seven thirty. The breeze was coming into the room from the open windows. Maria was still asleep. He got out of bed and went to the bathroom. When he came out, Maria was sitting up and looking at him.

"Good morning, Maria," Van said.

"Good morning, Van."

"Did you sleep well?"

"Yes, of course."

"I have a meeting with Carlos in a little while, but I'll be staying over again tonight. Can you come back and spend tonight with me? You were so wonderful."

"I think so. Can I call the housekeeper later this morning to let her know?" she asked, true elation in her heart.

"Yes, that will be okay. Just say the words *Yes* or *No*. She will know what the meaning will be."

"Van, last night you started to tell me something. I know you are feeling many things, and you can trust me. Please let me help you relieve your mind. I am so worried about you now. I feel your stress."

"I know. Things are very difficult, and I am thinking of some changes I must make in my life. I need freedom from some things I have done and freedom for the future. I am not sure how to attain what I need."

Maria moved out of the bed, stood next to him, held him close, and whispered, "Van, I don't know if I can help you, but I know I feel I love you and would do anything for you. You are special to me—so different and unique, and also so organized. But there is something very troubling to you, and now I am greatly worried for you."

"It is okay," he said as he stroked her hair and caressed her. "I need some time, and I think I can put things in place. And I think I love you too."

They tightened their arms around each other for a long moment. Finally, Van let her go and said, "I hope you can come back tonight, but please, always be careful. I will go and get some breakfast now, and you can leave for the day to your job. Please call."

He opened the door and walked down the hall to the small dining room, where the housekeeper served a typical Brazilian breakfast of fruit, bread, and coffee. He sat down and composed his thoughts for the meeting. It would be a very special one now.

After the door closed, Maria picked up her gown from the floor, put it on, and went into the bathroom. After she had showered and dressed, she put on her makeup and put a few things into the overnight bag she carried. She went out into the hall to the dining room and found Dorothea there, already eating.

"Dorothea, good morning. Did you have a nice night and a good rest?" Maria asked as she sat down.

"Yes, it was a wonderful time, and Carlos has asked me to come back tonight. Are you coming back to be with Van?"

"I don't know. I have to make some arrangements, but I want to. I think I love him."

"Maria, how wonderful! How does he feel?"

"He said the same to me. But I have no idea about the future."

"Well, let us hope and pray for you and him. I must get to work. Call me."

"Okay, I'll call later this afternoon."

Dorothea got up from the table, picked up her things by the doorway and went out calling "Ciao," as she left.

"Ciao, ciao," Maria responded.

She finished her breakfast in silence, wondering where Van and Carlos were—but she knew not to go looking. When she was done, she moved away from the table, picked up her bag, and went out the side door and down the steps to the street. Roberto was waiting with the car, and he drove her home in silence. As she rode, she felt the cool morning air and thought of why Van was so upset. Obviously he was involved in something not quite legal because of all the precautions he made in coming to Santa Rita on these visits. Was he in drugs? That would make her upset, and she couldn't stand that. Was he involved with the Mafia or the "Syndicato", as it was known in Brazil? Was he working for something bad? Why did he say he wanted his freedom? What did he mean by that?

She noticed she was almost home and now had to put these questions aside and get back to her own life for a while. *I must see him again tonight.*

CHAPTER 15

16 January 2001

Clarence van Dyke Jackson and Carl Durnbacher had been partners for almost ten years. They had been coming to Santa Rita for the last seven, each time to get away from the eyes and ears of the various police forces around the world that would like to hear the conversations and deals they made. Durnbacher had been to Santa Rita on a potential deal to buy a local business, and he found the guest house to be perfect for all his needs. And the local police were not a problem.

Jackson moved out to the backyard and up to the second level by the pool to meet with Durnbacher. He found looking at the cool water of the pool that reflected the mountains around Santa Rita to be comforting. How different this was from Wiggins, Mississippi!

Jackson saw Durnbacher emerge from the side entrance by the back wing to come through the lower garden and climb the steps to the pool level. He didn't notice anything unusual. Durnbacher was dressed in his usual tan slacks, silk shirt, and tan loafers—no bulges anywhere. Van didn't expect any, but one could never be too careful; he stayed alive because he was *very* observant.

Durnbacher waved as he came up the steps. He walked over to the other white, wrought-iron chair and pulled it out, but extended his hand to Van before he sat down. "Van, good morning to you. How are you today? Did you rest well?" Durnbacher inquired.

"Yes, quite well, thank you. And you?" Van asked.

"Excellent! I always enjoy coming here for the solitude and Dorothea. She is wonderful and makes me feel very good, indeed."

"Me too. I have enjoyed the rest and being with Maria."

"Good. Then we are both ready to cover some business items, now—unless you want to wait until this afternoon."

Van responded, "No, let's talk now while it is cool and pleasant and private for us. I did the usual checking with my government friends, and we are private until about ten thirty a.m."

"Good. Van, I have need of some additional armaments. This is the list. I will need them shipped by the usual method and destination within thirty days, if it can be arranged. There is a bonus for us if it makes Durban by March 25th. The list is not long, I think. What can you do?"

Jackson took the list from Durnbacher and studied it carefully. Although it was not long, and most of the items were easily procured from his source, he was actually trying to formulate the words to Durnbacher about something else: *his need to stop.*

He kept looking at the page, mentally making notes about the contacts needed and the arrangements to be made. Durnbacher just kept looking at him, but finally looked away toward the town.

"Carl, this is not too difficult, except for this rocket-launcher. This cannot be obtained from my usual sources. I don't know if I can get it to make this shipment. Otherwise, the thirty days is close, but we can get it to New Orleans and in the container easily enough, but I don't have any knowledge of the shipping schedules here. I think it can be done. What do you want done with the rocket-launcher if it must go separately, or if I can't get it?"

Carl turned back to look at Van as he spoke and looked carefully now at his partner. What was missing with him? Something started to sound alarms with Carl about his close partner in this business. He listened as Van told him about the shipment, but his eyes were on Van's eyes and face, studying him.

"Van, I want the shipment to go, with or without the launcher. If you cannot get it, okay, then forget it. If you can get it, but it will not make the container, then do not get it. I do not want to take the chance of it being sent separately. I have much more control over a full container than any partial shipments. What we put in the container will be relatively safe until it gets to the destination. I am sure you understand this."

"Yes, Carl, I do. We have been safe these past ten years because we set up a system and procedures that work all along the line. I agree completely. If I cannot get the launcher to make the container, I will not get it for us."

"Okay. What will the cost be for this one?"

"Our cost will be approximately $1,400,000 for the goods. Local payoff costs will be approximately another $200,000. Transportation and shipping will be around $100,000. How about costs after it ships from New Orleans?"

Carl looked up at the sky, noticed how blue it was, and thought for a minute, calculating costs for this shipment on his side. He had the same payoffs to make, especially at the destination port.

"Van, I think costs on my end will be about the usual $200,000 we have had in the past for one container. So that will make our total costs about $1,900,000, right?"

"Yes, $1,900,000."

"Why don't we charge them a round $4 million? I think we can get that quite readily. Is that figure okay with you?"

Jackson looked at the page of items again and thought of the continuing risks and how he wanted to get out and quit. But he could not at this moment. This would be the last one.

"I would like to get a little more from them for this one. How much is the bonus worth?"

Durnbacher replied, "It is another $1 million."

"Okay then—total $5 million, split usual fifty-fifty. We need 50% now to pay our costs, with the rest when it clears Durban. You will collect the money then?"

"Yes, I will wire transfer the $1,700,000 to your bank in Bermuda as usual in about five days. That will give you the funds to obtain the goods and make the shipment. When I get the rest in Durban in about a month when the container arrives, I will wire transfer you the remaining profit portion, $1,550,000. Agreed?"

"Agreed," Van responded.

"Okay, with that out of the way, there may be another deal for some of my longtime clients in India. Are you interested?"

"I'm not sure. The takes from this arsenal have to be reduced, and I may have to find another source or two. What will be needed?"

"Just some M-16 rifles, ammunition, some grenades, and C-4 plastic explosive. They are just doing some . . . how do we say it . . . a little local work."

Jackson looked straight into Carl's eyes. He saw the intensity of the man he had known, and he gave back the same intensity in return. Keep the mind on business. Don't let your guard down to Carl now, or you might not even make it back to Sao Paulo.

"Not much of a problem with that, but I don't think I can help for perhaps three months. Spring exercises coming and the items must be there for that. I have a friend in West Virginia that might be able to help, but it will still take a little time to set that one up. Do you have the time?"

Carl replied carefully, "Yes, I think so. But I'll let you know."

"Are you going to stay tonight?" asked Jackson, hoping he wasn't.

"Yes, I need the rest and the privacy. Shall we bring the ladies back for dinner and the evening?"

"Okay, I am in favor of that. I'll call Maria and she can get in touch with Dorothea."

"Great. I think I'm going to take Roberto and go play some golf this afternoon. Want to join us?" asked Carl.

"No, I think I will rest by the pool and catch up on some work I have. Tax time is coming for my business."

"Up to you. The course looked great when we drove by it, but I know you have many other items to attend to. So, I will see you for dinner about eight o'clock p.m." With that Carl got up and walked back down the steps and into the house. As he walked in, he looked back up to his friend and partner still sitting by the pool and decided then that he was right: Jackson wanted to get out. He couldn't have that happen just yet.

Durnbacher went in the house and found Roberto asleep in his room. He woke him up, and they began to get ready to go to the private golf club down in the valley just outside of Santa Rita.

With relief, Jackson watched Carl go down the steps. He had stayed cool, but he also saw Carl look back up. That was the giveaway. He knew Carl suspected something, so he must be even more on his guard and figure out the plans to get out of this business. His rage of all the years was wearing on him, and the guilt was beginning to eat at him now as he faced his own mortality.

CHAPTER 16
16 January 2001

Satellite NS47K was in its usual orbit with its medium-range-focus hearing and sight scope on. Very few people in the CIA knew of this particular satellite and two others that were launched by an early, *Enterprise* shuttle military mission. The satellite was monitored on a fifteen-minute basis by pulse download to the United States National Security Agency in Virginia. As good as Jackson's information was about satellite monitoring, he was unaware of this one.

At 10:37 a.m., Brazil time, it passed over central Brazil and continued out over the South Atlantic, headed toward Africa. Its arc of travel would take it upward over the ocean and then on a southeastward track, coming over the African coast at Angola, over the Calahari Desert, and then over South Africa and out into the Indian Ocean. This southern-hemisphere track and monitoring allowed this very particular satellite to monitor visually, electronically, and even vocally. It could see to a distance of six feet, and, although some of the technology was improved, it was a very successful resource of information gathering over some very "hot" areas of interest.

The download of data came in a scrambled rush at 0848 Eastern Standard Time. The data was decoded and transcribed. The tapes were sent over to two analysts, who had the job this shift of reviewing what NS47K saw and heard. Since this last download was from a pass over the jungles and hills of Brazil, there was not much interest. They were really waiting for the information in another hour from South Africa.

Jack James, a senior analyst, had the duty of reviewing the video tapes. As he was looking at them, shortly after 0915, he saw something interesting. Besides the usual people working in the coffee fields of Brazil, he noticed a quick pass with two persons sitting by a pool. He decided to have a close-up, computer enhancement done of this segment for review later. Intuition, as well as logical and tenacious analysis, was important in this job, and there was someone in that frame that looked interesting. He just couldn't explain it.

CHAPTER 17
16 January 2001

Maria received the call from Van. She contacted Dorothea and told her of the plans for tonight. Dorothea was excited about seeing Carl again as well as earning the additional money. They were to meet at Maria's at 7:30 p.m. for the walk to the hotel.

Van had returned to his room and made the call. He also talked with his bodyguard about the evening and night and went to his room. He put on his swim trunks and a T-shirt, got a towel, and pulled out a regular business folder from his briefcase. He went back outside and up the hill to the pool terrace and started to look over the accountant's reports for his company's taxes. After about an hour, he took off his T-shirt, and decided to get some sun, and have swim before lunch.

Carl and Roberto changed and left for the golf course. Arrangements were made, and now it was time for a little rest and play.

CHAPTER 18

16 January 2001

Carl Durnbacher and his bodyguard had played a very enjoyable game of golf. By the time they got back to the house in Santa Rita, it was already seven, but dinner was not for another hour so there was plenty of time to shower and get changed before meeting Van and the girls again. He thought about the conversation that morning for the first time since lunch. Yes, he would have to do something. Van was becoming a problem. How many people did Van use in getting the shipments made? Would they be a risk to him personally? He must explore that carefully with Van and see what he could learn. Before now, each one had kept their associates in this partnership a secret from each other as a means to protect the entire organization in case either one of them was caught; but he decided he must find out a little more tonight, or at least he might have to put some help on this.

Dinnertime came at eight o'clock p.m., and Carl walked down the hall to the small dining room and found Van at the bar with both of the bodyguards.

"Van, how are you this evening? Isn't it a beautiful one? I love it here." Carl said to Van as he looked at him and then to the guards.

"Carl, yes, I think it is very nice this evening. One more night in our private heaven, yes?" Van responded.

"Absolutely! Let's enjoy this one. We deserve it before we go back tomorrow to the real world out there. What time do Dorothea and Maria arrive? Were you able to make the arrangements?"

"Yes, they are supposed to arrive about nine thirty. They could not come to meet us for dinner," Van replied.

"Great. Let's take our drinks and go eat."

"Yes, good idea," Van said as the four of them continued to smile at each other and walk to the small dining room where dinner was laid out—grilled chicken, beef filets, rice, and fresh beans. Carl had picked up a bottle of cabernet from the wine rack at the bar and opened it. He poured the glasses after offering a taste to Van and seeing his head nod.

"Before we eat, please allow me to offer a small toast: To my good friend and business partner, I wish you good health and happiness, and may life go the way you want it to be," Carl said to the group.

"Thank you, and to you, my friend, let's move on and seek our peace and happiness," Van replied with his outstretched glass raised high.

The four men clinked their glasses and drained them dry for this toast. They sat down, and Carl poured the glasses full again, and they began the meal. As they talked about more daily life, Carl could tell that Van wanted out. He had given it away with his slip in the toast. That bit about peace and happiness, was it? Well, maybe Van might want peace for himself and many others, but the business and fortune Carl had made over the last twenty-five years was based on just the opposite—the greed, avariciousness, and warring side of mankind. All he had done was help to supply a few arms along to the needy. They would have gotten them anyway. And for the last three years, the source of funding from South Africa had been especially rewarding. Now was not the time to quit, just as things were moving forward.

As they finished, Carl began to look directly into Van's eyes. Yes, he could see the change. The hate that was there for all these past ten years was gone. *Where had it gone to and why so quickly?* he wondered. *Well, who cares, but I've got to do something.*

"Van, you know we have never talked to each other about our separate organizations that make us rich. And for good reason, don't you think?" Carl said as he tried to set up the conversation.

"Yes, I think that has been a wise position on both our parts. I have many friends that I work with who know nothing of you, and I'm sure the same is true for you. Right?"

"Yes, of course. Do you think we should continue this policy?"

"Yes, I do," Van replied, now fully on guard. He didn't particularly like this line of conversation.

"Good, I agree. But how do you obtain the products we need? Doesn't someone take an inventory once in a while. I would think that the US Army or whoever might find something missing now and then."

"Well, they do take an inventory each year. But the quartermasters have been paid off so that most of the items appear to have been scrapped over the twelve months or lost at summer encampment, or whatever. It is up to each quartermaster to fill out the paperwork for his responsibility. I never see it, and I don't care to."

"Okay, but do you get them locally or all over the US? Just a question, not prying really," Carl asked.

"From all over," Van lied.

Just as he finished this sentence, the doorbell rang and Van's guard went to go see who was there. Quiet ensued over the table quickly. He returned with the two women behind him, and he held the door for them to enter the small dining room.

"Dorothea and Maria! You two ladies look stunning this evening," Carl exclaimed as he got up from his chair and went to give them both hugs and a kiss on each cheek.

"Thank you, Carlos. It is good to see you again tonight. I'm very happy I could come back to be with you," Dorothea remarked, her smile warming toward him.

"Let us go outside up to the pool and enjoy the evening," Carl suggested. He wanted to get away from the confining atmosphere of the four persons now in the small dining room. He did not like to feel so caged.

The two couples walked out back and up the steps to the second level and the pool. The night was now well on them, and the stars were clear and bright with the blackness of the eternity beyond covering like a blanket. They looked up, each holding the hand of their lover, and remained quiet for several long and tender moments.

Dorothea and Maria had wondered, as they walked to the small hotel that evening, if this might be the last time. Maria was especially upset, as she was now very much in love with Van and did not want him to leave Brazil. She knew that she could not keep him there, but she thought there must be some way to see him again. *Tonight cannot possibly be the last. I can't stand if I have to never see him again. I've got to find a way to go to America and be with him if he will have me.* Desperately she tried to think of what to do, but knew the evening and night might give her opportunities. *I must make this night special for us,* she finally agreed with herself.

Dorothea, however, had come to realize that day that, even though she had some very strong feelings for Carl, she knew it was not love. As she walked with Maria, she pondered a thought that kept coming back to her from the previous night: *I wonder what kind of business he is in. It must be something sinister. And, he seems to have a wall around his feelings. Except for the moment he lapsed—but he is not caring enough.* Tonight for her was now only about the money.

Van decided that he seen enough of the stars. He had a plane to catch tomorrow evening from Sao Paulo and some business to attend there with another friend. This could not be a very late night, as he had to get up early and get back to the city.

Van looked into Maria's face and saw the beautiful eyes glowing with her feelings. They walked to the other end of the pool so they could have some privacy. He put both arms around her thin waist and pulled her close.

"I cannot stay long. I must return to Sao Paulo in the early morning," he whispered close to her ear. He brushed a kiss against her hair and could smell the sweet perfume. He became entranced now.

"Let us go to the bedroom. I want our time together to be special tonight. I need you," Maria whispered back to him. She pulled him closer and forced her lower abdomen tight against his. She felt his passion rising and could feel her own inside her doing the same.

"Carl and Dorothea, we are going to go inside to my room. Dorothea, I might not see you tomorrow as I have to leave early.

Carl, I will give you a call day after tomorrow at the usual place if I do not see you either tomorrow morning. Is that ok with you?" Van expressed as he walked around to them in the cool night air and the smell of the coffee beans.

"Yes, call me as usual for the arrangements. I will be leaving tomorrow about eleven a.m. for Sao Paulo. My flight is tomorrow afternoon to Germany. I wish you well, my friend."

Carl put out his hand for Van and embraced him with his other. Van was used to this and returned the manly embrace common in South America. He felt close to his partner and all that they had shared over the years. But this would be the last time they would embrace this way. Carl now had other thoughts concerning their partnership, but nothing different about Van's loyalty to him. As they split, he wondered if Van could discern what he was thinking. Too late, anyhow.

Van moved to Dorothea, held her in a friendly embrace, and kissed her lightly on the left cheek. "Dorothea, I wish you well in all you do. You are a beautiful woman and a special treasure. Take care of yourself. I hope to see you next year sometime."

"Van, you too." Dorothea wiped a tear from her eye. She knew his feelings were real.

Van walked toward the steps, and Maria moved that direction on the other side of the pool. She called out to Carl, "Carlos, be careful, and see you next year, I hope." And they left the couple standing at the pool and held hands as they walked down the steps to the house and Van's bedroom. They never looked back.

Carl and Dorothea watched them go. He led her over to a wrought-iron love seat, and they both sat down. He put his arms around her and held her. She put her head on his shoulder and her hands on the inside of his right thigh. She began to caress his leg and then moved her hand higher, feeling him growing with her touch. She looked up at him and kissed him fully and longingly. He kissed her back with all the urgency of his feelings. Now he wanted her.

Dorothea moved off the love seat and knelt on the walk around the pool. She pulled her blouse up from her skirt and unbuttoned it as Carl sat watching, his desire for her increasing with each passing second. She removed her bra, and now her breasts and nipples shown from the reflection of the starlight in the pool. She pulled the zipper down at the side of her skirt and pushed it down to her knees. She watched Carl's eyes with every move. She saw them study her breasts and then move down her body. She enjoyed the appreciation she was witnessing for herself from Carl. She felt very much in control now.

Dorothea pulled her panties down to her knees, then she stood up, and the skirt and panties fell to the ground. She stepped out of them and moved directly to Carl. His focus was now on her lower belly and the smooth curve. She put her wet fingers to his face, and he opened his mouth to accept them readily. She took his left hand and placed it inside her and felt his fingers probing while his palm slowly massaged the Venus. She held his shoulder tight with her other hand.

Now was the moment. She sensed him and his arousal. She dropped again to her knees and pulled at his belt. It came free, and she unclipped his slacks and pulled his zipper down. She reached inside and pulled his pants and undershorts off and reached for him. Slowly, she placed her lips around him and took him in.

The night air was silent. The pool shimmered in the light as the moon rose over the hill behind him. She was feeling wonderful as she looked up and saw the excitement building in him. She could feel his manliness harden and quiver. She wanted him.

She pulled him off of the love seat to the ground, and he knelt with his hands on her hips. She moved toward him and they came together. They thrust together, and their backs arched away from each other as the final moment came. She grasped his buttocks and pulled him to maximum penetration and kept him there. He cried in her ear, and she moved again several times to increase his pleasure and her own. The moment of her release burst forth with a pull to his head and a cry in his hair.

"Oh, my God, my God!"

"Dorothea, I love you," Carl said softly, still feeling her tight around him as his climax drifted away.

"Carlos, I love you too," she said with feeling, but not sincerity.

They remained this way for a few moments, and then they parted.

Dorothea got up, moved to the pool, and dove in. The water felt cold to her flush body, but the freshness was wonderful.

Carl dove in after her and swam up next to her at the other side. He moved against her and felt her against him. The cold of the pool would not necessarily revive their passion physically. The warmth of the two bodies together melted away the coolness of the water around them. Carl felt the years of stress slide out of him. He relaxed. He felt the woman next to him and holding him. He wanted to stay here, but he knew he couldn't. He must return tomorrow. He had much to do for this shipment, and the money was needed quickly.

Dorothea held Carlos tight against her. She could feel him relaxing in her embrace. She knew she still had control and she loved it.

"Carlos, let's go to our bedroom now. This is wonderful with you, but let's move to the bed."

"Yes, but just a few more minutes here in the pool."

With that he let go of her and swam several laps. This was like a tonic to his body. He felt rejuvenated. He stopped for a moment on the other side of the pool and saw the woman holding onto the wall. He always appreciated her beautiful charms and enjoyed the nights. As he stood there in the water, he knew what he would have to do. It would be difficult, but very necessary. The only question was how to arrange things and timing. After a couple of moments of thought, he swam over to Dorothea.

"Let's go, my sweet. The rest of the night waits for us."

She nodded her head. They got out of the pool, picked up their clothes, and put towels around themselves for the short walk back down to the house. Once inside, Carl locked the bedroom door and moved to Dorothea on the bed. The night was short for both of them as they enjoyed the love and pleasure each gave to the other freely.

Carl slept soundly. Dorothea woke first and moved to the bathroom to clean up and go to work. When she came back, Carlos was awake and watching her from the bed.

"Dorothea, come here," he called to her.

"Yes, Carlos, what do you want? I must go to work soon," she said as she walked across the red tile floor.

"I will miss you. You are truly wonderful. If I can send for you sometime, will you come to me?" he asked her sincerely.

"Yes, of course," she lied. She had seen something in him before tonight, and she knew she could not go to him. This last night had been for the feelings of control and the money. Something had changed in him in twenty-four hours. It was not the same as the previous night. Now she did not trust him.

"Good, I may ask for you to come to Germany in a few months—or perhaps Buenos Aires."

"Okay, I will come if I can take care of things here. My mother must be cared for—and what about my job? I don't know if I'll be able to take off for vacation."

"It is okay. I'll make arrangements and you will not need your job any longer. I want you to come and live with me."

She was surprised. "Carlos, I never expected this. I am very flattered. I do love you, but do you really want me to come and live with you?"

"I think so. My life is changing, and there will be more in the future. I have no other woman in my life, and you seem to understand me more than anyone I have met or been with in the past few years. I need your warmth and understanding. Last night proved to me that my feelings for you are real, and not just in the passion we shared. And now I want you to be with me. But I cannot take you with me today, and I have several major projects to complete in the next few months that will require much traveling and attention. It would not be fair to you to ask you to come now. And besides, this will perhaps give you some time to think about all this and make arrangements. What do you think?"

"Carlos, I do love you and have some very strong feelings about you. I think the idea is wonderful. And now I must leave. Please let me hear from you soon, my lover," she told him as she bent down to the bed and gave him a warm kiss good-bye.

They held each other for a long moment as the early morning sun awoke the town. The open windows let in the breeze, with the smell of the coffee beans from the hills. She would always remember this moment.

She let go of him, turned, walked to the door, and blew him a last kiss. "Take care of yourself, my love," she said as she closed the door behind her. She walked down the hallway and down the front steps and home. She thought that this past night had turned out much differently than she had thought it would some twelve hours earlier. She could not go to Germany or Buenos Aries to live with Carlos. He made her feel good, but, for her, this past night was not love—not like the night before. Carlos had changed and she wondered why.

CHAPTER 19

16 January 2001

Bryan Cummings completed the analysis of the pictures from the satellite. He was a recent graduate of James Madison University, with a degree in political science. He had been unable to find a job for the first seven months after graduation, and he became restless living at home with his parents. He had taken the civil-service exam and passed with an excellent score. The CIA reviewed the new applications and scores and offered him a job as a junior analyst in the infamous "Section 9," the far back end of the CIA complex in MacLean, Virginia—the section that had the tedious day-in-and-day-out task of reviewing satellite and communication data that was thought important by others. Most of the time, the junior analysts did not know what or why they were to look at something in particular, but they did so anyway. Most of them kept up with current briefings and readings, but were not that familiar with all they needed for the jobs. As was usually the case, sometimes the most important positions were left to those with the least experience.

On this particular day, Bryan had arrived early and was just about to go to lunch in the cafeteria with the new analyst down the hall—or rather line of cubicles—Miss Janet Simpson, a very attractive, recent graduate from Ohio University. Bryan was thinking of her and her legs when he went to work on the next project in his in-basket for the morning. It was some photos and an audiotape

Downfall and Freedom

from his supervisor, Jack James, of two men talking from a hillside in Brazil.

Bryan took the photos' blowups and compared them with the new computer enhancement. The pictures showed two males, a black and a white, talking by a pool. He listened to the audiotape and heard the snatch of conversation concerning the arms shipment. This was a clue he needed.

Next, Bryan went back to his computer and asked the database for pictures of all possible arms dealers. The computer would bring up the various pictures, and, by manipulating the program, it would take the frontal picture of the subject and move it in any three dimensional way to compare it with the pictures from the satellite.

"Great! I got a match," Bryan said to himself as the two pictures came together side by side on the split screen of his terminal. He pushed a *Ctrl-S*, and the screen showed him the data:

Subject: Carl Durnbacher
Home: Dusseldorf, Germany
Occupation: Owner, Manusafe Engineering GmbH
Suspicion: Arms trader with terrorists. Wanted for questioning.
Report findings to supervisor. Code Red—highly confidential.

Bryan Cummings read this and now was anxious. This was the first one he had seen with this designation. He called for Jack James.

"Mr. James, this is Bryan Cummings in Section 9, and I've got something here very unusual. The photos from the satellite that you sent me yesterday have resulted in a match. We have pictures of Carl Durnbacher, sir, and a small sampling of the audio. It concerns an apparent arms deal going down. The computer can't identify the other subject, the black male. What do you want me to do with this? It says to notify you with 'Code Red-Confidential.'"

"Bryan, good work. A first time, huh? Well, I'm sure you will see more of these in the next few months. Put the pix and tapes with the transcriptions and identifier numbers in a red envelope and send it to Intelligence Section Review, attention Mr. Mark Foster, with copy to me. Put a rush on it for delivery today. And thanks!" came the reply from James.

Cummings did not have any of the envelopes in which James had requested the information to be sent. He went to the administrative secretary's desk, but she had gone to lunch. He searched for a minute but couldn't find one. He was hungry himself, and his thoughts returned to Miss Simpson and the lovely legs. He needed to get to the cafeteria too, before she finished and went back to her own cubicle. He found a white envelope and wrote on it with a red pen:

RED ENVELOPE—CONFIDENTIAL
FROM: Bryan Cummings, Section 9
ATTN: Mr. Mark Foster, Intelligence Section Review
RUSH—DELIVERY TODAY SURE!!

He placed it in the out-basket of the secretary and went back to his cubicle. He closed his files and computer files, grabbed his sack lunch, and went off to find Ms. Simpson with the lovely legs.

CHAPTER 20
16 January 2001

Van and Maria made their way down the hallway and around the right to his bedroom, still holding hands. He felt her warmth and love come all the way through to him. He was thinking about her as they walked. *Should I explain anymore of my life to her? What should I do about our future together? Should there even be any future for us together?*

They arrived at the room and went in, and he closed and locked the door behind them. Maria went to the bathroom, and Van went over to the windows and opened them all the way to feel the night breeze. He looked at the lights of Santa Rita below and wondered what the next few days and weeks would bring to his life. He had to make a change. He had read the papers, and now what he had done had begun to kill people—not just whites, but other blacks like him. This he could not stand. *Enough!* This would be the last one.

He heard the door to the bathroom open and turned to see Maria standing there in the evening light. She was so beautiful in a cream-colored, silk nightgown that clung to her in all the right places. His eyes moved from her classic face with high cheekbones and bright, dark eyes down to her breasts and lower abdomen.

"Wow, you take my breath away," was all he could say.

Maria smiled the knowing smile of all women at this moment and walked over to Van and put her arms around him. She felt his buttocks and small of his back as she pulled him closer . . . and now the kiss—hungry, demanding, and full.

Van's hands went to her breasts, and he felt they were hard. They were not big, but when he touched her, she let out a small groan of joy. He pulled the straps of the nightgown over her shoulders, and it fell to the floor. He kissed her neck and smelled the sweet perfume she had put on. Her hands were now working quickly to get him out of his slacks. They fell to the floor, and she reached in his undershorts for him and pulled them down. She stroked him in a long kiss as he moved his hand to her womanhood. They were both high with the feelings of anticipation of each other now.

She pulled his shirt off, and, with a quick move, he reached down, picked her up in his arms, and carried her to the bed. She lay there as he began to use his tongue and lips to explore her and bring her to a peak. She felt the emotion building within her, and she cried out and raked her hands over his shoulders. Now, as she made it, she held his head tight to her, and he found all of her.

Maria wanted him. She wanted all of him. She loved him. She pulled on his shoulders, and he moved up over her. She reached down and found him ready for her. She inserted him in her. It was so good. He felt her all around him, and the heat between them made them feel like they were one in body and mind. He felt like this was heaven. As they moved together, their movements became as one body; twisting and in full synchronization and harmony. They worked at giving the other the fullest of pleasure that they each deserved. The more each gave, the more love and fulfillment each received in turn. Even during his twenty years of marriage, Van had never seemed to reach this kind of love peak. Now he knew what making love to and with a woman was all about. *Why had it taken this long?* he thought as the passion consumed him. *Oh, my god, this woman is truly wonderful, and we fit in a most beautiful way. I don't want this to ever end.*

First slowly and then quickly, they made love to each other. The moments passed as they worked the music of magic with each other. Never before had it been like this . . . never.

Van rolled over, and Maria followed—never losing each other. He placed his legs around her, and the movements now brought her to the first of several climaxes. She screamed in his ear with joy as the feelings vibrated every nerve in her body. The sensation was almost beyond bounds of comprehension. She trembled as she lost control and enjoyed the fullest of the pleasure as her climax swept over her, again and again. The high just kept on going to new levels. Oh, how this man made her feel so wonderful!

He groaned, and she could sense his increased tension as he moved toward his climax. She let go and worked to bring him and herself to the moment together.

"Van, now, I need you. Let me have all of you, my dear; give me all of you," she whispered in his ear.

And the moment came. He could hold it no longer. He lost his control, and she held him tightly as she too reached the pinnacle. They shuddered together. They looked and kissed for long moments, tasting each other in this joyful embrace of a man and woman. Ever so slowly, the tension began to subside, and she could feel him slowly retreating from her. She moved off of him and laid beside him, holding him as he held her. She put her head in his upper left arm and looked at him, and they kept kissing each other.

"Oh, my God, I just can't believe this is so wonderful. Van, I love you so much. Please don't ever leave me. I know you must go tomorrow, but I know I must be with you. What can we do?"

"Maria, I love you too. That was the most wonderful moments of my life. I don't even have the words to tell you how terrific you have made me feel," Van replied softly.

"It is not necessary. Your body and embrace told me everything. I felt all of you, and you made me feel more loved and so completely, I think these two days—and especially this night—was God's plan. Yes, I do believe this. I love you." She moved on top of him again and kissed his face and ears and neck.

"Oh, Maria, you taste so good. And your love is so sweet and wonderful. Yes, I must find a way for us to be together, always. Will you come to America and marry me?" The words almost jumped out of his mouth before he knew it, yet this was how he truly felt.

"Van! Oh yes, my darling! I will come to America and marry you." The joy filled her face and body. She trembled again and cried softly, and they embraced this way for a long time. Finally, she gave him another kiss and left him and moved to the bathroom. She ran the shower and felt the warm water glide over all of her. It was wonderful, but not as good as feeling Van insid of her, the passions of each other rising and ebbing and returning with even more intensity. She dried herself off with the big, soft towel and put on her camisole and tap pants. She found the powder in her overnight bag and put some on. When she walked back into the bedroom, Van was asleep. She crawled into the bed beside him, and he stirred as she put her arm around him. When she gave him a kiss, he awoke.

"Maria, you smell like an angel. Oh, my God, this is so heavenly," Van said softly to her. And then he kissed her again, and she kissed him back. They tasted the warmth and love of each other. The kisses would not stop. She could feel herself becoming aroused again, and with her leg, she felt him, too. She wanted him again.

Maria sat up on the bed and pulled the camisole off. She reached for the tap pants, and felt Van's hands join hers, and they went down and off her legs. She reached for him and moved down to take him. He tasted wonderful to her. She kissed him all around and moved up and over him and placed him inside her. She put all of her body on him, and they began the rhythm of a man and a woman together. Again they moved, each wanting only to increase the pleasure of the other.

He could feel his passion rising now quickly. The sensation for him was almost unbearably great.

"Van, come to me, my love. Give me all of you. I want to feel all of you. I love you!" Maria cried into the night.

"Maria, this is so great! Oh, my God, you are terrific!"

The moment came. He moved and was lost in her. He let go with a shudder that rocked them both. He lost control as he held her buttocks next to his lower abdomen and felt the weight of her move to him. She felt his shudder and wanted to kiss him. She moved her body back to feel his lower abdomen on her buttocks. Oh, he felt so good!

He let go of her and fell onto the bed. She turned to him, and, for the second time this night, they embraced longingly. They had enjoyed the love each had given so willingly and fully without holding back—total, unconditional love.

"Maria, I love you."

"Van, I love you too, my sweet."

They stayed this way, just holding each other and letting the passions subside for a while.

"Maria, I'm going to clean up and come back to bed with you. But I must go to sleep and get some rest now. You have drained me, I think, for a while." He smiled.

"Yes, I know. I'll be here when you return, and I'll let you rest. I don't want you to leave tomorrow, but I know you must. Go now."

He got out of the bed where they had made their storms and went to the bathroom. When he returned, he found her standing by the window, gazing out at Santa Rita.

"What are you looking at?" he asked as he came up behind her and placed his arms around her waist

"My home. The city is beautiful this time of year. But I want to leave it for you," she said. She turned around and embraced him and gave him a kiss.

When the kiss ended—and they both thought it might not ever—he said, "I must go to bed. I love you."

"I know, and I love you. Go on and I'll be back in a few minutes."

Maria went into the bathroom and, when she returned, Van was asleep soundly. She got into bed again and put her left arm around him. She relaxed and fell into the sleep of total comfort and peace. She was with the man she loved.

CHAPTER 21

17 January 2001

Jackson awoke to the sound of his travel alarm. It was 5:30 a.m. He opened his eyes some more and could see the first light of morning coming over the hills outside the open window. He felt Maria's arm across his waist and the warm heat of her body curled next to him in sleep. She did not stir with the sound of the alarm. He turned over to face her and held her and kissed her on her cheek and hair. Now she moved some and nuzzled his neck and kissed him.

"Maria, I must leave. Stay here and rest, my love. I'll be back in a few minutes," he whispered.

She nodded her head and turned over.

He got out of bed, made his way to the bathroom, and shaved and showered. He was fully awake now, and he wanted to leave without seeing Carl. He got dressed in the small dressing area next to the bathroom and put on some light tan slacks, a white polo shirt, a blue blazer, and brown loafers. He packed his toilet gear and the clothes he had out back in his overnight bag. He checked his briefcase, determined that nothing had been disturbed, and locked it, removing his passport before he did so. He grabbed the two bags and went back into the bedroom and put them down by the door and walked back to the bed.

"Maria, I must go now," he said to her as he sat down on the bed and stroked her hair.

"Van, I know, I love you. When will I hear from you? Please make it soon," Maria said as she turned over and faced up at him.

"It will be soon. Perhaps in a couple of days. I have a lot to do, but I will call. I love you too. Take care, my wonderful lover. Last night was terrific! I'll be thinking of you all the time. I must go."

And with that, he bent down and kissed her tenderly. She held him close and smelled his cologne. She wanted to remember this moment. She let him go and watched him walk to the door, pick up his bag and briefcase, and leave without looking back. That was his way—never look back.

She looked at the clock and decided it was time for her to get up and go home for breakfast with her mother and her kids before she must leave for work. As she showered, she remembered her feelings for Van and their lovemaking the night before, and she wanted him again. But their time together would have to wait.

She dried off and dressed and put her spare things and makeup in her own small bag before she left. She walked to the front door without seeing anyone, and then she went down the steps quickly and headed home.

CHAPTER 22

17 January 2001

Carl woke up about three thirty and left Dorothea to go outside and check with Roberto. He found him close by in the inner hallway, wide awake, as expected.

"Anything going on, Roberto?" Carl asked his trusted bodyguard in Brazil.

"No, boss, nothing. Van and the woman are asleep. They made love as expected, but both are now out for the night. No problems. The police made a round about an hour ago and looked over the car. But no problems there either. The thousand dollars I paid the police captain a week ago should insure that."

"Anything from Van's bodyguard?"

"No, he is out back by the pool with a good view of the house, as he and I arranged for tonight. He was walking around the lower courtyard about a half-hour ago, but did not come in. He went to the front corner, but no further. He did not come near your room."

Roberto wanted to ask his boss how it had been with the woman, Dorothea, but he knew not to intrude on this private matter. He was paid well to be awake when his boss was sleeping and watch out for trouble all the time Carl was in Brazil. He was paid very well indeed! Still, he wouldn't have minded spending some time with Dorothea himself, but not today, for sure.

"Okay, it seems all is well for now. Have things ready for us to leave about seven. I want to be back in Sao Paulo by eleven at the latest. Pay the housekeeper and bring some coffee for us for the ride in the car. I am going back to bed for awhile."

"No problem. See you at seven."

Carl went back down the hall to the first bedroom—the one that faced the front of the house—and went in. Dorothea was still asleep, and he went to his side of the bed and got back in next to her. He didn't want her now; he just wanted to rest some more. His mind was racing with some plans, but he closed them off and closed his eyes and reached out for the naked woman beside him. He moved closer to her, and she responded in her slumber by backing up to him. He could feel her warmth with him in the cool sheets. Sleep came again to him this way.

His alarm sounded like a small chime. He had been dreaming of a big clock, but the sound coming from it was so small; and he awoke. He reached out for the alarm and turned it off—6:00 a.m. Dorothea woke up and turned over to face him. She gave him a smile and a kiss and got out of bed and walked to the bathroom, leaving him in the bed watching her. She enjoyed the thought of his eyes on her naked back and the curve of her buttocks.

She was quick in the bathroom and began to dress when he came in. He gave her a quick kiss before he removed his shorts and began to shower. She put on her makeup and packed the carry bag with her camisole and tap pants and the blouse, skirt, and underwear from yesterday, and then went into the bedroom to wait for him. She hoped it would not be long, as she now wanted to get to work.

Carl emerged from the dressing area in about ten minutes. He was dressed in a light gray summer suit with a blue shirt and red, printed, silk tie. She thought he looked very handsome. The suit and shirt accented his light gray hair and his blue, very clear eyes. She smiled a genuine, warm smile as he approached her.

"Carl, I must say you look very handsome today. I hope you enjoyed last night and had a good sleep. I enjoyed our moments together very much. I will not forget them. You made me feel so alive and so good. Thank you."

"It was not I, but you who made the evening and night so special. Here is the money for last night. You were terrific; and even more, I have thought I would like you to come to Germany to live with me. Please think about this. I will be in touch in a few days. I hope the rest of the week is good for you. Please expect to hear from me and think things over."

"Yes, I will," she replied, knowing what the answer was already.

"Good, then I must go." He moved closer to her and embraced her. She held him, and they kissed lightly, and then strongly for one last time. She pulled away from him and smiled directly into his eyes.

"I must go too. Be safe and good health. I hope to hear from you soon." She picked up her bags, opened the door, and closed it behind her. She walked down the hall, turned right, and went out the back door to the lower level patio and down the steps to the side street. She walked a block and then hailed a passing taxi to take her to work. The money was safely in her bag, which she held close. As she rode, she thought that this was probably the last time she would see him. She didn't know why she suddenly had that vision, but it was real, and she cried a small tear. She really liked him, but the second evening was different, and there was no love. When she got to work, she pulled out the money and put it in the company safe, with the envelope of money from the previous evening. Today she would make the arrangements for her own deposit and transfer of her funds to the bank in Houston. She felt safe.

As soon as the door closed behind Dorothea, Carl went back to the bathroom and finished his packing. When he was done, he picked up his bags and walked down the hall to the entryway and found Roberto in the small dining room eating some breakfast rolls and drinking dark, heavy coffee in a very small Brazilian cup.

"Roberto, are you ready?"

"Yes, boss, I am ready. Do you want a cup of coffee now before we go? It is very fresh and delicious."

"Yes, I will have one cup and a roll, and then let us go. Have Van and the other woman left?" Carl inquired.

"Yes, he left about a half hour ago. The woman, Maria, left just a few moments before Dorothea. Maria went out the front, and Dorothea went out the back and down the side street. Only we are left along with the housekeeper."

"Good."

Carl held the coffee cup as Roberto poured the dark brew. The aroma was so strong that one almost didn't need to drink it. Carl liked this coffee. He placed three spoonfuls of sugar in the small cup. This was necessary to even drink it. He stirred the mixture that was almost like syrup and tasted it. *Wow,* he thought. *This really wakes you up!* He drank the rest and placed the cup on the table.

"Let us go," Carl announced to Roberto.

"Okay, I am ready, and the car is ready."

Roberto picked up the bag and Carl's briefcase, and they went out the back and down to the side street to the BMW. Roberto put both bags in the trunk as Carl got into the passenger seat. Roberto moved around the car and got in, and they began the drive out of Santa Rita. As they rounded the turn heading up into the hills, Carl looked back at the city nestled among the coffee beans. He thought there were worse places to live. Perhaps he might move here after the new plan was done. This was a quiet place, the food was great, the golf good, and Sao Paulo was close by. And with the money in several bank accounts, one bank in Sao Paulo would be enough to make the transfers and live. *Perhaps I might do this.*

The drive for them was uneventful. Carl actually went to sleep in the car and woke up just as they entered the freeway around Sao Paulo.

CHAPTER 23

17 January 2001

Roberto dropped Carl off at a small office just off of Avenida Paulista in the center of the business section of the massive city. The area was surrounded by many new banks and office buildings. Roberto was under instructions to return that afternoon about two o'clock p.m. to pick up Carl. Roberto drove to his small house and went to sleep after setting the alarm for one o'clock.

Carl made his way to the elevator and went to the seventh floor. He had a small office here that was useful for many things. He had a secretary, Margaretta Monte, who was medium color, slender, and very smart. She did all the money transfers for Carl, and she knew where all the funds were. Carl paid her very well and insured her loyalty by having Roberto look over the work and keep and eye on her.

Margaretta was expecting her boss. "Good afternoon, Señor Carl," she said as he entered the office.

"Margaretta, a pleasant day to you. How have you been?"

"Good. The work is not too hard, and I went to Rio last weekend with some friends. We had a very good time, but the gangs are getting worse. If you go there, be very careful."

"Thanks, but I am not going this trip. In fact I am on the afternoon plane back to Frankfurt and Dusseldorf. I have some arrangements I need you to make today and tomorrow for me."

He went into his small office and unpacked his briefcase. He pulled out a small book filled with coded numbers as Margaretta walked in with a ledger from the safe and a notebook. She knew the procedure well. Carl would detail what transfers he wanted from which account, this would all be given to her in code, and she would make the telex and bank transfers the following day.

Carl went over his own book of numbers and wrote down in her notebook what he wanted done. He explained a particular transfer and wanted that one verbally confirmed and written confirmation on same day. Margaretta knew what to do.

"I think that will take care of all for now. Do you have any questions, Margaretta?" Carl asked when they finished their work.

"No, I have everything, and it will be done as you want. If I have any problems, can I contact you?"

"Yes, but do so by the daily code-book. If you do not get me on the phone the first time, leave the message on the recorder with the code words, and I will call you as soon as I get it. If it is an emergency, use this number."

He took her notebook back and wrote something inside the back cover.

"Whomever answers this, just tell them the 'shipment is behind schedule,' and they will know to get in touch with me immediately, and I will contact you. Do not go out of town again until all these transfers are accomplished and confirmed. I want to be able to contact you immediately if I need to. The next few days are critical. And after this one is done, I will see about a bonus for you, and then you can go on vacation for a while."

"Yes, Carl. I understand, and I will take care of it all."

He got up from the desk and put the books and papers back in the briefcase. He walked around the desk and gave Margaretta a hug and kiss.

"You know you are very special. I could not handle all my affairs alone," he said as he held her for a moment and looked directly into her eyes. What he was trying to detect was any hint of treachery from her. He found none.

"Carl, I thank you for everything. You have my full loyalty. When will I see you again?" she responded.

"Soon. Perhaps in a few weeks. I will have to let you know. I might even stay for a while. But now, I really must go. Ciao,

Margaretta," he said to her as he released her from the embrace and walked out the door.

Margaretta looked at him leave and returned to the notebook. She went to work typing up the few faxes that would be needed and phoning the local bank's senior vice president downstairs to tell him that she needed an appointment within two hours to go over some urgent transfers for her boss. The senior vice president was most willing to meet with her, as this client provided some very nice commission income to the bank and himself for the large company money transfers.

Margaretta was now ready. She locked everything in the safe, walked out, locked the door, and went to lunch.

Durnbacher got downstairs and went to the side street of the building entrance. He found the BMW and Roberto waiting about a half block further down the street. He got in the car, and Roberto drove to the new international airport.

Just before Carl got out of the car at the terminal he said to Roberto, "I feel confident about the woman, Margaretta, but I also want you to watch her the next few days. They are very important to me. Listen to the office phone tapes and see if anything should be followed up. Call me as usual if you see or hear of problems. Also, I may need you to work in the US, so keep a bag packed."

"Okay, boss. No problem."

They were now at the terminal, and Carl and Roberto both got out. Roberto opened the trunk of the BMW and removed the hanging bag for Carl.

"Here it is. I think you have everything. Do you need me to come in?" Roberto asked.

"No, I do not want you in the terminal with me; too many cameras and security. No need for us to be seen together. I will call you in a few days. Remember to contact me if the need is urgent or an emergency. Ciao, Roberto." Carl waved to his friend and bodyguard as he walked to the terminal door.

"Ciao, boss." Roberto got back in the BMW and drove off back to the office.

Carl walked up to the Lufthansa counter and checked in. He was flying business class again back to Frankfurt. Normally, he might take a flight to Buenos Aires and stay there a day or two before going back to Dusseldorf, but, on this trip, there was not enough time. He had to take a few chances that he didn't like taking, but events in South Africa were moving quickly, and this shipment needed to get on the water. He wanted the shipment made, get it received, and then keep the money. He also had to begin to work on some new plans regarding his partnership with Jackson.

He found a seat in the Lufthansa VIP lounge in the back, where he could see everyone come and go. The flight was called about an hour later, and, after the walk to the gate, he was finally on and settled in his seat. The giant 747 took off and turned out over the Atlantic for the long flight back to his own country. It would be good to get home. He felt safe there. He had many friends there to protect him.

* * *

Jackson arrived at the same airport about an hour after Carl. They didn't see each other, since Jackson was flying on the American Airlines flight to Miami that evening. He was returning to New Orleans via the fastest route, and he knew he was taking some risks. But he too had work to do, and there was not time to take a more circuitous route. After he checked in, he went directly through the Brazilian customs area and to the gate. He knew the police didn't want him, but he felt that everyone seemed to be under watchful eyes these days.

His flight was called, and he boarded with the first group. He took his seat on the aisle near the front of business class and stowed the bag and briefcase. Now came the interminable wait to see who and what kind of person might take the seat next to him. He always hoped that the seat might be open, but the flights had been full for several months now.

Then he saw him. He was coming down the aisle very confidently. The man was about forty-five, white, and wearing tan slacks, a polo shirt, and a sweater. He carried a briefcase and hanging bag that seemed not too full. He looked directly at Jackson as he arrived at the seat.

"Hi, I have 13-K. Please excuse me."

"No problem," replied Jackson as he got out of the seat.

The man put his hanging bag in the overhead compartment and slid the briefcase under the seat in front of him and sat down by the window.

"My name is Doug Edwards. What is yours? Looks like we will be seatmates."

Jackson sat back down and responded, "Clarence Jackson, but most people call me Van. What business are you in?"

"I'm in the heavy-construction-equipment business. Just wrapped up a nice deal with Vilares. But I'm tired and plan to sleep just as soon as I can get a drink and some dinner. Hope you don't mind."

Jackson was now relieved. Great, not an all-night talker. He needed the rest too. "Okay with me. I think I'll do the same."

After take off, they talked about the weather in Brazil and the football playoffs in the US. Finally, after each made a trip to the lavatory, both put on their eyeshades, put in their earplugs, covered up with their blankets—carefully keeping their seatbelts on top so it would be visible to a flight attendant if needed, and they went to sleep.

After a brief breakfast before the very early arrival in Miami, they talked for a while more, but only about sports again and the college basketball season. Finally, they landed on time in Miami.

Jackson said good-bye to Edwards as they walked to the US Customs area. Both headed for the blue lane—a new, special lane for US citizens where their personal information had already been partially processed from information sent by the airline while they were flying. Jackson was only asked how long he was gone, and he was through. He went down the escalator to the baggage-claim area, where it seemed pandemonium reigned all the time. Since he was carrying both of his bags, he did not have to wait for the checked baggage from the flight. He walked directly to the final customs inspector, who, after giving his form a close inspection, waved him on to the exit door.

Jackson went outside into the lower area of the Miami terminal and took the escalator back up to the ticketing level, where he checked in for the New Orleans flight. He walked down the D concourse to Gate 16 and waited. As he sat there, he thought about all the international flights he had taken. Most people thought that international travel was glamorous, but mostly it was tedious, with much waiting.

The flight boarded on time and was rather uneventful back to the Crescent City and home. He was glad when it arrived; he was tired.

He walked out to the parking garage and found his car on the third level. He drove straight home, looked at the mail for a moment, and decided to take a shower and a nap. The bed felt great! There was now a lot to do, but he was really tired from this trip. He fell asleep within minutes.

* * *

Carl arrived in Frankfurt at 7:30 a.m. The flight was long—over thirteen hours, but uneventful. He had slept for almost seven and felt rested by the time the plane landed. He had sketched out some ideas in his mind during the flight. It was actually a good time to do that kind of thing, since there were no phones, no faxes, and no interruptions—just the dull sound of the engines whining.

Carrying his two bags, he made his way off the plane with all the passengers and looked at the terminal screens to see that he had to go to C-36 for his flight to Dusseldorf. He walked toward the customs official, a very young man seated behind the counter, wearing the uniform of an olive drab shirt and dark green pants. He gave most of the passengers only a very quick look at their passport, but, as Carl moved closer, he noticed that the other customs guard—the one standing next to the enclosure and caring the automatic rifle—was staring at him. Carl tried not to appear unnerved, but he could feel his heart begin to quicken. Was he imagining this? Why couldn't he handle this type of pressure anymore? Was he getting too old for this? He knew he was wanted for questioning by Interpol, but would border guards look that carefully? Which passport should he show? Now was the time to make a move, but if he made one too quickly, the one with the rifle might call for assistance. *No scene now. Just stay cool. Play out the hand*, he thought.

Carl moved forward, and the one with the rifle moved closer to the customs kiosk and maintained his stare. The official inside was looking at the papers of the person in line ahead of Carl, and now, another morning 747 had arrived spilling out its load of passengers, all tired and looking very weary and impatient. The line behind Carl was growing rapidly in length.

The man ahead picked up his briefcase and went around the kiosk out of sight. Carl picked up his bag and moved forward. He gave his passport to the official with a tired smile.

"Good morning," Carl offered.

"Umm," came the bored reply.

The one with the rifle shuffled his weight on his feet but kept looking at Carl, as if to see if he could find some important feature. There was none on Carl that could be seen.

"Where have you been, Mr. Durnbacher?" came the question. The official was not entering the name in the computer—just looking at the passport pages with the same bored expression.

"Only to Brazil. I went there to visit my office."

"I didn't ask you why, only where you went. You do not need to offer anything more than just answer the questions asked. Please don't take up my time further. Welcome back."

"Thank you," Carl replied and moved around the kiosk counter. He never looked at the man with the rifle, but the man kept looking at him.

As Carl moved on down the hallway toward Terminal C, the rifle guard opened the door to the kiosk and asked his friend, "Who was that man? What was his name? He looks familiar for some reason."

"Some Mr. Durnser. His passport was fully in order. Please, Jurgen, leave me alone and watch for trouble among the passengers in line. I'll take care of the passports. Look at all these people out there. Why not walk to the end of the line and look them over. Next!"

The rifle guard moved his head out of the kiosk and closed the door. He did not like to be told what to do by this corporal, but his duty today was clear. He decided to forget about the interesting man and get on with his job. He moved down the line, but he couldn't get it out of his mind. He kept trying to figure out what made him interesting, but couldn't quite put his finger on it. He decided to talk with his sergeant at the break. There was something there.

Carl was now almost to Terminal C by the time the private had made his decision to talk with another supervisor. The passage through security was easy. Carl moved to the gate area and checked in. He went inside and found the breakfast bags and coffee that Lufthansa provided. The flight was called, and he flew on to Dusseldorf. When he arrived, his male housekeeper and bodyguard were outside waiting with his dark-brown Mercedes 300SE, the motor running and the car warm inside. They exchanged quick greetings and a handshake, the bags were placed in the trunk, and Carl moved into the backseat to read the morning paper during the ride to his home.

Later that same afternoon, after he showered and changed, he went to his engineering company office. Now it was time to make the arrangements and put some new plans in place.

He worked at his computer and made out a fax to send to a small private security company in Durban. The fax read:

TO: Mr. David Mbutu
Managing Director
Sentry Security Services Pty. Ltd.
Durban, South Africa

FROM: C. Durnbacher
Manusafe GmbH
Dusseldorf, Germany

DATE: 18 January 2001
SUBJECT: Shipment 15 February

Please wire transfer amount of USD 2,500,000 immediately to account in Bahamas Third International Bank, account no. TZ-64-57098. Upon receipt and bank confirmation, shipment will proceed with your P.O. 5576 for container of various machine parts per our discussion and agreement of 12 Dec 2000. Once the container is loaded, we will advise complete shipping details and furnish via courier the bill of lading for you to claim goods at port. These documents will be sent upon confirmation of receipt of final payment of USD 2,500,000 at time of shipment.

Regards.

He faxed this after reading it over several times. He was always taking a chance this way, but it was necessary to have a few documents in place for possible inspection. Generally, he didn't worry, as the German customs officials and the police force did not necessarily look at these transmissions. He dialed the number, watched the fax machine move the original through, and received confirmation of receipt on the other end. He put this all together in a small file in a safe behind his desk.

Next he made a local call to a close friend of his. They decided to meet the next day at the fountain by the large convention center near the airport. Since there was a furniture trade show in progress, they would give the appearance of two businessmen having a discussion.

He made a call to Tampa. The woman on the other end was surprised to hear from him. Carl wanted her to go to New Orleans, but he wanted her to drive there so she would not have to fly and rent a car. He had a very special job for her. She would find the instructions when she arrived at the Hilton out by the New Orleans airport; they would be sent by courier. She agreed to leave later that day after making some arrangements. She would be in New Orleans late the following evening.

Carl leaned back in his chair and looked out at the river, the gray Rhein, and at the snow falling. He loved it here, but his thoughts went back to the warmth and beauty and privacy of Santa Rita. He would go back. He packed everything into his briefcase and went home.

CHAPTER 24

16 January 2001

About 1:20 p.m., the mail clerk came by the secretary's desk and found the envelope in the out-basket. He was observant and saw the address and message, so he knew this was hot and placed it in the "code-red" area of his mail cart before going on to the next stations. After he returned to the sorting room, he took all the code-red envelopes, including the only white one among them, and walked them over to the Intelligence and Operations wing. He dropped the others off as noted and found Mr. Foster's office.

"Mr. Foster, I've got a code red for you from Section 9—Mr. Cummings. It's not in a red envelope per regulations, but someone has written on it that this is what it is supposed to be," the mailperson said to Foster.

Foster looked up from the piles on his desk and replied, "Thank you. Please put on top of this third stack."

About four o'clock p.m., Foster came back from the men's room and saw the envelope still waiting for him. He picked it up as he sat down and looked over the contents.

"Wow, Durnbacher himself. What the hell is he doing in Brazil, making a deal? And who is that with him? A black. Brazilian? African? American? Indian?" he said to the walls. He called in Kelly Tegarro from across the hall. "Kelly, what do you think of our boy, Durnbacher? Any ideas?" Foster asked.

"Must be something going down again or getting ready to. I think we should contact Brazilian customs and get a reading on who has been there for the past few days. We must make it look like a routine inquiry. We don't want them to know about the satellite. I think Mr. D. has got himself a friend, and somehow a deal is working. I wonder for whom."

Foster replied, "I'll send a fax to Brazilian customs—our contact Antonio Guerra."

"What else?" asked Tegarro

"Let's put a direct tracer on Durnbacher's office line."

"We can't do that! The German government will never allow us without more hard evidence. You know how they feel," Tegarro said.

"Did I say anything about telling or asking the German government?" Foster replied, giving Tegarro an interesting smile.

"Mark, you just can't. This one will come back to us, and we'll find ourselves doing farming in the enclosed area of the federal penitentiary in Marion, Illinois, for a few years. Do you want to risk that?"

"Yeah, I think I would for this guy. We've got a big file on him, a lot to go on for suspicion, but no hard proof. And this time might just be what we need to get a smoking gun and nail the bastard and at least find out who is paying him. Yeah, it's worth it this time. Call Peterson in Ops and have him do it. Let's get a tap on the lines and get his faxes and phone calls both. Let's put a modem close by and feed direct to our EPXZ47 satellite. I'll send you an e-mail now to cover you. Okay?"

"Okay," Tegarro replied, very reluctantly. "I still don't like this, but if you will cover me in case of the fall, I do agree it might be worth it for Durnbacher and who is paying him. I'll get on it."

"Terrific. Let me know when the tap is made. Ask Peterson to have the raw info sent to us for review. This is too hot for Section 9. I'll tell the chief what is going on, but I'll protect him. Let's make it happen."

Tegarro left and sent the e-mail to Peterson. The next day, the order went out to a small company in Essen to go to Dusseldorf and do another job for the CIA. By midnight, the tap was in, and the satellite uplink in place. Data began downloading on the third day to NSA at Fort Meade, Maryland. Direct transmittal to Foster was accomplished within two hours of download.

It was Sunday when the data was transmitted via confidential secure link to Foster's computer terminal. A copy was also sent to Tegarro across the hall.

Monday was a holiday. No one there. Foster woke up that day with cramps in his stomach. He was getting the flu. *Dammit, he thought, what a shitty time for this.* He stayed in bed between his trips to the bathroom, and, when Tuesday morning came, he knew he just couldn't make it in. He called the administrative secretary and told her he would try to be in the next couple of days. He didn't come back until Thursday.

Tegarro got a call on Monday night at home from Peterson. He was needed in Miami to stake out a drug lord. He flew down on the early morning American flight from Reagan National Airport and was out of his office until the following Monday.

The piles were higher now on this Thursday for Foster. He worked the in-basket first, since it held several new code reds. About ten thirty, Foster finally decided to review the e-mails. As he booted up and typed in his password, he waited with expectation for the usual "You have XXX e-mails." He was rewarded with the message now he only had forty-four to get through. Not bad for only four days.

He scanned them and saw the data-message transmittal from Langley about data from the Durnbacher tap. He opened a file and loaded the data directly to it for review later and then went onto the rest of the e-mail messages. At one p.m., Peterson called him to come over for a briefing, and he was there all afternoon. When he returned, he felt too tired to continue this day and closed up his files.

Friday morning, he came in feeling much better. He had already decided to take a look at the Durnbacher info first thing. As he read through the raw phone conversations, he saw that a deal was in progress and how the money was being transferred. He needed to get a handle on the transfers out of Bermuda, and that would give him a clue as to who was receiving the funds. But it was clear now who was paying for this one: a security firm in Durban. This had to be arms for the KwaZulu.

"Greg, this is Jack. We got a hit on the risk tap with Durnbacher," Jack phoned immediately to Peterson. "It's the KwaZulu in Natal for this container. No real information where it is originating from in this data. However, there is an interesting phone call to a Nina Carlton in Tampa. He wants her to go to New Orleans and take care of a few 'loose ends,' as he said. Isn't she a hit-woman for the mob in Miami?"

"Yes, she was in on the job to knock off Carlos Esteban last year for them. A great-looking woman, and very slick with the night rifle, so we hear," Peterson replied.

"I think we ought to see where she turns up in the Crescent City. Okay if I call Preau down there and let him go to work on it?"

Peterson said, "No problem. Call him and give him some background. Let him know Durnbacher is involved. Have him do the usual checks to see when our Miss Carlton shows up and what she does to keep herself out of trouble."

"Done. Anything else? Can we get to the records in Bermuda for the funds transfer? Know anyone there that can help?" Foster asked again.

"That's a tough one. I don't think so. Let's do at least an analysis of the funds going in. And we do know where the money is coming from originally. I think we should let a few of our new friends in South Africa know about this one and let them work on it. What do you think?" Peterson inquired.

"I agree. I'll send a message to the embassy in Pretoria to make another contact with the new Mandela government and see if they want to move on this. It will be difficult though if they do. Mandela has to keep the KwaZulu happy, and he has several of them in the cabinet. I feel sure that if we go too far with this, someone there will get wind, and the deal will stop. This is our chance to nail Durnbacher—especially the next time he comes to our shores. Okay with you?"

"Yes," Peterson said. "You're right on target. I think this is the chance to get Mr. D., if we have all our ducks in a row. I've got to go, so talk with you Monday unless anything comes up this weekend. Get some more rest too. Bye."

Foster put the phone down and made out a secure fax to intelligence head in Pretoria, advising him of the developing situation and to not disclose it to the Mandela government until authorized later. He also sent an e-mail to Larry Preau in New Orleans about Nina Carlton.

As he went out to his car in the vast parking lot, he thought about what he had learned: there was a deal going on now with Durnbacher, a hit-woman was being sent to New Orleans for some reason, and a security firm in Durban was placing the order and the money. Who was going to be hit by Carlton and why? Would Durnbacher come to the US before they had enough on him? And the biggest question of all—where was this arms shipment coming from? He drove home thinking about all these, but there just wasn't any sense to it yet.

Monday, Foster returned to the office, but there was no real new information in the latest download from NSA. He put the files in his hold basket and went on to the rest of his work.

Just before noon, Tegarro stopped by and asked Foster about the Durnbacher information. They talked about it, but neither one could come to any conclusions just yet. They both agreed the Carlton involvement was not good for someone, but the question was whether it had anything to do with the shipment, or whether it was related to another deal of Durnbacher's that had gone somewhat sour.

CHAPTER 25
19 January 2001

Van Dyke Jackson arrived at his office building on Magazine Street a little before seven a.m. He greeted everyone there and in his contracting operations area by name before moving to his office.

After reviewing the weekly operations log, sales report, collections report, and work schedule, he could now work on the special project that was the reason for his visit to Santa Rita and meeting with Durnbacher. As he dialed the first number, he thought to himself that this would be the last time for sure.

"Jake, this is Van. How ya doin', my man?" Van asked when the phone was answered.

"Van! Great. You just caught me goin' out the door. Another two minutes, and I would have missed you. I got a short run today to Mobile, and the load is waitin'," Jake Briscoe replied.

"Can you let it go for a few minutes? I need to see you about a project uptown. Can you meet in half an hour in the parking lot next to the McDonald's at Clearview and Jeff Highway?"

"Yeah, man, no problem. I'll see you there." Jake hung up the phone. He knew it was a special deal.

Jackson next called Bobby Jeff Littleton in Meridian. Bobby Jeff was not in at his office. Jackson left word that he would call in the afternoon, and he left to go meet Jake.

Jackson drove out to I-10, got off at Clearview, and went south toward the Huey P. Long Bridge over the Mississippi. Just before the bridge ramp, there was a McDonald's on the west side of the street in front of a small shopping center. He drove in the parking lot and saw a black Porsche parked so it could look out at the traffic making its way through the intersection and up on the bridge. Jackson backed his Jaguar into the space next to the driver's side and rolled down the window.

"Jake, how is the world treating you today?" Jackson asked with a big smile.

"Like I said, man, any better, and I would have to take a bad pill. What's up?"

"I got a project worth a hundred bills—half now and half at delivery. Just a short little run like the last time, but maybe no waiting time on this end. Same place, same destination. Okay?"

"Got it. Tell me when."

"I don't have that arranged yet. I'll just get back to you, but it will be in the next ten days for sure. Here's the first part." He handed across the short distance a large plain envelope with the $50,000.

"Great, try to give me a least five days in order to get my schedule worked out. But if not, I can do it with perhaps two hours minimum. Okay?"

"No problem. I'll call soon. See ya!" Jackson said to Jake as he waved good bye, put the car back in gear, and drove out.

Jake looked in the envelope and decided to go downtown to his deposit box at the security center. This would take another hour before he could get in the truck for the trip to Mobile, but it was worth it. Maybe he would reduce the rate a little for the guy since, he would not get to Mobile now before 4:00 p.m. He drove away smiling. *Another $100K! Yes!*

Jackson returned to the office after making a stop at city hall for a bid and lunch with his lawyer. He called Bobby Jeff and was connected quickly.

"Bobby Jeff, what's goin' on up there in beautiful Meridian these days? Are you stayin' out of trouble?" Jackson asked of his grade-school friend.

"Van, I'm takin' it easy like I always did, you know that. And I stay away from trouble. It comes searchin' for me. I don't have to go lookin' for it," He laughed.

"Meet me in Slidell tonight if you can. We need to catch up on a couple of things." This last line was a prearranged code between them that Jackson needed Bobby Jeff Littleton to work a deal at the armory.

"Gotcha. How about the Wal-Mart parking lot on Gause Boulevard about eight p.m.? If I'm late, just wait. I'll get there. Okay?"

"Okay, see you then. Bye." Jackson hung up.

Jackson worked until six thirty, and then drove to Slidell, about twenty miles east of downtown New Orleans. He pulled into the Wal-Mart parking lot and saw the blue Olds in a row by the east side of the big lot. He pulled into the spot next to his friend and got out. Bobby Jeff got out at the same time.

"Hey, bro, how's it goin?" Bobby Jeff asked and gave Jackson a firm handshake. Bobby Jeff was about six foot four, two hundred and fifty pounds, and all muscle. He was an Afro American like Jackson and had gone to school with him. They had been friends for over fifty years. Together, Bobby Jeff almost overwhelmed the smaller Jackson, but they had never fought—never.

"Got a special deal. Same as last time. You'll need some help. Do you need me to get someone from home to help you?"

"No, man, I can handle it. I'll use Fred Jenkins. He helped the last time, and we can trust him. I'll need the cash for the big boss though, ASAP; know what I mean?" Bobby replied.

"I'll have it in about five days, but we need to load in less than ten. I don't know the exact date, but how much time do you need?"

"I've got to have minimum of two days; no way with less than that, and no way on a weekend for sure, as you know."

"Gotcha. I'll bring the money to Hattiesburg, and we can meet in the Gulf truck-stop parking lot. Will that work?" Jackson asked.

"Works like a greased skillet, man. No problem. Anything else I ought to know about?"

"No, not really, but this might be the last. What do you think about that?"

"It's okay with me. These are hard, mostly, but the money is good, and everyone gets well, you know, for a while. I have saved most of mine, so it don't really matter one way or another to me."

"Good, I'm glad for you, my friend."

They talked for a while more and walked to the front of Wal-Mart and each bought a Dr. Pepper from the machine. They drank the cold drinks, leaning against Bobby Jeff's car and talking about mutual friends in Wiggins and Hattiesburg. Finally, they shook hands, got in their cars, and headed home.

As Jackson drove back to New Orleans, he thought of the friends he had and how Bobby Jeff had always been there for him—just like Jake, but Jake was white. It was not the same.

Jackson got home about nine thirty p.m. and went to bed. This had been a big day, with more like it to come.

CHAPTER 26

23 January 2001

Four days later, when Jackson got into the office, he had a fax from Brazil. The money was transferred to the account he kept for this at Hibernia. He would have to go downtown.

He walked into the central office of Hibernia Bank on Common Street and went up to the receptionist. He asked to see Mr. William Blevins, the senior vice president. She made a phone call and took him back to the executive offices.

The meeting with Blevins was short. The money had been transferred, confirmation received. Jackson wrote out a draft and gave it to Blevins. Blevins took it and walked over to the head cashier, waited, and came back with a small briefcase the bank had furnished many customers like Jackson for this amount of cash. One would think the withdrawal of $400,000 did not happen often in this day and age of telex and telegraphic and computer transfers of money, yet, in New Orleans and several other port cities, it happened frequently. Cash made the shipping of goods always go easier, and cash in New Orleans was a staple item in the local food chain of the economy.

Blevins counted out the funds and smiled at Jackson. He knew that, when he got home, his wife would be holding onto an envelope with $20,000. Another year at Tulane for his daughter was paid by someone else for just doing his job and keeping his mouth shut. Not a bad job at the bank.

Jackson took the briefcase, shook hands with Blevins, and left. He went down the street to the Security Center and put all but $20,000 in the box. That he put into an envelope that he took uptown to Blevins wife.

Back at the office, he called Bobby Jeff. "Bobby, we are ready. Meet me in Hattiesburg tonight?"

"Yeah, I'll be there about nine thirty. See you there." Bobby hung up.

About six p.m., Jackson drove back downtown and got $250,000 out of the security center. He drove up to Hattiesburg in the evening rush hour traffic out of the city, but by the time he got to Picayune, Mississippi, he could go about seventy miles per hour without any trouble. After another hour's drive, he got to the big Gulf truck stop north of town. He didn't see Bobby Jeff's car, so he waited and listened to the radio.

About 9:40 p.m., Bobby Jeff drove in and parked next to Jackson. They got out of the cars and shook hands strongly, with an arm on each other's shoulder.

"It's in the car. $250,000 now and another $250,000 after the container is on the boat. Okay?" said Jackson.

"That will work, my man. Everything set for the fifth. Lock and load! Let's get this done," Bobby Jeff said.

"I agree with that, man. Here it is. Take care." Jackson gave Bobby the small briefcase with the money. They smiled, and shook hands again, got back in their cars, and left in opposite directions on I-59 for home.

Jackson called Jake the next morning. "Jake, all set. February 5. See you later."

"Got it. Get the container at J&B, same as last time?" Jake asked.

"Yea. That is all set too. Be careful."

"I will. Talk with you on the sixth. Bye."

Jackson got up from his desk and walked to the window. He looked out on the traffic on Magazine Street and could feel the hate somehow leaving him. His own business was doing well, and he had the money he needed to retire. It was time to arrange some personal things in his life. He sat back down, called his lawyer, and made an appointment for that afternoon. He called Maria at her office and told her to come up to New Orleans by the end of March. He would have a ticket for her to pick up at the American Express Office at the airport in Sao Paulo. He wanted to get his life in order again. The guilt of all these years was eating at him; it was time to release himself from his pain of over forty years. He needed to feel free. He needed to feel good.

CHAPTER 27

5 February 2001

Jake Briscoe backed his tractor and hitched up to the empty cargo container at the J&B Freight Forwarders warehouse on France Road, along the Industrial Canal in New Orleans. He had made this little run twice before. The money this time would be enough to buy that condo over on Destin Beach he wanted. He already had the first payment for this run of $50,000 in the special safety deposit box at the security center in downtown New Orleans. This was a place where they would ask your name only once, and the numbered box and account were very private. Access was guaranteed twenty-four hours a day.

He pulled the forty-foot container on its trailer out onto the main avenue and the entrance ramp to eastbound I-10. Slowly he made his way up the high-rise bridge over the Industrial Canal as the sun turned orange in the clouds behind him. He gathered speed now for the run through East New Orleans, past the car lots, the almost abandoned shopping center, and the bayou. Quickly he crossed the five-mile bridge over the Chef Menteur that was the link between the Gulf of Mexico and Lake Pontchartrain. As he passed the midpoint in the bridge, he looked into his side rearview mirror and could see the brilliantly smoldering red sun now setting in the lake horizon. *Wow!* he thought. *This is beautiful. I love it living here and I'm going to love that new condo. Why, I might even retire from this job of driving for a living.*

Jake Briscoe was from Hattiesburg, Mississippi. He was about six foot one, two hundred and twenty pounds, and was developing that paunch in his middle. He had medium brown eyes and a small scar on the left lower part of his chin. His hair was beginning to gray, but it was still full. He exercised regularly to keep himself fit, and he tried to avoid drinking too much beer. That part of his regimen was very hard.

Jake had been driving a truck since he learned this trade in his ten years in the army. He knew plenty of people in the local southern Mississippi and Louisiana areas. He could count on his close friend, ol' Van Dyke Jackson, to give him a little boost now and then. Jake had served in the quartermaster corps unit that Jackson had commanded, and he and the old man had become close—even if Jackson was black and Briscoe was white. They had drunk more than a few bottles of beer and sometimes bourbon whiskey at a joint near Alexandria, Louisiana, when the unit was stationed at Fort Polk. It was in those interesting evenings together that Briscoe and Van Dyke partied and developed a bond. Now, Jake was working a little special job for Van Dyke. The money was good, and everyone got some. "Win-win, all the way, I always say," was Briscoe's favorite line.

The terrain changed as he left I-10 and headed northeast on I-59 for his destination, Meridian, Mississippi, still some four hours away. *Great, that will put me there on schedule about midnight,* he thought. *Then another quick four to five hours back to Desire Street Docks and unload the container about dawn.* The ship was to sail on the 10:30 a.m. tide down the Mississippi River to the Gulf of Mexico, to Charleston, South Carolina, and next stop, Durban, South Africa.

About 9:35 p.m., he decided to take a break at the large truck stop just at the north edge of Hattiesburg. Here he might see one of his old buddies for a coffee, followed by just another two and a half hours to Meridian. He pulled into the big Gulf Oil truck stop and was almost run over as he got out of the truck by a small station wagon. It was full of girls—"Judies," everyone called them. These were the local truck-stop prostitutes that would spend from fifteen minutes to all night in your truck bed with you, depending only on how much a driver wanted to spend. A quick "half-and-half"—a short suck and short, quick fuck—was thirty to fifty dollars, depending on the time of night and how good a negotiator one was. An all-nighter was more like two hundred. The station wagon had the windows rolled down, and a woman in the back left recognized Briscoe.

"Jake, honey! How about a date tonight? I think I really need you and that big one you got," she called out to him laughingly.

"Not tonight, Janey," he said with a huge smile on his face. *Why spend a little money on pussy when I can make some big ones myself,* he thought. *There will be plenty of time for action later.*

"Aw, Jake, I need it and the bread. Can't you just spend a few short minutes with me? You know I'll give you the best head in Hattiesburg. Why, maybe the best in all Mississippi!"

"Nope. And Janey, you take care, you hear?"

"Okay, baby, come back and find me some night. See ya."

The station wagon started moving again, with the girls looking around for prospective johns for their nightly work.

Jake walked to the big building that served as the center of the truck stop and went in. His first destination was the restroom for some relief from that earlier coffee. He washed up and went out into the main dining room and saw his cousin, W.W. Grayson, over at the counter.

"Hi, Dub, how you doin', boy? How's your ma? Has she gotten over that flu?" he asked as he sat down on the stool next to Grayson.

"Why, Jake, how you doin'? Thanks. My ma is okay now and back home from the hospital. What brings you up this way tonight?"

"Just a short run around the ol' state tonight. Back home tomorrow. Where you headed?" Jake asked.

"I'm workin' a load up to Louisville. Got some lumber for a floorin' mill up there. Some nice money, and it's maybe goin' to get steady. At least I hope so. The rest of the work around here ain't so hot."

"Well, I hope you do well."

The coffee was served, and they sat there for a few minutes and talked about local neighbors and friends. Jake had been two grades ahead of his cousin, and had always called him Dub, which in these parts was correct for someone that had the two initials of *W*. This was common in the South. Their mothers were sisters and very close, and Jake and Dub grew up together. As a result they saw and did things with each other; they had learned to swim at the same YMCA in town, and, when Dub finally got to high school, it was his big cousin and senior, Jake, who had taught him the ropes about how to get around, meet the girls that were fun and the ones that were even more fun, and how to stay out of trouble. Dub would always be grateful and close to Jake for the education of those years—education that didn't come in the classroom!

Finally, Jake pulled the last gulp on his second cup and laid three dollars on the counter. He yelled to the waitress, "Peggy, I got to go. Here is some money, and you keep the rest. See you soon."

"Bye, Jake, take care of yourself. Let me know when we might go to the honky-tonk over in Beaumont for some dancin' and action. Okay?"

"You bet. Dub, I'll give you a holler next week and see if you're in. You take care too. Tell your ma I said hey." Jake got to his feet, giving Dub a strong handshake and pat on the arm with his other hand. Both smiled as he left. He felt very good now.

The truck started up right away, and, after checking the tires and hoses all around, Jake got back in and pulled out onto the service road and up to the stop sign at the intersection. He waited for a big, long Mayflower moving van to cross, and then he moved ahead, through the intersection, and down the entrance ramp, back onto northbound highway I-59.

At 12:30 p.m., Jake Briscoe pulled off I-59 at exit 91. He went along the service road about a mile and turned to the right down a very nicely paved two-lane street. He could see clearly his first destination on this trip, the local Mississippi National Guard Armory up ahead in a tree clearing. The building only had one window and was surrounded by asphalt. He could see some infantry carriers, trucks, miscellaneous vehicles, and five Humvees at the back perimeter. He stopped the truck and turned off the lights about three hundred yards from the gate. Around the entire edge of the perimeter was a twelve-foot-high fence with two feet of razor wire on top of that. The gate was imposing for an NG location. It was backed up by a concrete barrier that was now raised, but could be lowered in the ground by the duty officer, if there was one. Tonight, that would be—Bobby Jeff Littleton, another close friend of Mr. Clarence van Dyke Jackson.

Briscoe flashed his lights four times very quickly and waited, ready to back the truck into the small dirt road just behind the trailer in case someone might come along unexpectedly. If needed, he would always say he was lost and just trying to get this dammed thing turned around and back out to the main highway. He had a fake move order from the forwarder for a load of heaters from a manufacturing plant about another klick up the side road.

But tonight, plan B would not be necessary. A flashlight now spoke its quick message with three short flicks and one long one. Jake put the lights back on and moved toward the fence. He could see the concrete barrier now dropping into the ground and the gate beginning to open. He put out the truck lights and the trailer running lights. *This is the tricky part,* he thought. *I have to get this little bird inside the fence and backed up to the loading dock in total darkness. Don't want the Mississippi Highway Patrol that just might be wanderin' around to see this truck movin'. No problem once I'm parked. Keep cool, Jake,* he said to himself. *You've done it twice before, you know where the marker point is to begin your backup, so look for that big pine by the corner.*

Jake pulled the truck all the way into the lot and could see the fence gate closing behind him and the barrier rising back into position. He turned the wheel left and swung the truck and trailer around and stopped. He was pointed at the big pine by the corner. Now he looked in his side rearview mirror and could see the truck dock and loading door. He shifted into reverse and maneuvered it back slowly. He knew he was almost there. After driving a truck for all these years, the really good drivers can almost feel the dock before the truck hits it, even though there is almost fifty feet separating them. He felt it, and he rode the clutch with just a bare movement of the truck and trailer. *Thud.* Home free so far. He left the engine in idle, set the brake, and put the truck in neutral. He got out of the cab and walked backed to the dock and up the steps by the side to the small, heavy, steel door on the side of the building. He knocked and waited. The door opened, and a light was put directly on his face.

"You got business here tonight?" came the question from behind the light.

"Mr. Clap sent me," was Briscoe's answer. *Clap*, of course, was old army slang for VD, venereal disease, and now it conveniently referred to "V.D." Jackson.

"Okay, the goods are ready," the voice answered.

This was the signal for Jake to go and open up the trailer doors and go back to the truck cab.

He sat there for about half an hour. He could hear the goods being loaded in the container. It didn't take a rocket scientist to figure out what was probably going in there, but he really didn't want to know. And he didn't care where it was headed. The money was just too damn good to care.

Jake heard the doors being closed and locked by someone. A voice called out again, "Okay, come on back here now and put your lock on this. It is supposed to have a double-safety lock and identification tag. I'll put the light down low so you can see what you are doing."

Jake got out of the cab again and walked back to the end of the container. He carried his big Master Lock and a stainless-steel identification tag. He walked up the steps and could see well, because of the flashlight shining on the loading dock area. He moved to the back doors of the container, found the open lock nest, put his lock through it, and closed it. Next came the identification tag. It was looped through both locks, closed, and clamped shut. This identification tag was not actually his number, but was a fake driver ID.

Clarence van Dyke Jackson was the only person, so far, who knew this number. He had impressed the tag himself earlier that afternoon in his workshop and taken it in a sealed envelope out to B&J.

Briscoe's job was now half over. He walked back to the truck, put it in gear, and released the clutch. The loaded container and truck now drove significantly different than it had on the run up from New Orleans. He could feel the weight of the load strain the engine, but this truck had the power for almost anything. He moved forward slowly, turning the wheel to the left again to head out of the armory. He saw the barrier down and the gate open, so he moved ahead in the gears and picked up a little more speed. He was out beyond the fence now and could see the gate and barrier moving back into position. He continued up the street and stopped at the main road before turning right.

His nervous state got to him now. He just had to take a quick leak. He got out of the truck again, moved around to the back, and stood there, relieving himself on the new spring vegetation by the ditch. *Ah, yes, this is necessary,* he felt.

Afterward, he went back to the cab, climbed in, and built speed back up along the main road. A couple of klicks later, at an intersection, Briscoe turned the truck to the left. He followed this about three miles and came back to the interstate. No entrance here, but the service road along the north side of the interstate would take him back to exit 91 in another four miles. *Just one big circle route,* he thought. *Now to get this mother back to New Orleans without trouble.* He cruised along carefully here, not exceeding the speed limit of forty-five miles per hour. He reached the intersection that made exit 91 on the interstate, went through it after a careful stop, and back on southbound I-59.

"Rock 'n' roll!" he yelled to no one as put in his current favorite, *Best of Fleetwood Mac.* He felt good, like luck was with him for this one. He felt like this would be the last one of these. The money was great, but maybe just one more to set the ol' IRA fund with a little extra. *No, too many chances.* A couple more years of driving legit, and he would be able to retire to Destin and go fishin' all year round. *Yeah! That is the plan,* he thought to himself.

It was now almost one thirty a.m., and there was not much traffic on I-59, just the usual group of trucks and a few cars. He pulled a Coke and a sandwich he had made from his carryall ice chest. The Coke tasted great. He usually had one for breakfast and wondered how many people didn't. Almost everyone he knew either had a Coke or Dr. Pepper in the morning. Coffee was not a big thing where he came from, but he guessed that most of the USA and maybe most of the world started with coffee. He really didn't care for it, but he had it last night, as he knew the particular brew at the truck stop would definitely keep him alert and awake for the rest of this trip.

He clipped along now, keeping up with group of three J.B. Hunt trucks that were traveling in a convoy. He could hear the drivers' exchange stories on his CB radio while he listened to Fleetwood Mac.

Jake was unsure of his load weight, but he had to chance the inspection at the Mississippi state line by Picayune. He followed the Hunt trucks up the ramp to the weigh station and waited his turn to cross the scales. The light went from red to green, and he moved forward just staring straight ahead. He didn't want to look into the booth with the state trooper. He actually might know who was on duty. Anyhow, the new bar-code readers would automatically record the truck, the trailer, the time, date and weight. If he was over, the next light would turn yellow or red and he would have to turn right into the inspection lane and wait for a trooper to make a personal review of his log book, move orders, and possibly of the load.

The light went green! He moved into the next range of gears and caught up with the group of Hunt trucks. They moved quicker now, and the speeds went up as they crossed the line into Louisiana. The word on the radio was that the road was clear all the way to New Orleans except for a police car doing radar on I-610 near Elysian Fields exit. Speeds now moved over sixty-five toward seventy. Jake decided he would back off to sixty for now and let those Hunt guys go ahead and break their speed-control governors. He needed to be more careful with this one.

As he came across the five-mile, twin-span bridge back home, he saw the early morning twilight behind him. The lake was glimmering like a smooth pool. After coming into the city, he stayed on I-610 and slowed down. He wanted to get off at Louisa Street and go south toward the river and downtown. No problems so far. The exit came quickly after the high-rise bridge. He made the turn to the right and came back around to the light at Gentilly Boulevard. He turned right, drove to Louisa Street, and turned south. When he arrived at Chartres Street and the river, he turned the big truck and its loaded trailer to the east and proceeded along Chartres Street toward his destination—the new big, container-ship-loading terminal at Desire Street docks. He drove along this narrow, one-way street and looked to his left at the houses that had once been very nice but were now falling into various states of disrepair. This area, the Ninth Ward, as it was known, was once very safe. Now, it was one of the centers of drugs and the almost nightly murders and killings in New Orleans.

He wondered if it might ever change back to the way it was. He used to have some relatives in this area of town and remembered coming here as kid and playing baseball at the recreation field at Royal and Louisa Streets. *Too bad,* he thought. The many thousands of tourists never saw this, even though it was only a very short mile and a half from the French Quarter.

Jake passed the new Louisa Street and Piety Street docks and could now see the big cranes up ahead at the Desire Street Dock that would load the container behind him directly onto the ship. This pick-up had been timed to allow for a direct movement from the truck to the boat instead of the more normal unloading of the container to a storage yard for later. He drove up to the gate and found he was only fourth in line. *Great,* he thought. Sometimes when he had done it this way, the waiting time was over twelve hours, but luckily, not today.

The line of trucks moved forward as each driver had to present all the papers necessary to the guard and then to another dispatcher office inside the gate. All the papers for Jake's load were reviewed and stamped. He got back in the truck and drove to loading point number four alongside the huge container ship. Here again he had to wait, but only two trucks were in front of him, their containers being taken off the trailers and loaded aboard the ship.

Jake was waved forward and stopped. He placed the truck in neutral, set the brake, and climbed out. Legally, the container still belonged to the forwarder and shipper, and Jake felt it was his responsibility to at least oversee the loading of this one as he did for all his shipments. The sun was now moving well into the early morning sky with the promise of a beautiful, late-winter day in New Orleans. He watched carefully as the loading crew removed the various locks and tie-down straps that held the container to the truck. The giant, bright-yellow crane moved overhead, and he could see that a loader had climbed up to the top of the container on his truck to place the hooks. With this done, and after a quick wave from the foreman alongside Jake, the crane pulled the container off the truck and moved it up very high before it began the horizontal travel to the location where the process would be repeated in reverse.

Jake watched for a minute as container number XRTZ46593 was moved over the ship's edge and lowered into place.

With a sigh of relief, he climbed back into his rig and moved out of the loading position and to the dock exit. The shipping documents were beside him on the seat. He drove down Desire Street to Saint Claude Avenue and right to France Avenue. He wanted to return the empty trailer back to D&J Forwarding. While he was driving, he thought of this special load again and agreed with his earlier decision—perhaps only once more. The money was good, but now he wondered for the first time if perhaps this load might not be destined for someplace where good American boys might get hurt or killed. And that was definitely something he would not like to have on his conscience.

When he arrived at D&J Forwarding, the gate guard immediately recognized the rig and opened the big steel chain gate. Jake drove in and found a spot for the empty trailer. He backed the rig into position, got out of his truck, and unhooked the cables. He got down and lowered the trailer stationary legs, and then he moved back into the truck and pulled it away from the trailer. The gate guard watched this and now walked toward him.

"Hey, Jake, you seem to be working mighty early this morning. Where you been with the empty?"

"Marvin, I just had a little run and dropped the container off about a half hour ago. Easy piece of cake, you know," Jake responded.

"Well, now I suppose you done for the day?"

"Yep, I'm headed for home and some sleep. I might go out later tonight, but for now, the bed sounds real good."

"Yeah, me too. I get off in another hour, and I'm ready to hit it for a few hours. I hate this night duty, though. Makes it real tough to sleep during the day. I feel like I'm missing something with the graveyard shift and going to bed at ten a.m. in the morning."

"Me too, sometimes. But I've been drivin' for such a long time now that it almost seems natural to start at about midnight and work until eight or nine o'clock before taking a rest for a while. Anyhow, I'm outta here. See ya!"

Downfall and Freedom

"Take care, Jake," yelled the guard, Marvin Wilson, as Jake moved the truck out of the big yard.

Jake drove back onto I-10 and headed west. When he came to the Williams Street exit in Kenner, the far western suburb of New Orleans, he got off I-10 and turned south again toward the river. He didn't have to go far. He was headed for his trucking company yard to park his truck, get in his car, and go home. The truck yard was two blocks to the west of Williams Street and four blocks south of Veterans Highway. It faced the access road to the New Orleans airport and was surrounded by a chain-link fence. The office and maintenance building were at the back part of the big yard. When he got to the gate, he had to get out and unlock it himself, open it, get back in the truck, and drive into the yard. He parked it in his usual spot and turned off the engine. As he sat there, he could watch the cars move along the access road to and from the New Orleans airport and even watch the planes land and take off. He pulled his log book down from a shelf over the bed in the back and recorded his mileage and time. He was very careful and meticulous about this, as he had been stopped many times at the weigh stations around the country, but had never been fined for not having his log book up to date and in order.

Finally, Jake Briscoe could call this a day and go home. He locked the truck as he got out and walked over to his 1986 Porsche 944 and drove it outside. He got out of the car, closed the gate, and locked it. Now, time to go home.

Jake lived in a condominium off of Jefferson Highway in Metairie. It was a nice area of town called River Ridge. He liked it because it was close to the truck office, although he was usually gone so much it might not have mattered all that much. But he kept such unusual hours that it was nice to be only fifteen minutes away. The condominiums were on the river side of Jefferson Highway. This was the quieter side of the road, and they were mixed in with some single and duplex family homes. The condominiums were relatively new—only five years old. Jake had moved into this one two years ago from an apartment complex up the road after his divorce became final.

He arrived home and parked the car in the garage attached to the side of his condominium. He closed the garage door, went around to the front door, unlocked it, and went inside. He looked up at his alarm system and read that all was in order. He closed the door and headed for the bathroom first for some needed relief.

After he came out of his shower, he changed into a pair of slacks and polo shirt. Time for a little breakfast and then some sack time.

Just as he was putting the bacon in the skillet, he heard the front door buzzer. He looked through the peephole and saw a familiar face on the step—none other than Clarence van Dyke Jackson. He turned the lock and opened the door to his friend with a big smile.

"Van, how you doin' this mornin'? I just got back about a half-hour ago, you know," Jake said to Van as he shook his hand and pulled him inside and closed the door.

"I know. I have watched you every step of the way since you arrived at the dock with the load. How did it go at the loading point? Any problems?"

"Nope, didn't see anyone there, as usual. All seemed to go real smooth. I was worried about those Mississippi State Police comin' up on me while I was there, but it didn't happen. And then I was worried about the weight when I got down to the weigh station at Picayune, but no problems there either. Rest was a piece of cake."

"Great. Here is the rest I owe you. Want to count it?"

"Nope, I trust you."

"Thanks. By the way, are you interested in doing this again for me? Maybe one more trip?" Van asked carefully.

"I don't know. Can you tell me where this is goin'? I sure would be upset if this stuff was goin' somewhere that some GIs might get harmed or killed."

Van was more cautious now. He didn't want to arouse any undue suspicions, but he had to keep the trust of Jake.

"No, I can't tell you. I'm sorry. But I can assure you that this load is not going anywhere that USA GIs might be involved. This is for some folks that need to put back in order some rights to their lives from some oppressors of many years. You are on the right side of the good guys with this one. Okay?" Van explained.

"Okay, I get it. Well, maybe one more. When?" Jake asked.
"I'm not sure just yet. I'll call you if it becomes real. Okay?"
"You bet. Hey, want to stay for breakfast?"
"No, I got to be movin'," Van replied and walked slowly back toward the front door from his position in the hallway.

Jake moved around him and opened the door.

"Okay, boss, I'll look out for your call. Take care and keep your head down," Jake said as Van moved back out onto the steps.

"You bet. And you take care too. See you soon."

Van turned and walked toward his car at the end of the small street and waved to his friend one more time. He got inside and drove to the airport to make a call.

Jake watched his friend leave, and then he closed the door, locked it, reset the alarm system, and went back to his bacon and eggs breakfast. He put the envelope with the fifty thousand dollars in cash in a small drawer in a table in the hall. He decided while he was finishing breakfast to take the money downtown and put it away in his safety deposit box at the security center. No use leaving it around the house where someone might steal it.

After he finished his breakfast, he put the dishes and skillet in the sink to soak, took the money out of the drawer, unlocked the front door, and left the house. He locked the door and opened the garage, got in the car, and started it. He backed it out of the garage and pushed the automatic door-closing button in the car, watched it close, and then drove off toward downtown on Jefferson Highway.

Jake arrived at the Security Center on Common Street about thirty minutes later. He found a place to park on Poydras and walked to the Center.

After he entered, he registered with the receptionist and waited to go to the back, get the box, and go to the private room. He was called in a couple of minutes, and he went back with the very cute-looking blond with the great legs. He placed his key in the lock after she had done so with hers, and he opened the door and pulled out the box. He took it to a private room and made sure the rest of the contents were in order before he placed the envelope with the new fifty thousand dollars inside. He then took the box back to the storage location, closed the door, and removed his key. Safe and sound at last!

He walked back to his car in the mid-morning sunlight and marveled at how warm it seemed to be for a February day. But that was the way it always was in New Orleans this time of year. It could just as easily be thirty degrees as seventy-five. It all depended on the winter cold fronts. But today it was warm and beautiful. A day to enjoy. Not a day to sleep, even though he was tired from the overnight trip. He decided to head for the lakefront and just relax for a while.

Jake drove back on Poydras Street toward the river and then turned on Magazine Street toward Canal Street. He crossed Canal and the street changed names to Decatur Street. New Orleans fooled many this way. One side of Canal Street the streets had one name, and another on the other side. *Tourists could never figure this one out,* he thought.

He drove down Decatur and watched the early morning tourists in the French Quarter walk along, staring at the balconies and taking pictures in Jackson Square. He turned to the left as Decatur Street ended just past the old French Market and drove toward the lakefront on Elysian Fields. His car moved along swiftly, but he tried deftly to avoid the new chuckholes that seemed to reappear every winter.

He arrived at the lakefront and drove around the circle where the amusement park and beach used to be when he was a kid and his mom brought him to New Orleans to visit relatives. He loved it here and decided to make it his home after he got out of the service. The only problem was that, after too many days away from home, his wife, Betsy, found someone that she thought was at least a little more permanent and around more than he was. As he drove, he thought about her, his love of her scent at night next to him, and the nights that their lovemaking never seemed to end. But that all ended four years ago, and he realized it was really his fault, not hers. He missed her, even though the divorce had not been entirely a friendly one. *They never are,* he thought. He had too many friends who had ended up the same as him and Betsy, and each divorce was not pleasant. Some were better than others. *Well, that is life,* he considered for another moment before pulling the Porsche over to a parking place and getting out. He stood there looking at the lake for a long time.

Lake Pontchartrain is a very large lake, some twenty-two to twenty-eight miles across and almost forty miles in length before it empties into the Gulf of Mexico just east of New Orleans. It is very shallow, and the color of the water can change quickly depending on the surface winds that can stir up the lake bottom easily. Today, the winds were light, the lake had just a few ripple waves, and the color was a deep royal blue, much like the color in the English guards' uniforms.

Jake sat down on the seawall and just looked out. The lake had a calming effect on him. He could sense the tension leaving and began to relax. He felt tired, closed his eyes, moved his body back from the seawall a few feet, and lay down on the grass. Within minutes he was asleep—a very peaceful and needed sleep.

CHAPTER 28
6 February 2001

Jake Briscoe was dreaming. It was dark, and somewhere someone had left a door open. He saw himself lying down as a robed person was getting ready to sprinkle water on his forehead; he was about to be baptized. He felt the drops and panicked when the pitcher started to pour all the water out. He was soaked!

Briscoe woke up with a start. He was still on the lakefront, and it was raining hard—one of those early spring storms that would come up off of Lake Ponchatrain and move inland quickly without much warning. He ran to the car and got in, shielding his face and eyes from the sudden torrent. He didn't notice the small, blue Corsica a few meters away.

The woman inside had been watching him all the time he was on the lakefront after having marked him outside the security center on Commons. Nina Carlton was playing her game her way. She had plenty of time, according to the message from Durnbacher, and she would not be in a rush. She was too careful and intelligent. Nina Carlton was five foot seven, with dark brown, almost black hair that was cut to her shoulders. Her dark eyes were from her father, a Cuban who had come to America in late 1958, just before Castro took over. Although she looked thin, she was an accomplished black belt in karate and could shoot small arms, but was especially good at using a night scope, .30-caliber rifle with special muzzle—better than her other "friends" in the Miami mafia. She had been recruited by a close girlfriend after she had dropped out of the University of Florida in 1990. The recruitment process was not long, and she decided the money and freedom of travel and action was just what she wanted. She did not have a conscience about the hits she had made. All three had been drug lords involved with the Miami group; for one reason or another, the boss wanted them hit. She never failed.

Durnbacher had heard about Nina Carlton from a friend of his in Miami who knew about the last hit. He wanted her for his new plan, and he asked Doguro, the second-in-command in Miami, if they would let her do a freelance job for him. Doguro agreed, as it was always good to have Durnbacher as a friend and owing you a favor. The call to Nina was over in two minutes. She knew who and where; she did not know why, and she did not want to know.

Nina had packed her things and drove to the Tampa airport. After parking her black Miata in the long-term lot, she went into the terminal and walked down to rental cars. Avis gave her one for a two-week rental with free mileage, and she drove it off, up to I-75 and then west on I-10 to New Orleans. It was a long drive, almost nine hours, but this way she had the car, she didn't have any air ticket or security trail, and she was operating on her own time and schedule. This was the freedom she always wanted. After arriving in the city, she decided to stay at a small motor inn on Chartres Street, just a few blocks down from the cathedral. The motor inn was furnished with antiques, very private, with an outside entrance for each room and two entrances and exits. She placed her bag in the room, changed, and went out to begin locating her subjects.

Briscoe was first on the list. She found his condo off Jefferson Highway and took a few pictures of the area. This would not be a good spot, as there was no decent location for her to spot herself, and any quick getaway would be too risky—too much openness. His car wasn't there. After checking the garage, she saw it wasn't in there either. A walk around the block and into the back alley gave her a chance to look in the backyard. She could see the security system monitor through the kitchen window—an excellent one, top of the line. She decided not to try to defeat this one.

Carlton returned to the car, which she had left by the gas station across the street, and she drove back downtown. Not much more to do today. Time for dinner and some rest. Tomorrow she would check out the offices of Jackson and his home in east New Orleans.

Two days later, Nina Carlton had all the information she needed. She was on to Jackson's general daily schedule and had gotten near his house the previous day. But it was the same system there; it just wasn't worth it for this plan. She spent the rest of the day as a typical tourist in the French Quarter, shopping, having lunch at a restaurant on a corner of Jackson Square, and visiting the museum. She kept a close watch around her and knew of the many plainclothes police who worked the Quarter, but she didn't notice anything unusual.

* * *

Jake was soaking wet. He pulled out a towel from his workout bag in the backseat and dried himself off a little. The rain pounded his car as he drove home to take a shower and change. Nina followed him from a distance, but not too closely. She figured he was headed home.

Once inside, Jake turned on the security system and stripped off the wet clothes in the bathroom. The hot water from the shower was exactly what he needed. After he got dressed, he went downstairs to the kitchen to make a hamburger—one of his specialties, with secret sauce from his daddy's recipe. As he got out the skillet and food, he noticed, through the mirror in the dining room, a blue Corsica parked across the street at the gas station. He knew he had seen it before, but he couldn't place it just yet.

After he ate, he went upstairs to the front guest bedroom with his binoculars. He thought *I'm involved in a special deal right now. Might as well be careful.* He saw the car, but no one was in it for now. *Umm, I think I'll call a friend and see if anyone knows anything.* He went back to his bedroom and closed the curtain.

"Marty, this is Jake. How you doin'?"

"Jake, my man, I'm super today. What's happenin' with you?" asked Martin Corcenta, a local sub-don with the New Orleans mafia and a very old friend of Jake Briscoe.

"Hey, Marty, I'm workin' on a special deal, you know, and I just wanted to know if you might know of anything goin' on about me. I feel like I'm bein' watched, but not sure. Just a feelin'."

"Jake, I'll do some checkin' around. Stay cool. Want to call for some assistance on your retainer?" Marty asked. Jake Briscoe knew everyone around the docks, and to make friends and also protect himself, he had been paying a thousand dollars each month for the last ten years to one of Marty's runners for information and protection. Jake was certainly on the good side of the New Orleans mob. And that was just the way he wanted it. Jake had also given ten thousand dollars each year to the Policemen's Benevolent Fund, and he had several drinking buddies on the force. Jake had friends in New Orleans on both sides of the law, and now might be a great time to call in a few favors.

"Marty, I would appreciate anything you can find out for me. Call me on my mobile phone. Don't call at home or leave any messages. Okay?"

"Got it. I'll get back to you soon. Just stay cool." The first call was done.

Briscoe placed another call to his best buddy on the New Orleans Police Department, Lieutenant Christopher Garzetti. Garzetti was also well connected to the local crime family, since his uncle was a don. But each respected the other, and, as with all things in the Big Easy, each tried to stay out of the way of the other. Garzetti readily agreed to find out if Jake was being worked by someone.

Jake decided to go visit his girlfriend, Carol Dobbs, and he gave her a call. She had just come in from work and asked him to come over after she ate dinner and relaxed. Carol was a nurse supervisor at the big Ochsner Hospital on Jeff Highway.

He watched the news but looked out the window every fifteen minutes or so. The car had not left, but there was still no one in it. He finally began to figure someone had just left this one for some mechanical work at the station. His mobile phone rang.

"Jake, I got something. A hit woman from the Miami group may be here on a freelance job. It is for some dude in Germany with lots of dinero and a few connections to the right folks, if you know what I mean. They don't know nothin' more. Want some cover?" Marty asked.

"Yeah, give me some cover for the next week or two if you can. I'm just a little nervous."

"No problem. I'll ask Lucas Marcello and Patrick Escenau to give you a little assistance. You know them from the poker game a couple of months ago, right? We'll see what happens. Let me know if you see anything we should check out. Bye."

Jake was unsure whether to feel comforted or not. *Perhaps I need to ask a few subtle questions of Van. I wonder if he knows any German guy.*

He left the condo and drove the car out of the garage to Carol's. He did not spend the night, and, when he returned about midnight, the blue Corsica was gone.

* * *

On Tuesday, Nina Carlton drove the blue Corsica she had rented from Avis in Tampa out to the New Orleans airport and parked it in the big, long-term, remote parking garage. She took the shuttle bus to the departure level. After entering the terminal, she went to the west end, rode the escalator down to the baggage-claim level and walked up to the Hertz counter. The sign on the desk said "Cars available."

After a brief wait, she was on the Hertz shuttle bus and soon in a new, dark-gray Taurus. She drove out to Jefferson Highway and toward Jake Briscoe's condo. As she came down the street, she saw the silver 944 come out of the street and go toward town. What luck! She only had to follow now, staying behind about six car lengths.

Jake turned onto Clearview and headed north toward the lake. Caught at the light, she lost him. She decided to return to the apartment she had rented down Jefferson Highway from Jake's condo and wait for his return. She knew he had no deliveries for today, and so she decided to wait it out for him there.

Nina parked the Taurus on the side street from the apartment and walked around the corner, to the small building that held the furnished apartment. Down the block, Patrick Escenau took pictures of all this from his dark-green Thunderbird with the fully darkened windows. He had staked out the intersection of Jake's condo and Jefferson Highway and was taking pictures of everyone who walked or stopped in this area. He was almost at the end of this roll of film.

Nina entered the apartment, and, after her usual quick look to see if anyone had been there, she went to the window that faced up the street with a view of Jake's condo and garage. She noticed the Thunderbird farther up Jefferson Highway, but she could not see anyone inside because the front glass was so dark. She turned on the infrared sensor aimed at the condo and lay back on the bed for a rest. The sensor would go off automatically when someone entered Jake's condo.

* * *

It is just as well that Nina Carlton lost Jake Briscoe. He went downtown to the security center, withdrew the money from the deposit box, and drove the four hours to Destin, Florida. There he met with a real estate friend from high school. He paid her a hundred thousand dollars in cash for the closing and ownership on a condo directly on the beach. He finally had something he had always wanted. He drove back to New Orleans and returned to his old condo at about midnight, very tired from the full day's drive. There was a message on the machine to call Garzetti, no matter what the time was. Jake pulled out his mobile phone and hit the buttons for the call.

"Garzetti," the sleepy voice sounded from the answering phone.

"Chris, this is Jake. What did you want? I'm sorry to call so late, but I've been out all day."

"Jake," said Garzetti, now awake, "there is definitely something going on, but I don't know if you're the target. Our friends all around say a new hit woman is in town, but no one knows much about her or who she is staking out. She might even be staking out someone to get to someone else. The source was good, but didn't know many specifics. She did know that the contract is for excellent dough—maybe two big ones—and the marching orders are not from her normal bosses in Miami. She is supposedly good-looking, but very quick with a knife and a .357."

"All right, that is good confirmation. Marty has the same story," Jake said.

"Hey, man, watch your game, okay? This broad's very classy and very good, at least from what I've heard. I'm out. Call me if I can help. I'm back to the rack for tonight. Bye." Garzetti went back to his bed.

Jake turned off the phone and went up to his bedroom after checking all the doors, windows, and the security system. As he got into bed, he decided he needed a personal, private meeting with Jackson tomorrow.

* * *

When Jake entered his condo, the sensor alarm began its low buzz, and it woke up Nina Carlton. She got up and put on the night scope to take a look. She saw Jake talking on his mobile phone, but she didn't have one of the new, high-powered scope microphones that can overhear conversations right through glass at over five hundred meters. She was a hit woman, not a private detective. As she watched, she saw the conversation end, and she kept an eye on the upstairs bedroom for Jake. After the light went out, she knew it was time to go to work on the real subject of her visit, Clarence van Dyke Jackson. She did not want to go to New Orleans East at this time of night; it was just not good for a woman alone who would stand out there easily. She left the rental apartment and drove back downtown to her room at the motor inn. She set the alarm for 6:00 a.m. *Need an early start tomorrow,* she thought. *A lot to do at Jackson's place.*

* * *

Even in the dark, Lucas Marcello noticed the woman who came out of the small apartment building and walk around the corner. He got some great frontal pictures of her using the new night camera and super-speed film. In New Orleans, it was still not all that unusual for a woman alone to be out walking around in this neighborhood at this time of night. It was only 12:25 a.m.—still early yet for many. He had just started a new roll of film. After taking a few more pictures of the area and vehicles parked around it, he got out of the car and walked around the block, just to see if there was anything interesting going on. Things were uneventful. He returned to his car, opened up his thermos, and settled in for the night to keep a watch on Jake's. Although he didn't like the night shift, Jake was a personal friend of his, and besides, a friend of the "family." He would want someone else to do the same for him if needed. Besides, Jake had paid over the years for protection without ever asking for any help, so, no problem.

At 7:00 a.m. on the dot, Patrick Escenau drove up in his Thunderbird and parked behind the black Olds that belonged to Lucas. He got into Lucas's car.

"How did it go last night? Anything interesting?" Patrick inquired.

"Mornin', Pat. No, not much. Pretty quiet. Jake came back about midnight and went to bed about twenty-minutes later. At 12:25 p.m., the chick you told me about in the apartment came out, went to her car, and drove off. No sign of her since."

"Anything else?" Patrick asked of his partner.

"No, only the tall, white, cowboy-type guy in the small house on the other side of the Exxon station left about one a.m. He came back about three. Nobody else walking around, except for the usual bunch over at the convenience store. I think that is it. Do you know who we are looking for yet?"

"Not a good description, but the woman sounds interesting. Supposedly the hitter is a woman from Miami. I think I might check out that apartment of hers today. See you tonight. Get some rest."

"You bet. Ciao," said Lucas as Patrick exited the car and shut the door.

Patrick walked over to the convenience store and got a cup of fresh coffee, a doughnut, and a *Times-Picayune* newspaper. He went back to the car and studied the paper for a while. He saw Jake's car pull out onto Jeff Highway about eight fifteen a.m. Nothing else seemed interesting.

At 9:05 a.m., he decided to go take a look at the woman's apartment. He drove the car around the side street and parked in almost the same location where he saw the Taurus park yesterday. He got out and walked around the street to the small apartment building. It was only two stories, with a one-level brick facade on the front. The sides and upper front were painted a medium-blue color that he thought went very well with the red in the brick. He found the front door and walked into the dark hallway.

There were two doors to the two downstairs apartments as soon as you entered the hallway. A stairway went up to a landing where there were two more doors on either side for the two upstairs apartments. *Now,* he wondered, *which one?*

He went back outside again and looked up the street toward Jake's condo. *If I wanted to watch what was going on, where would I be?* he asked himself. He could see clearly that the upstairs left had to be the one. The downstairs apartment would not have a good view due to the magnolia by the front, side window in the yard of the house next door.

Patrick went inside again and up the stairs. He found his cheat key and forced the lock without any effort. He entered and found a cheap, furnished apartment—one of those with furniture from one of those stores that advertise in the Sunday TV magazines for only $599. He walked carefully over to the bedroom and saw the infrared sensor detector mounted on one tripod and a camera with a night scope mounted on another. *Bingo!*

He left quickly and went back to the car to phone this in to Marty.

"Marty, this is Patrick. I checked out that woman's apartment on a gut feel just now, and we hit it. She's got a motion sensor and camera with night scope up there trained on Jake's place. What do you want me to do?"

"Patrick, great work. Stay put and call Lucas if she returns. Tell him about it tonight. I'll get to Jake and let him know. But you are now to stick close to Jake wherever he goes. Got it?"

"Got it, boss. Jake has already left. Let me know if you find him, and I'll get to him. Okay?"

"Okay, I'll get back to you." Marty then called for Jake on the mobile phone. "Jake, this is Marty. We have a bingo there. Some doe down the street in a furnished apartment driving a Taurus is keeping a close eye on you. Where are you now? I want Patrick to get to you and stay close. You are at least marked by her. We'll have pix in about an hour."

"Marty, thanks. I'm in the car almost to Williams and I-10. I'm going over to the office for a while. Patrick can get there in fifteen minutes and I'll still be there. Have him check with me after he arrives. Talk with you later. Bye."

"Okay, he'll be there soon. Bye," came the reply from Marty.

As Jake drove off the exit ramp, he was now bothered by what he had heard. This deal had gone down well, and he had his money, but now there was a new element. He thought about the conversation with his old buddy, Jackson, that morning after he arrived at his office.

"Van, can I see you for a few minutes?" Jake inquired, sticking his head in Jackson's small but impressive office on the second floor of the building.

"Hey, Jake, sure. I've always got time for you. Business or personal?"

"Both, man. Maybe we should go take a walk around the block or out on the floor to look at some of the new equipment for the casino you are working on," Jake offered.

"You bet. Let's go for a walk on the floor."

They headed down the stairway and went out on the main work floor, where electricians were completing a control panel for the new casino to be built. They walked up to one of the panels and pretended to look it over.

"What's up?" Van inquired, looking intensely at his friend.

"Someone is dogging us, man—a woman. She's a trigger from Miami and is looking over me, and maybe you. She is supposedly working for a German guy, not involved with the family down there, but obviously well connected enough to hire her. He must know them too to get their approval for whatever is going on. Any ideas?" Jake asked.

"Hmmmm. Yes. I'll be frank with you, as I always have. My partner for many years is a German. We got involved for different reasons, but with the same goals—to assist others under oppression to free themselves. We met recently and are finalizing the deal you just completed and were paid for. I decided on my own—and you are only the second person to know this—I have decided to quit this personal business. My conscience is getting to me, especially after reading about what happened in Rwanda. I am afraid that what we have done in another country in Africa will also have disastrous consequences. I want out. He doesn't know that yet, but now I think he definitely suspects something is up. Our last conversation was pleasant, cordial, and businesslike, as it always has been. But he is a very perceptive person, and he may have gotten some vibes from me about my future intentions. What I want to do only crystallized on the second day of our meeting. Well, what do you have going for you? How did you find out if you can tell me?"

"Van, I have some good friends in town with the local family and some friends on the police force. A couple of phone calls have given me some initial, but so far unconfirmed, information. I wanted to check with you today to see if there was any connection, and now it appears there is. What will you do?"

"I think I'll ask a friend of mine on the force to give me a little protection for now. Plus, I'll have the house checked again. I have a friend coming in from Brazil in a few days. I want you to meet her and have some fun with us. And I think I'll make a call to a friend of mine up in Virginia. He might be interested in some information on my soon to be ex-partner if I can be protected. In any event, let's stay in touch, and let me know what you are doing and where you are, and I'll do the same. Will that work?" Van asked of his friend.

"Yeah, that works for me. I'm going out to the office for the rest of today to work on some future load contracts. I'll give you a holler later. Take care."

"Yeah, man, let's watch our backs real careful for a while. See you later," Van replied.

They shook hands, and Jake walked out on the loading dock and down the street to his car. Jackson stood there, looking thoughtfully at the panel, but not really seeing it as he thought through what he had just heard. The pieces were now falling in place. Although the money to pay for everything had been sent along with his share, he sensed again that the last meeting with Carl had been a foretelling. He wondered how he might have given any of his feelings away.

But it was too late now. His feelings were correct, and apparently Carl had decided to do something about it. He needed to check everything out now. He walked back up to his office and decided to make some calls after lunch from the mobile phone.

All this Jake considered as he drove the short distance up Williams and over to his office. After he went inside, he pulled out the new contracts and looked them over for any changes. He heard a knock on the door and looked up to see Patrick Escenau's smiling face in the doorway.

"Hey, big guy, what's happening?" Patrick asked. He came in, shook Jake's hand, and sat down. He had a smile on his face and was waiting for Jake to answer.

"Pat, things are difficult out there, aren't they? What's with all this business with the hitter?" Jake asked.

"She's definitely bad news. She did a job about two months ago, according to family sources down in Miami, and she was not even fingered. Super slick. Knows her business. But this time, we know that she is here. Question is whether you are the target, one of several targets, or just a lead dog to the final target. What do you think?" Patrick inquired.

"Possible I might be a target. But I think the primary target is Van Dyke Jackson—you know, the contractor in town. He's a good friend of mine, and we have been involved in a couple of personal deals. He told me this morning that his partner is a German. It looks like a possibility he may be the contractor for the woman, but Jackson doesn't really know for sure. He just has a strong hunch so far. What do I need to do?"

Patrick's reply was quick and to the point: "Okay, Jake, I'll give it to you straight. You are entitled to the best we got in protection. That means one or two of us close at all times—outside and inside; that's to protect you in case the hitter gets inside somewhere you are going and can get you before we follow you inside. Outside, all is fair. We will stay real close. Keep the mobile phone in your hand, charged, and on. If you are going over to Carol's, let us know in advance so we can check it out. We will keep the hitter's lookout post under watch and see if she returns. If she does, we will mark her. We can't touch her, though, unless she makes a move toward you. Family agreements, you know. Marty was going to call his counterpart in Miami this morning, since we found out she is at least looking at you close, and determine if we have to avoid her or just what the deal is. He doesn't think there will be a problem, since she is relatively freelance, and she's here probably under contract from the German. However, she is still part of the Miami family, so we need to be careful and ethical. What's Jackson got going for protection?"

"He is covered by plenty of friends downtown on the force. They may even make a formal show just to warn her off if she is after him. He's not scared so far," Jake said.

"Well, I'm the man with you until about six. I can call for some soldiers anytime I think I need help. Marty has already squared it away with the boss."

"Okay, just make yourself at home, I guess. I've got some work to do here rest of the morning, and then a few errands. Since I'm here, why not take a look around the neighborhood and see if there is anything interesting. Is Lucas or someone watching her apartment now?"

"Yeah, Vincent is over at your place down the street, watching for her. I think I will take a look around. Here is my number. Okay? See you later," Patrick told him and walked out the door and out the building.

Jake watched him go and programmed Patrick's number into his mobile phone. He wondered whether to call Carol or not, and he decided not to for now. No need to worry her. He looked out the window and watched the traffic coming and going to and from the airport on the access road. There were so many visitors now. They seemed to come all the time, not just for Mardi Gras, Jazz Fest, and the conventions, but just to be here and enjoy the food and the music—and now the gambling. He wondered if Jackson's German partner would be coming to New Orleans.

Jake looked back at his desk, and the moment was gone. He had to get this work done now. He still had his trucking business to run.

* * *

By 7:20 a.m. the same day, Nina Carlton was in the car and pulling out onto Chartres Street, headed for New Orleans East and the house of Clarence van Dyke Jackson. It took her about thirty-five minutes, as she was going against the inbound traffic, which was already backed up, trying to get over the high-rise bridge over the Industrial Canal. She exited at Morrison and went east on Chef Menteur Highway to Jackson's street. It was straight with intersections and circle drives for each of the houses. All had large palm trees and plants in the center of the circles and along the houses.

It was easy to spot Jackson's house. Each house on the street had the street number painted on the curb. She drove past and gave it a quick look-over. At the end of the block, she turned right and went up the alley and then back down the opposite way. She found his garage tucked neatly between two large magnolias. The alley was narrow, so there would be no room here to park. She continued onto the street and turned right again. After the stop sign, she went across the street and parked the car, got out, and walked down the street to Jackson's house.

Nina rang the bell, not really expecting anyone to be there. She knew Jackson had left. As she waited at the door, she looked around. The two windows to the right were for the living room, and the one on the left for the dining room. She only wanted to get in for a few minutes to place a couple of bugs to her scanner phone. She had decided on the first day in New Orleans that the house would not be the place for the hit. She wanted a more open setting with greater options.

After a few minutes, it was apparent that no one was there. She walked back to the corner and down the alley. Beside the garage was a small door to the backyard. Nina pulled her key-lock opener from her purse and quickly used it to open the gate. She was in.

Nina went to the garage door that opened to the yard and tried it after putting on her cotton gloves. It was open. She went in and used her key-lock opener again to get into the house. She looked for the security alarm and found it in the pantry closet. It was one she knew well, and she disarmed it with only a push of two buttons.

The house was quiet. Nina wanted to get done and get out of there. She went to the master bedroom first and placed a bug under the nightstand. The second one went under the kitchen counter above and behind some cooking pans. This one might not be quite as useful because of kitchen noise, but she had assumed that Jackson would probably either be in the bedroom or the kitchen when he was there. She already knew from a local source that he did not have a girlfriend at the moment, so that was not a problem. After looking around again, she turned on the alarm and was out and in the alley. She quickly walked to the street and back to her car. She felt safe now, and she started to drive back downtown, but decided to go on out to the Briscoe's condo to see if he was there.

When Nina arrived on Jefferson Highway, she parked in her usual place on the side street and walked around the corner to the front door of the apartment. She noticed the green T-bird on Jefferson Highway, but couldn't see anyone in it. As she entered the apartment, she went to the bedroom and checked the sensor—no one there. After a couple of minutes, she went into the kitchen, fixed herself some iced tea, and began to think about the hit. She had a couple of places to scout out, but she knew that Durnbacher was due in town on Saturday evening. It would have to be that night or Sunday, and it would have to be very clean. She couldn't afford to get crosswise with the local family. This hit was still on their turf, and she had to minimize exposure hype and the impact in local coverage. She decided on a plan. Now she just had to pick one of two or three possible spots and work out the logistics.

Nina looked at her watch—lunch time. She left and went downtown to the motor inn, parked the car in the back lot, walked over to Decatur Street, and found a cute cafe with mufalletas, the local specialty sandwich. She ate outside watching the passing parade of tourists and locals.

Lucas Marcello walked up and sat down at a table next to her. He had marked her from the moment she walked up the street to the apartment on Jefferson Highway and called in for backup help from his boss, Marty. They kept in contact via open car phones and tracked her back to town. Now they knew at least where she was staying.

Lucas was very appreciative of Nina's good looks. *I wonder where she packs the hitter,* he thought. *There aren't many places on her to hide one. At least with what she's wearing today.* As he watched her, he also noticed his other partner, Vincent Gaultier, walk on the other side of Decatur and find a table where he could see them both, drink coffee, and ostensibly read the paper. She was covered.

* * *

Jake and Patrick left and went to lunch. They knew that Lucas had marked the woman. Jake was interested in seeing her in person, but Lucas advised against it for now. They drove over to Veteran's Boulevard and went down to Houston's. It was crowded, and Marty met them there.

"Jake, good to see you," Marty said as Jake and Patrick walked up to the table where Marty was waiting. All exchanged handshakes and sat down. They waited for the order to be taken before any other conversation.

"Marty, what do you think now about all this?" Jake asked.

"Man, I don't know. She is downtown in the Quarter, having lunch alone. Lucas is literally right next to her at another table and Vincent across the street. We've got her, and I don't think she knows it yet. We've got to be very careful, as Patrick explained. She's got full rights to be here, and we've got to protect you first, but second priority is her. Difficult, if you know what I mean. Conflicts make the world go round, don't they?" Marty replied.

"Yeah, they sure do. What is the plan now that you have her?" asked Jake.

"We will keep close contact with her. We are also going to stay with you. Same plan, except now we have her covered. If she finds out about us, she might make a call or two, and then she might be told what the deal is with you. Remember, your buddy, Jackson, is third in line for protection priority from us. If he is the target and not you, then we will have to let her go. We can only interfere if you are threatened. *Capice?*"

"I got it," Jake said.

The food arrived, and the conversation turned to the casinos now expanding in New Orleans, along with the new flood of tourists.

After lunch, they went outside to the cars and talked a few more minutes.

"Marty, should I tell Carol about this?" Jake asked his friend.

"Yeah, I think I would now. But be careful. I would only let her know that you might be in a little danger and that we are watching you for protection. Do you think she can handle that?"

"Yes, I know she can. I'll tell her tonight. I got to go, so talk with you later." Jake left with Patrick.

Marty watched them leave and decided to make another call to Miami. The one earlier in the morning had not gone as well as expected, and he needed some cover for himself. In fact, this was getting so complicated, he needed to get the boss in on this one so that all the bases could be covered. It might get very dicey very quickly.

* * *

Lunch was great. Nina Carlton had enjoyed this one. It was a great day, the weather pleasant, the humidity low, and the sun was very nice for late February. She had noticed the guy across the street reading the paper, but she gave no looks at Lucas seated just three feet from her. She paid the bill and walked back to the motor inn, but the guy across the street stayed put.

As soon as she turned the corner, she was visually picked up by Maryanne Delgado, who was pretending to look at sweatshirts just inside a shop on the side street. As Nina walked by, Maryanne went out and began to follow her, but crossed the street and stopped in front of another store for a minute to let Nina get a little further away and become comfortable. She saw her turn into the motor inn entrance, and she walked closer. She went by the entrance as Nina went into her room on the second floor. *Now we really have her.* Maryanne walked to the end of the block, ducked in a courtyard doorway, and phoned in.

Lucas showed up in a couple of minutes with the car, and now the waiting for the two of them began. It would be a long afternoon.

CHAPTER 29
6 March 2001

Friday, a new piece of information came in the morning satellite download at NSA—a very important piece. It was a fax from Durnbacher to Brazil with the coded transfers for the money from Bermuda to Jackson. The fax and the other phone calls were to be sent via e-mail, as usual, to Foster and Tegarro. But the operator, after making a transmittal letter for the files to be carried under, sent the e-mail to his own special memo file. There it would remain. Foster and Tegarro never did get this one.

CHAPTER 30

10 March 2001

The container vessel, *Crystal River*, owned by the Lykes Shipping Group, arrived Durban on schedule on March 10. The captain, Mr. Antonio Christofo, was told to wait outside the breakwater entrance to the channel harbor for one day until the berth at container dock number four was opened. The delay was caused by a faulty crane that had necessitated repairs. The harbor board promised to make up the lost time and get the vessel back on schedule, sailing on the tide on the fourteenth.

The next day, clearance was granted, and the pilot was sent aboard. The large vessel moved easily through the channel and into the main harbor area of Durban. Two tugs were called and *Crystal River* was moored alongside container dock number four by noon. Within the hour, the cranes were moving over the ship like giant spiders, picking the containers off the ship and either loading them on the dock, where they were moved again to a storage area, or directly onto trailers for immediate delivery.

Container number XRTZ46593 was unloaded at 6:33 p.m. directly to a waiting trailer. The driver, Richard Mbele, had been waiting for two days for this. He was a member of the KwaZulu Organizing Committee for a Free Natal. He was also a driver for the Natal Shipping Co. Ltd. It made it easy. His brother was the assistant managing director of Sentry Security Services Pty. Ltd. of Durban, the purchaser of this particular container of "security hardware."

Mbele drove the truck to the dispatch office. He stopped for a minute and went inside to obtain the bill-of-lading papers for the container and shipping documents. He was ready to go through customs.

This was the tricky part of his pick-up. The payoffs had been made to all who were concerned, but there was always the chance that the wrong person might be sick or called away or gone for some other reason, and then he might have to have the entire shipment checked. This was one that many people did not want that to happen.

His instructions were to drive to lane number six and make sure that his friend, Ian Grotta, would be the customs inspector in charge. He drove down the long concrete, double-wide land road toward the customs office and inspection station. He moved the truck and trailer into line for lane number six and began the wait. There were four other trucks ahead of him. The wait could be as short as an hour or as much as four if customs decided to make a search of each one. He shut off the engine and lit a cigarette.

Richard Mbele moved the truck and container #XRTZ46593 into the brightly lit inspection area at 8:40 p.m. He got out of the cab and was met be the customs inspector in charge, Mr. John Glaxon. This was not who it was supposed to be.

"Mr. Glaxon, pleasure to meet you. I'm Richard Mbele, driver for Natal Shipping. Here are the papers for the load," Richard said to the inspector with all the confidence he could muster.

"Thank you, Mr. Mbele. Let me take a look at these for a minute. Would you please wait by the rear trailer doors? I'll be back in a minute or two. Did you pick this up from the yard, or was it delivered directly from the vessel?"

"Directly delivered, sir. All prearranged, and those were my instructions from my boss and dispatcher."

"Thank you," Glaxon said and walked away to the inspector's office, looking through the sheaf of papers.

Mbele lit another cigarette, and then another. He stood by the doors of the container and waited, trying to keep from becoming too nervous and visible about it. He saw Glaxon emerge from the office with two other officers, and he knew he was in trouble.

"Mr. Mbele, would you please open the doors? We will witness the removal of the original seal and lock. This is Mr. Watson and Mr. McGordon. Please proceed," Glaxon directed.

Mbele pulled out a set of cutter pliers from his back pocket and cut the shippers' seal. He gave this to Glaxon. The numbers matched with the bill of lading. Glaxon nodded to proceed.

From the documents' envelope, Mbele found the keys for the locks and unlocked and removed them. He wanted to run, but that would give it all away. He must be strong and have courage—remember what he was fighting for. He opened the doors.

Glaxon and the two white customs officers moved closer. The shipment was supposed to contain security alarms and special sensors. They looked at the crates on the pallets at the edge of the door. Each was marked with the name of the shipper and the name and address of the purchaser.

Shipper: Southeastern Security Alarms, Inc.
1616 Great Piney Road
Meridian, MS 43424

Ship to: Sentry Security Services Pty. Ltd.
Long Blackson Street
Durban, Natal, RSA

"Mr. McGordon, have that fork truck over there get the box from the top pallet and move the other pallets below it off to the side. I want to inspect the top crate and the bottom one," Glaxon ordered.

"Yes, sir," McGordon responded. He walked over to inspection station number three and ordered a customs worker with a fork truck to come over and remove all the end pallets—three of them—for inspection of the top and bottom ones. The fork truck-driver did as he was told and, within a couple of minutes, the three crates were on the concrete area behind the truck. Glaxon peered inside with his flashlight and saw the same markings on the next set of crates.

The tops to the two crates were removed and the contents reviewed. The first crate contained seventy-two security alarms. The second crate contained another seventy-two units.

"Okay, Mr. McGordon, close them up and reload. This is cleared," Glaxon remarked after reviewing the contents and the documents one more time.

Mbele watched the reloading of the pallets carefully. He closed the door, and the two officers signed the bill of lading and inspection forms, indicating they had removed the original shippers' seal, inspected the cargo, and cleared it for entry into South Africa. Mbele's heart was still pounding, but he was under control.

He got back in the truck after the paperwork was handed to him by Mr. Watson. He put the truck in gear and moved out smartly from the customs inspection station and to the main highway, N2. He went north toward Newark.

"James, this is Mbele. I have the goods. Are you ready at the delivery point? I'll be there in about a half-hour," Mbele said over his mobile phone. He had called James Mdelthe, the region commander. This shipment was destined for delivery to a local group. He had picked up and delivered previous shipments all along the Natal coast and to some interior rendezvous points.

"Mbele, I have it. I will have the people meet you at the old sugar mill. It is a change from the agreed point," Mdelthe responded.

"Okay, but which one?"

"The Dominion Mill on Goodman's Road, just up from Tugela. Do you know where it is?"

"Yes, I know it."

"Good. Bring the load around to the rear of the mill to the supply loading dock. Back the truck in there and wait for us if there is no one when you get there. I am on my way now," Mdelthe said.

"Got it."

Mbele continued driving north on the N2. He passed Uhlanga Rocks and could see the Indian Ocean off to his right. There was a very famous restaurant there, but he had never been to it. For many years, only whites were allowed; but now, he knew that he could go if he wanted. And more changes would come soon, he hoped.

Mdelthe made two more calls to local unit commanders to meet him at the Dominion Mill in one hour. He wanted Mbele to get there and be alone for a while. This would give him time to have the units check all the surrounding area for possible followers of the container and any others who should have no business being there. Also, he wanted Mbele to wait and stew. He needed some further testing. He had already had a phone call from the customs inspection station concerning the inspection of the cargo on the container and Mbele's actions there.

Glaxon was in on the deal. He had received his payment of twenty thousand dollars into a Swiss account established for him two years ago by Durnbacher. This was his fourth shipment, and now that account held over ninety thousand dollars from the monies and interest. He knew there would be more to come.

Glaxon was worried most about this inspection of this container when his supervisor, Mr. Grotta, had called him to his office and gave him the special instructions.

"Mr. Glaxon, there will be a container coming in tomorrow, number XRTZ45693, with some security equipment. It is for some friends of ours. We will have to inspect some of the goods, and unfortunately, Mr. Watson and Mr. McGordon will be asked to assist you. They are new, and my boss, inspector general for Durban, Mr. McQuaid, has appointed them as new assistants. I don't know if they are working for the secret service or not. We cannot take any chances, though. Here are your instructions for the container. Read and destroy them here."

"Yes, sir, Mr. Grotta," said Glaxon, and he began to read a confidential fax.

> Grotta, XRTZ45693 will arrive on Crystal River. If need to check contents, check only top and bottom pallets. All others are special equipment. Do not fail.
>
> Carl

"Sir, I understand," said Glaxon, and he gave the fax back to Grotta.

Grotta took it, placed it in an ashtray, lit a match, and then lit the fax. It was ash in a matter of moments.

"Okay, get going. I will be out tomorrow. Also, after the container is gone, call this number and report the driver's reactions to the man that answers. You are only to give your name at the beginning of the conversation. You are only to report on whether the driver seemed scared and showed it, or any other strange actions. Do you understand this?" Grotta asked.

Glaxon read the paper with the number and memorized it.

"Yes, sir, I understand. It will be done as you have requested without problems. Anything further, sir?"

"No. That is it for today. I'll see you on Thursday," Grotta replied and turned back to the papers on his desk as Glaxon turned and left the room.

* * *

Now with the inspection complete, Glaxon made the phone call from his mobile phone outside of his office. There was the background noise of the trucks, but he felt it would be safer there than from his office. He dialed the number given to him by Grotta the previous day, and the call was answered on the second ring.

"Yes," came the voice at the other end of the call.

"This is Glaxon at Durban Inspection. The container is through. The driver, Mbele, showed he was scared as we unloaded the pallets. Anything else?"

"No, thank you."

The call was over. Glaxon was clean, and so he went back to his office.

* * *

Mbele was waiting at the dock. He had no trouble in finding the old sugar mill. But now it was so quiet. He had been waiting for almost a half-hour and was wondering if he was at the right spot when he saw a small van approach from the west road entrance to the mill.

The van pulled up to the truck, the doors opened, and several men got out, all with new AK-47s slung around their shoulders.

He recognized the man coming up to him as Mdelthe, but he did not see the small pistol that Mdelthe had behind his back in his right hand. As soon as Mdelthe had a clear view at Mbele, he brought the pistol up and fired. The shot hit Mbele directly in the forehead, and he dropped to the ground beside his truck, already dead before he hit the earth. After the call from Glaxon, Mdelthe made a decision to eliminate Mbele, as he would be too much of a risk now and in the future for this container, because he showed his emotions at the inspection station, risks that the African Freedom Party could not afford.

"Get him out of the way, and get this container unloaded quickly," Mdelthe ordered to the men that were now walking toward the fallen man and the truck.

Mdelthe pulled his phone from his jacket pocket and made a call. He checked with his sub-unit commander that had investigated the perimeter of the mill and was now guarding it and the two roads leading to the old Dominion Company mill. Everything was okay so far.

Two large trucks pulled in from the east road. They backed up to the dock next to the container, and the men began to transfer the pallets from the container to the two trucks. A steady rain began to fall, and the drops came down like large, wet beetles on the men. Within minutes, they were soaked through, but they continued silently as Mdlethe watched.

After a half-hour, the job was done. The trucks drove off back out the west road entrance. One of the unloaders got in the truck with the now-empty container and started it up. He would drive it back to the forwarder in Durban, get a signed receipt for the return, and be picked up there for his ride back to Tugela and headquarters.

Mdelthe got back into the small van with his driver and the remainder of his unit. He placed a call again to his sub-commander, and now they all went back into their hiding places in this heavily treed and sub-jungle area of Natal. They would melt back in quickly.

The trucks were driven to an old school near Brutatan and were unloaded in the dead of night by another sub-unit of Mdelthe's. The next evening, the arms were distributed in three shifts of two hours each to six units, beginning at 10:00 p.m. They already had their orders. The attack would start at 4:00 a.m. on Sunday, 1 April. The official alarm would go out at 3:00 a.m.

CHAPTER 31

30 March 2001

Larry Preau had seen stranger cases come across his desk than the request for information and a tail on Nina Carlton. He called in two of his agents, Jeffrey Blackstone and Oliver Ferguson, and let them know the details, which were not much. Blackstone and Ferguson left and looked at each other as they walked back to their office.

"Jeffrey, I think I'll do a little checking with some of my old friends in the Irish Channel about this. Why don't you try Garzetti downtown to see if he knows anything. Do you think he'll help," Oliver said as they sat down.

"Yeah, I'll see what he knows. I have another contact uptown at St. Charles and Jefferson Highway that might know something. I'll talk at you later. I'm gone. Good luck on this one," Blackstone answered his partner, and he left.

Blackstone made the call to Garzetti from the car. The New Orleans police captain was out, but the sergeant on duty gave him Garzetti's mobile phone number. He redialed and was rewarded with, "Sorry, the person you are calling is not available or within the calling area. Please try your call again." *Ouch.* Blackstone hated this, but with nothing else to do, he drove uptown to a small bar frequented by college kids from Tulane and several of his former classmates. He tried Garzetti again after parking the car, but he got the same voice.

Garzetti's phone was off for a very good reason. He was in an apartment in North Claiborne with his mistress in the middle of the sunny afternoon in Crescent City. He would be there for another two very important hours.

Ferguson remained back at the office, and he called his brother at a furniture store in Harahan.

"Benny, this is Oliver. How you doin'?" Ferguson asked.

"Olive." That was what Oliver's older brother had always called him since he was born. "I'm Okay. What's happenin' downtown that you need me today?"

"I'm lookin' for some information on a special woman in town. She is from Tampa, and has some good friends in Miami, and maybe here too. Heard of anything from your friends?"

"Nope, not yet. But I'll give a call or two and get back at you. Need the info soon?"

"Yeah, real soon. This has some high visibility, if you get me."

"I got you. I'll call you back in an hour or two. Office or mobile?"

"Mobile. I'm going out for a while. Take care, Benny."

"Okay, Olive. I'll get back to you."

Ferguson wasn't sure what to do, but staying in the office was too confining for now. He needed some other help and decided to go see a snitch down in the Gentilly area of New Orleans.

Blackstone's sources at the bar on Saint Charles didn't know anything. He returned to the car and called for Garzetti again—same message. He decided to call his partner, but after a short conversation with Ferguson, they both realized they were getting nowhere fast trying to locate Nina Carlton.

About 3:30PM, Blackstone decided to stop at Sal and Sam's on Veterans Highway, a favorite bar and restaurant of his. The bar was always crowded in late afternoon, with sales reps and a few late diners still there from lunch. It was a place for contacts and trading information, business and otherwise.

He saw another classmate of his from Loyola, Joe Proctor, at the bar sitting alone and nursing a martini. He said hello and sat down next to him. They were at the end of the bar, away from the door with some privacy.

"Joe, it's good to see you. What are you doing here this afternoon?" Blackstone said as they shook hands to open the conversation.

"Jeff, I'm just celebrating my divorce. It was final this morning. What brings you here in the middle of the afternoon?"

"Just thought I would stop by for a minute. I don't have any other appointments this afternoon." Almost all Blackstone's friends thought he was a marketing manager for a local manufacturer.

"Well, good to see you," Proctor replied, and he went on to talk about the past two years and the divorce. Blackstone listened patiently and ordered another beer. This was part of the job too, he supposed. It was all about information, and for what he needed, he had to wait for the right opening. Finally, there seemed to be an end to Proctor's story, and, sensing the moment, Blackstone jumped in.

"Joe, you know a lot of people in town that I don't, and perhaps you might have heard about something going on. Supposedly there is a woman in town, Carlton's the name, and several friends are interested in her. Do you know anything?"

"Yeah, I heard about her from a friend over in Kenner. She is here to do a deal for someone out of town, but not from Miami. Right?"

"Yes, you got the information right. Anyone know where she is staying, or can you find out?"

"I can make a call or two. Back in a minute." Proctor left and went to the phone by the men's room. Blackstone watched and knew he would have a full report of who was called and what was said by ten p.m. This phone was tapped by the FBI. Proctor returned to his seat at the bar and looked around the room suspiciously. What he had just heard had given him a feeling of not wanting to really get involved; but he would tell what he heard and then leave. He figured the phone in Sal and Sam's was tapped.

"She was at the motor inn down in Chartres in the 800 block. That was last information. However, she may have moved this morning, but everyone is still looking. Haven't found her yet," Proctor told the CIA agent.

"Thanks, man, that is good news. I'll leave you alone to keep celebrating."

"Okay, but don't let anyone know where that info came from. I've got some friends to protect too. Okay?" Proctor asked.

"No problem. Take care and see you later."

They shook hands again, and Blackstone went out to the car and drove away. He called the office and Ferguson's mobile phone, to give him the news. Both headed for the motor inn on Chartres, but they would not find Nina Carlton there. She was already under watch at the Holiday Inn in Metairie, just two miles from where Blackstone had the beer with Proctor. The CIA was behind the current timeline by almost six hours, and the local agents would never catch up.

After Ferguson and Blackstone ran into the very cold, dead end at the motor inn, Ferguson tried a call again to Garzetti.

The phone answered, "Garzetti."

"Frank, this is Ferguson. I've been trying to get you all afternoon. What's goin' on, man?" Ferguson asked while smiling at his partner in the car.

"I've been working an undercover case. Had to keep the phone off. It was a big deal for a while. But I think all is quiet now. What do you need?"

"What's with the hitter in town, Carlton. You have the word on this? Uptown is lookin' for some answers from us, and we have come to a dead end down here on Chartes at the motor inn. She's gone," Ferguson told the New Orleans police captain. He was not surprised at this, as he already knew she had sneaked out quickly and left everyone looking in all the wrong places. He figured correctly, but he didn't really know at the time that the local family would be the closest to knowing where she was, but he couldn't tap into that information source just yet. And even when he did, he was not going to give the local CIA guys any strong leads. People in New Orleans tried to protect each other, and, even though he and Ferguson's brother played football on the same high-school team and were still friends, that didn't mean he had to let the CIA know everything he knew, when he knew it.

"Yeah, I think she may have left town, but I don't know. We are keeping an eye out for her in case she turns up somewhere. Sure are a lot of people interested in the chick. What do you think?"

"Yeah, I agree with that. Well, if you hear anything, give us a holler, will you?" Ferguson asked, but he already knew the answer.

"Not a problem. Tell that bro of yours to call me sometime, and we'll go get a beer or two. See you around. Bye."

Ferguson looked at his partner, and they decided it was time for a little dinner out at a Chinese restaurant on Veterans Highway in Metairie. They called in and found out that no one in the office knew anything, except for Kelly Tegarro from CIA Headquarters, who was flying in tomorrow morning and wanted them to pick him up at 11:30 a.m. The message was received and they made a note of the time and flight. Now the weekend was shot, since tomorrow was Saturday, and now they supposed they would have to be at the beck and call of this guy from CIA. It was meant to be.

CHAPTER 32

15 March 2001

Maria had not heard from Van for six weeks. She began to wonder if he still remembered his promise. She decided to call her friend Dorothea to see if she had heard from Carlos.

"Dorothea, this is Maria. How are you?"

"Maria, it is good to hear you. I am fine. Very busy. How are you? Have you heard from Van yet? I know he will call you. I am sure of it."

"No, I haven't heard from him. Have you had a communication with Carlos? I was wondering."

"No. And I don't expect to."

"Why," Maria asked.

"Because he changed from the first night we were there to the second. He was a terrific lover both nights, and on the second night, he talked to me about wanting to return to Santa Rita and loving me. But I didn't believe him. He just had a different, faraway look about him, and I sensed some change in him. He had a different look in his eyes. Much harder. More intense. A real distance. I decided I was not interested in seeing him again. That is not what I told him, of course, but it is how I feel. If he comes back to Santa Rita, I am not going to see him. I don't trust being with him anymore. I believe with all my heart now that, if he ever thought I knew anything about his business, whatever it is, because I don't know anything, then he would kill me. I don't want to take the risk of being with him. I don't want to know anymore about him."

"Dorothea, I can understand how you feel. I too have felt that way sometimes with some of the men I have been with. And now I don't take any chances either. I want to leave this life I have, though. I have not told anyone else about this. But I must stop this being with all these men. I am beginning to have nightmares, and I am afraid for my life and my children. What if I were to be with some man that would hurt me or become angry if I was not satisfying him, or perhaps he might want to do dangerous things. No more. I want to be with Van, if he will have me. He said he wanted me too, and I believed him. Do you think I should have?"

"Maria, believe what is in your heart. What does your heart say about him and how he feels for you?"

"My heart is what is keeping me going these past eight weeks since he left. I love him. I know I can love him even more than I did my first husband. And I want to be with him all my life, if he will have me. He said he was going to send for me, but I haven't heard from him. And now I am worried about him. I am scared for him. He wants to quit part of his business—the part that is causing him so much mental pain and guilt. I don't know what it is, but I think it has to do with Carlos, and that makes me even more scared. Carlos seems like he can be very cruel if he wants to be. Perhaps that is what you felt."

"Yes, I think that is part of what I felt in that change with him that second night. I am scared his anger could become cruel and hurtful quickly. And I don't want any part of him anymore. I hope you will understand that, if they return. I just cannot be with him again. I hope Van calls or writes. It must be so wonderful to really love someone. I never have. Maybe I never will. I don't trust men all that much. I have never understood why. It must be something within me—something from my past. But I enjoy the love and sex they can give. But I feel they can be deceitful and can hurt you as quickly as care for you. I need to find some man that is true and kind, always, not just some of the time, someone I can trust to be with forever. Do you think that will ever happen?" Dorothea asked almost pleadingly to Maria.

"Dorothea, yes, of course it will happen. However, you must open your eyes and your heart for it. Love will not find you unless your heart is open to it. Caution with most men is always advisable, but I believe, because I have now been in love twice in my life, that there really are kind, gentle, strong, and caring men that can love a woman and make her feel special. I believe you will have that love one day. I do."

"Oh, Maria, I love you. You are such a special friend to me. Here you called me to find out if I had heard from Carlos because you are concerned about your love, and you end up cheering me up about my own lack of true love in my life. I must go and get back to work. Please call me if you hear from Van. I want to share your feelings. And I believe he will call and help you escape this life of being with all these men. He will take you for his wife. I saw the look in his eyes when we walked up to the pool that last night, and I did see the love he has for you. Take care. Bye."

"Goodbye, Dorothea. I'll call in a few days."

Maria went back to work in the accounting office. She was not really interested anymore in the many columns of figures she was entering into the computer. She could only think of Van and how sweet he was that last night and the words he said to her. She would just have to be patient.

Lunch came, and Maria made a quick decision. She would go to the church, light a candle, and pray. Perhaps Mary would help. She needed the peace of mind, and she needed to hear from Van. He was her only hope now for a new life—a life without being a whore; a life of caring and loving for one man, bringing into this world his children and caring for them if he wanted them, and sharing the joys and pain of life together.

She walked to the church nearest her office, which was on a corner and made of dark brick from the local clay surrounding Santa Rita. It was not her regular church, but she had been here before on holy days and for confession, since the priest would not recognize her voice.

Maria entered and went to the right side and walked up to the side altar with the statue of Mary and the candles. She took a match from the container and lit it from one of the candles already burning and lit another one in the rack. She kneeled and began her prayer: "Oh, most Holy Mary, Mother of God, please pray for me now and at the hour of my death. Oh, Mary, my namesake, I beg your forgiveness and that of Jesus, my Savior, for all my sins. I promise to repent and live a new life, if it be thy will. I pray to you with all my heart and soul that you will listen and help me. Van needs peace from his life. He has so much guilt for whatever he has done. Please forgive him and give him your peace, the peace of mind that only you can give. I love him so, and he deserves a chance to begin again too. I don't know if he has ever confessed what he has done, but I know you know what is in his heart. And I know too. He wants to give up his guilt and truly live again. I want to be with him and give him all my love for the rest of our lives. Please listen to my prayer, I beg of you. I know what will happen will only be your will, and I will try to accept that. But I will make a change in my life beginning now. Please forgive me. Amen."

She pulled out her rosary from her purse and said it silently, moving the beads one by one through her clasped hands. Their smoothness and the rhythm of the prayers calmed her. She felt a quiet peace falling over her.

When she was done, she went directly to the front aisle and genuflected deeply in front of the huge cross with Jesus on it, behind the heavy, wooden altar. After making the sign of the cross, she stood fully upright and said to the statue, "Please hear my prayer, O Holy Jesus." She turned and walked out into the bright sunlight of the summer day in Santa Rita. She felt so relieved. She might never hear from Van again, but she knew she was truly going to change her life. She would no longer be a whore. She felt forgiven, and that was enough for now.

Three days later, in mid-afternoon, the phone rang in her office. She answered it and began to cry softly after she heard Van's voice.

"Maria, this is Van. How are you?"

"Van, I am fine. I am much better now that you have called. I have been so worried about you since you left. Are you all right?"

"Yes, I have been very busy at my business, finishing up one last project. I want you to come to stay with me for a few days here in New Orleans. I think we need to talk about our lives. I know I love you and want you here. Can you get away soon? How about the boys? What can you do about them so you can come?"

"Van, I will make some arrangements. The boys can stay at my mother's house. They love her dearly, and I know she will enjoy having them there with her. They are out of school, as you know, since it is summer here, so they will keep busy with their soccer games and swimming. How long do you think I will be there, though, until I can return? I will have to give my mother some answer when she asks me."

"Tell your mother you will be gone a week. I am sure, in that time, we can talk about all our dreams and hopes for the future. I know I need you and want you with me. I have missed you so much since I left. I hope you have missed me too."

"Oh, Van, I *have* missed you—all of you. And now that you have called, I want to leave quickly. How soon can you make the arrangements?"

"Maria, I have already made them. You will fly up to Miami on an American Airlines flight in a week from tomorrow night. My friend Jason will come and pick you up next Thursday afternoon about four o'clock to take you to Sao Paulo Airport. You must go to the US Consulate in Sao Paulo to get your visa. Jason will come tomorrow to pick up you up and take you there. I have already sent the invitation to the commercial attaché. He is a good friend of mine, and you will have your visa in about an hour, so just wait, and Jason will take you back home. You will be safe with him. Do not worry."

"Okay, I will be ready. What should I tell my boss here?"

"Just tell him that you have to go to America to visit a very close friend for a week and that, if he needs a temp for the work while you are gone, you will pay for one. That should take any concern he has away. I will pay for the temporary person, of course, if needed."

"Van, I don't know what to say, except that I am so thrilled to come and see you. I know I love you and want so badly to talk with you too about our lives."

"Take care, my love, and I will meet you at the gate in New Orleans. If there are any problems along the way, just call my mobile phone number, and I will have it with me all the time. I can hardly wait to see you and hold you in my arms again. I love you, Maria."

"Van, I love you too."

"See you soon. And call if you need anything. Bye."

"Bye," she said. She put the phone down and cried softly again as she said another silent prayer, "O God and Mary, I thank you for this. I am ready to go and change my life. I love him so."

* * *

Jason, Van Dyke Jackson's bodyguard and assistant in Brazil, arrived in Santa Rita about ten a.m. to pick up Maria and take her to the US Consulate in Sao Paulo. She was ready and excited. The three-hour trip back to Sao Paulo was uneventful, except for one special conversation between the two persons in the car.

"Jason, how long have you known Van?" Maria asked as she looked out the window at the passing hills.

"Maria, I have known him for almost five years. I would give my life for him. He saved mine many years ago."

"I won't ask about that, but it obviously left strong feelings with you for Van. Do you know much about his life outside of Brazil. You know I'm going to New Orleans now to meet with him and talk about our future together. We love each other."

"I know. You will find his life there much different than what he has perhaps let you know. He owns a business in New Orleans and is very successful. He has many friends in the USA, not only in the New Orleans area, but also all over, from his experience in the US Army for ten years. Many people owe him favors, and he gives favors in return," Jason said.

"What kind of partnership does he have with Carlos?"

"That I cannot tell you. He has not given me approval to talk about it with you or anyone. I really don't know much, except that they have been partners in some business ventures for over ten years."

"What do you think of Carlos, or whatever his name is," Maria continued with her questions.

"He is very intense. I mean, he has very strong opinions and is very controlled. I don't trust him, especially after their meetings eight weeks ago here."

"Why? Will you tell me what you feel?" Maria pressed.

"Yes, I will tell you what I feel. The day of their discussion, while you were at work, something happened between them, either during the discussion, or later. But, Carl, that is his real name, changed. Van noticed it too, and we both were more careful that second evening and since."

"I know. Dorothea, the woman with me that was with Carl both nights, told me four days ago that she noticed a difference in Carl from the first night to the next. In fact, she is now scared of him, and, if he returns to Santa Rita, she will not be with him for any amount of money. She said he seemed lost in thought, and, although they had a very nice night together, she became scared. And she has scared me now for Van. What is Van's real name? Can you tell me now? I think I have to put it on the visa form."

"Yes, Maria. His name is Clarence van Dyke Jackson. He is from a small town in southern Mississippi, a state close to New Orleans, where he now makes his home. His mother is still alive and lives in his hometown. His father died several years ago, before I knew him," Jason responded with honesty.

Maria asked, "Do you think there will be problems between Van and Carl? I know Van is very upset. He told me about his feelings of guilt and how he wants to get out of his business arrangement with Carl. He is scared that Carl may not want to, and may try to do something to him. Is this true from what you know?"

"Yes, very possible. I think you should be very careful in New Orleans, and watch for Van's safety too. I don't trust Carl," came the warning from Jason.

"I will, you know. I love him," Maria said after some pause.

They continued on in silence for most of the rest of the journey. When they arrived at the consulate, Jason let her out of the car, and Maria went inside. She saw the window for visa applications and addressed the clerk behind the counter.

"Sir, my name is Maria Bonaventure, from Santa Rita, Minas Gerais. I am here to apply for a visa to go to the United States. There is supposed to be an invitation here for me from my sponsor, Mr. Clarence van Dyke Jackson of New Orleans. Do you have it? Here is my application form."

The clerk took the forms and studied them. He asked her to wait for a minute and he called the commercial attaché, Clark Richardson. In a few more minutes, Richardson arrived in the waiting area and asked Maria to come with him to his office.

"Ms. Bonaventure, I have your application here, and I also have a letter of invitation from Mr. Van Dyke Jackson. If you do not mind, I have several questions that I would like to ask you. Is that all right with you?" Richardson asked very politely. He knew what he needed to know, and he knew he would also grant the visa. His boss had told him to do it. Mr. Jackson apparently had many friends in the State Department, and the phone call that morning from Washington was quite clear.

"It is okay. Please ask me, and I will answer truthfully for sure."

"What is your reason for visiting the US?"

"I have been asked to come by Mr. Van Dyke Jackson. He was here about eight weeks ago, as well as several times the past five years. I have known him for all that time. I think we are in love," she said with a smile and flush on her face.

"How long do you plan to be in the US?"

"I don't know. Perhaps a week or more."

"Do you still have family here in Brazil?"

"Yes, my mother and two sons live in Santa Rita."

"Do you plan to return to Brazil? What if Mr. Van Dyke Jackson asks you to stay?"

"I will return, no matter what. If he asks me to stay, I will return to see my mother and sons, collect them, and then return to America."

"In that case, we will grant you a visa for a temporary visit for thirty days. If you plan to stay longer, you must contact the Immigration and Naturalization Service in New Orleans, Miami, or Houston in order to be granted an extension. Do you understand this?"

"Yes, I understand. Thank you very much," Maria said most sincerely. She had become worried during these few questions that the attaché might not grant the visa to her. And she must get to New Orleans and see Van. She missed him so.

"Thank you for your honesty. If you will return to the waiting area, I will have your visa and passport returned in a few minutes. Goodbye, Ms. Bonaventure, and good luck to you."

"*Obrigato, senor*," she said and left.

The waiting seemed endless, but Maria looked at her watch, and it was only thirty minutes until her name was called and her passport with the visa returned. She paid the fees, collected her passport, and left the consulate. Jason was waiting outside for her, and they walked to the parked car. All the time they walked, Jason never stopped looking around and gauging the people on the street. It was natural for him, and he never knew who might have found out something concerning his boss and now his boss's new lover. He was paid to protect, and that is exactly what he did—and did it well.

The drive home was uneventful, and, the next day, Maria told her employer that she was going away for a few days. He was upset with this news and told her that if she did not return in a week, she would be considered fired, because he needed someone to handle his accounting. She agreed to this condition and finished her work for the day before she left. That night Maria had a long talk with her mother and two sons about why she was going to America. She talked about how she felt she loved this man she knew as Van, and that she needed to go to him. After the boys went to bed, she finally told her mother of her other life and her need to stop. She wanted a new beginning, and this might be her chance.

Maria's mother was shocked, and she cried when she heard the news about her daughter's life of prostitution, but she had always suspected something. She moved across the room and held Maria close and told her the boys would be okay and to go see if her love was true. Maria went to sleep that night full of concern, but she remembered the final evening and night with Van and how he needed her. She was convinced that somehow all would work out.

Five days later, in mid-afternoon, Jason returned and picked her up. He drove her to the Sao Paulo International Airport and took her to the American Airlines check-in counter. As Maria moved from the counter toward the customs-clearance area, Jason talked to her for a minute.

"Maria, I hope you have very pleasant journey. Van will meet you at the gate in New Orleans. Here is some US money for you, in case you need it." He gave Maria ten new twenty dollar bills folded over.

"Thank you, Jason. I will return this to you when I come back."

"There is no need. It is from Van to you. He wanted you to have some money already in case of an emergency. Please be very careful. I have heard from another source of mine that Carl may come to America for another meeting with Van. That doesn't sound right to me, as I think Carl may be wanted by the police. It is a big risk for him. You must be very careful and trust only the people that Van trusts and keeps close to him. Do you understand this clearly?"

"Yes, Jason, I understand. I must go now. Please be careful yourself. Ciao," said Maria as she waved to Jason.

American Airlines flight number 66 was full. Maria had a seat in first class and was able so sleep after dinner was served. She was awakened by a flight attendant for breakfast about two hours before the Boeing 767 landed in Miami at 6:30 a.m. Maria was fully awake as it landed in the early dawn.

Maria went through the US Customs entry formalities with only a few questions asked of her. She did not even have to open her baggage.

After exiting customs, Maria found herself on the lower level of the giant Miami terminal. She followed the sign and took the escalator up to the departure and ticketing level and found herself immediately in front of the large American Airlines check-in desk area. She checked in for the New Orleans flight in the first-class lane and was directed to gate D-17. She passed through the security check point and walked the long departure corridor to the gate.

Her wait was not long, and the flight boarded and took off. As the plane flew out over Miami Beach before making the hard left turn back to a northwest direction, she looked down and saw the water and beach. She thought of the days when she was young and lived in Salvador, Bahia, with her family, and of all the days they used to spend at the beach swimming and playing. She wondered now what New Orleans would be like and how she would find Van. What kind of mood would he be in? What will we do our first night? Will we make love? Will he take me out, or will we stay at home? What kind of danger is he in? And will we decide to get married?

Maria let her mind wander as the flight moved over the Everglades and then out over the Gulf of Mexico and the final leg of her journey to her hoped-for new life.

The plane circled the city from the north side over Lake Pontchartrain and landed smoothly to the south on the north-south runway. She could see the houses, the water canals, the hotels and buildings of downtown, and the shopping center almost as she landed. *It seems so flat*, she thought. *But I'm here.*

She walked off the plane, turned the corner and saw Van off to the right in the main departure gate area. He smiled and she ran to him and embraced him tightly. While she was in his arms and holding him, she could hardly believe she was here. It was a dream. *God, please don't let me wake up!*

"Maria, you look beautiful, my sweet."

She stood back, still holding him, and said, "Van, you look great. I have missed you so. Thank you for having me come here. It all seems like a dream to me."

"Come. Let's get your bags and go. I'm going to take you to my home, where you can rest from your journey. I still have some work to do today, so I will leave you there at my house and then return tonight, and we will go out to dinner."

With this said, he picked up her small traveling bag, and they left, looking like the many lovers who came to New Orleans for romance and love.

They talked of a few things during the half-hour drive to Jackson's home in East New Orleans—mostly about her kids and how things had been in getting the visa. She was fascinated by the greenery, even though it was only mid-March. It was still supposed to be winter in America, but New Orleans was very much in the South, where spring really begins in early March. And it was so flat. She was not used to this.

After they arrived at the house, Van put her bags in the bedroom and showed her around, helping her to get used to his home.

He made some tea and sat down in the kitchen to talk for a few minutes before he left.

"Maria, there may be trouble. You must not worry, as the house is being watched by the police—some very good friends of mine. There is a woman from Florida in town, supposedly looking for me. She is a known killer and works for the syndicato in Miami sometimes. She is not here for them. She has been hired by someone else, but I don't know who. I am worried it might by my partner, Carl. I tell you this so that you will know. All this happened only three days ago. Tonight, we will have dinner with a close friend of mine, a person I trust now very much. He will bring along his girlfriend. I know we will have a very nice time, and I don't want you to worry. I needed to tell you though, as there will be some police and some other persons around close for me, all watching out for our safety. We know what the woman looks like and where she is staying. She is being watched, so we feel more comfortable about keeping up with her movements. I must leave now, so make yourself at home here. My office number is on the pad, and you already have my mobile number. I should be back about five thirty, and then we will go meet my friend, Jake Briscoe, about seven thirty."

He got up from the table and gave her a long kiss. She kissed him back, and he began to wonder why he was going back to work. They could spend a long afternoon together. But then he remembered why he was going back, and he pulled away from Maria.

"Van, I wish you didn't have to go, but I understand. I will get some rest and be ready for your return. I can hardly wait." Maria kissed him again.

He went out the back door to the garage and his car while she watched him go. She locked the doors, walked back to the bedroom, and removed her clothes. She looked in the mirror as the bath water filled the tub. She thought, *I look good. And I will give him the best tonight!*

Nina Carlton heard the bath water running from the microphone in the bedroom and turned off her recorder. *So they know where I am, do they? Well, it is time I took that situation and showed them the professional I really am. I have been too lax these past few days. So it's time to make another move.* She packed her bags, her radio-listening relay devices, and her recorders. She opened the door, walked straight to the car, and drove away out on to Chartres Street.

* * *

Carl Durnbacher was having dinner in his home about this time. He knew it was time to contact Nina Carlton for a meet in the next few days. He had decided to go to New Orleans. He needed to talk with her about what was going on. He called the motor inn and asked for her room. The phone rang and rang and rang, with no answer. No, he could not leave a message. He hung up. He was unsure what to do. He decided to call a local friend and go out for a while. Perhaps they would know another way to contact Nina.

* * *

Lucas Marcello watched Nina Carlton leave the hotel from his car in the back of the motor inn parking lot. He did not try to follow her, but he picked up his mobile phone and called Maryanne Delgado, who was parked down Chartres in another car. Delgado spotted her and began the quiet chase of following her while Lucas left and drove to Esplanade to begin a two-car follow pattern. He made another quick call to his boss and told him that Nina was on the move, with her bags. His boss called Jackson and Briscoe and let them know to be doubly careful.

Nina drove back up Royale Street and turned right onto Canal. She drove directly into the Marriott garage entrance, got the bags out of the car, and left it for the valet parking. Marcello drove into the garage in time to see her walk into the hotel lobby. He got out of the car, walked inside, and began the search for Carlton. She was nowhere to be seen. He went over to the concierge and asked if he had seen her. He showed him the picture of Nina taken at lunch a couple of days earlier. No luck—she had not checked in. She was gone.

Marcello went back out to the garage, retrieved his car, and made the calls. Everyone on the other end of each call was not happy. She had gotten away. The word went out on the street for everyone involved with the family to look for her. A bonus was involved for the first spotter and the person that could keep her under observation until one of Marty's lieutenants could get a confirmed and stable watch on her.

* * *

Carlton sensed the eyes on her as she left the hotel room. After entering the Marriott, she dropped all the bags but two at a spot by a planter in the central lounge area, and then she walked directly out the front door to flag a taxi on Canal. She went to the airport and then to Hertz to get another car. With this done, she drove to the Holiday Inn at I-10 and Causeway Boulevard in Metairie, a western suburb of New Orleans. She had no problem getting a room. She set up the sensor equipment and went the short distance to Lakeside Mall. She needed a few things now that she had left her clothes back in the Marriott, and she was able to get everything she would need for the next few days in about an hour. Nina returned to the hotel, parked in the back lot, and entered by the service entrance. As she came inside, she saw the laundry area, where several people were finishing up for the day. A tall, black man by the name of Maurice Gedson looked up from the large laundry basket and saw the white, very good-looking woman walk past. Something struck him about her looks. He would check on a picture in the employee break room later. Now he had to get this last load underway.

Nina went to her room. The sensors for the Jackson home were on, the recorders running. *Must be the woman from Brazil roaming around the house.* She listened for a couple of minutes and didn't hear anything worth a continuing effort. Nina went to the bathroom, took a shower, and laid down on the bed for a nap. This could be an interesting evening. Time to get some rest.

At 4:35 p.m., Maurice Gedson was done. He could go home. He remembered the woman and wanted to check the picture before he left. *Well, why not?* It would only take a couple of minutes. He stared at the picture for at least that much before he decided to make a phone call.

"Mr. Marty, please; this is Maurice Gedson out at Holiday Inn, Metairie," Maurice said to the person that answered the number under the picture.

"Just a minute, please," came the impersonal response on the other end of the line.

"Mr. Gedson, this is Marty. What can I do for you?" Marty asked.

"Mr. Marty, I'm in the laundry here, and I saw a woman come in the service entrance this afternoon that sure looks like the woman in the picture that Mr. Vincent dropped off early this afternoon. Do I gets the reward?"

"We'll see, Mr. Gedson. Stay put if you can. I'll have Vincent there in ten minutes. Thanks." The line went dead.

Gedson really needed to get home, but the reward of a thousand dollars cash was worth a little wait for Mr. Vincent.

Vincent Gaultier arrived in his dark-gray T-bird in exactly ten minutes. He had been at Jake's office, so it was a short drive down I-10 to Causeway Boulevard from Williams. He went inside the service entrance and found Mr. Gedson standing by the door.

"Mr. Gedson, I'm Vincent Gaultier. Do you know me?"

"Yes, sir. I know you well. Anyhow, I'm just tryin' to help out and get that reward. I saw her come in about four p.m. She was carryin' some shopping bags. She looked into our work area back there—the door was open because of the humidity today in there—and I looked up jus' as she passed by. I got a real good look, and it is her."

"Any idea which room she might be in?" Vincent asked.

"Nope. None. I didn't follow her."

"Okay, good work. We will start a watch here, as this is our first real lead this afternoon. If we confirm it is her, then you will get the money for sure, I promise you. Okay?"

"Yes sir. I'm off tomorrow, but I'm back in on Sunday. Thanks. Can I leave now?"

"Yes, and thanks."

Gedson went out to the back parking lot to his car and saw the new, green Ford Escort in the parking lot. The hotel wasn't that full, and there were plenty of spots out front and along the east side. He walked back in and found Gaultier on the phone in the hallway. Gaultier saw him coming and hung up from the call.

"Mr. Vincent, there is a car out back that don't belong to none of us workers. It's a green Ford Escort. Just thought you ought to know. Okay?"

"Okay, that is great. Thanks again, Gedson. And if it is her, and that is her car, I'll give you an extra five hundred dollars for the watchful eye and taking the time to come back in and tell me. I'll see you Sunday." Vincent stuck out his hand and shook Gedson's. Gedson turned around and went out to his car with a huge smile now. *Wow! Fifteen hundred for the information. I sure hope it is her,* he thought as he drove out the entrance onto the service road.

Vincent Gaultier called again to Marty and gave him the new bit of news. Vincent went back to his car and drove around to the front parking lot, where he could watch the hotel entrance. There was only one way in and out from the back parking lot. He spotted Maryanne's car come into the lot, and she drove over to the gray T-bird.

"Vincent, I'll go to the other end of the back lot and keep an eye on the car. You watch the front entrance. Call for help if you see her come out and take a taxi. She might not use the car again."

"Got it, Maryanne," Vincent replied and rolled up the window.

Maryanne drove around to the rear of the hotel and parked at the far end of the employees' parking lot. She got a good look at the green Escort and got out and walked around to get the license number: BCA-457. She wrote it down on the pad on her dash and called Vincent with this information.

After taking this call from Maryanne, Vincent called in.

"Marty, Vincent here. Maryanne here too. We have the car covered and the front covered. License number is BCA-457. Hertz sticker on the car."

"Vincent, good work. Don't lose her this time if it is her. Otherwise, you had best go to Texas, my friend. Capiche?"

"Got it, boss. We won't lose her. I'll call in as soon as she is on the move."

"Okay, get her. We have a big reputation on the line. If we fail on this one, we will lose a lot of protection money—and that is not what we want to happen. I'll check you later." Marty hung up the phone.

Marty's second call a few days earlier to Miami was very informative. The New Orleans family was cleared to take action on Nina Carlton only if she made a move on Jake and Jackson in the open; and she would have to make the move first. Otherwise, she was not to be touched. She was freelance, for sure, but she had Miami family overall protection. This would be difficult. Marty promised himself that, no matter what might happen, Jake would not get hurt. The debt was an honorable one for all his payments, and he must be protected. They had honor.

CHAPTER 33

28 March 2001

The MD-11 was ready to go. American Airlines flight number AA81 from Frankfurt to Dallas had been fully fueled, the bags were in the final stages of loading, and the passengers were now filing on. Carl Durnbacher would be among them this Wednesday.

He had arrived at Frankfurt Airport after driving from Dusseldorf. During this past week, he had become increasingly concerned that events he needed Nina Carlton make happen in New Orleans warranted his personal involvement, even though the risk was high. It was a risk he had to take, because the bigger risk was now full exposure by his partner.

"Mr. Durnser, welcome to American Airlines. I have a few questions for you today, and I hope this will not inconvenience you," said the very lovely assistant gate agent as she examined Carl's ticket and passport. "Do you have any bags checked? I see that you have none."

"No, I have only my briefcase and my traveling bag," replied Carl.

"Okay, did you pack the bags yourself, and when was that done?"

"I packed the bags last night and this morning."

"Have they been out of your possession since that time, and has anyone given you anything to bring with you?"

"No, they have not been out of my possession, and no one has given me anything."

"Anything electrical in the bags?"

"No, only my computer in my briefcase and my electric razor in the hanging bag."

"Very good. I see that your final destination today is New Orleans. You know you will have to clear US Immigration and Customs authorities in Dallas. Here are the forms for you to use upon arrival. Please have them filled out before you get there. Have a good trip, and thank you for flying with American." And the short interrogation was over.

"Thank you," Carl responded and picked up his bag and went through the second security screening. The holding lounge was now almost empty. He had decided carefully to arrive just at the time of boarding so that he would lessen his chances of perhaps being recognized by the occasional FBI or CIA operative traveling. He moved down the jet way and onto the plane with smiles for all. He found his seat, 11B, near the front of business class and on the aisle. He settled in and said a quick hello to his seatmate, a young woman in black tights and a roll-neck, black, cotton sweater. He sized her up quickly as a young businesswoman, but not worth his time today. He wanted to be rested when he arrived in Dallas and for the rest of the journey to New Orleans.

His flight was very typical, with drinks and lunch being served after takeoff. The eleven-hour flight would give him plenty of time for rest and sleep after the service was completed. The shades were pulled down, and everyone seemed to settle himself or herself even more for the long flight to Texas. He got up to allow the young woman out, and glanced over at her bag on the floor for a quick look. She had a business card in a clear plastic holder attached to it: "Ms. Cynthia Gordon, Director of Marketing, HSA Hospitals, Austin, Texas."

Pretty innocuous, he thought.

When she returned, he got up and went to the lavatory himself. As he returned to his seat, he saw that his seatmate had pulled up a blanket, put on an eyeshade, and was trying to go to sleep. *Great,* he thought. *Time to do the same thing.*

CHAPTER 34

1 April 2001

Michael awoke with a quick start. What was that beeping tone? As he rubbed the sleep from his eyes and focused his mind on the small but continuous sound coming from the closet, he realized the monitor had sounded, and so he got out of bed and moved to the closet and opened it. He turned off the monitor and turned on the radio. He could hear clearly the commands going to different units located in the Transvaal and Capetown areas. They didn't have much time—they always knew they would not.

As he stood there, a cold shiver ran through his entire body. The questions in his mind now came too quickly for answers. His usual thinking mode of analysis and careful consideration of all the facts before he made a decision was under assault from the need to implement their escape plan. He shook off the anxiety and realized that only common sense and quickness might save him and Carter from the impending terrors and possible death to come. They might be killed or captured at any step along the way of their escape, but at least they would die trying to save themselves rather than wait for the inevitable.

Michael immediately went back to the bedroom and awakened Carter. When she looked up at him with that sleepy look of wonder, he said, "Carter, we have to go now. The attack has started in south Jo'burg. We don't have much time. Please get up and get dressed so we can go."

Carter felt the rush of adrenalin throughout her whole body.

"Michael, I'm scared."

She put out her arms, and they held each other for a very long minute. They could feel the heat of the flush of the adrenalin working, and now they were both awake. She looked at Michael longingly, but there definitely was no time for love now.

Carter got out of bed and went to the bathroom. Within five minutes, she was washed and dressed. She finished putting the final cans of food and supplies into the sea bag and her travel clothes into another duffel bag. Michael dressed in jeans and his dark, navy-blue pullover. He took his own partially packed bag from the closet, where the radio was still broadcasting the commands and chatter from the units of the ALFM, and placed it on the bed and finished putting his last few items in the bag.

Now that the packing was done, Michael went to the closet and turned off the radio. He dialed a different frequency, unplugged the monitor, and put it on the floor behind his shoes. Carter looked around the apartment for any major items not to leave behind. She remembered the small picture of her mom and dad in her dresser, and she went there and found it. She was looking at it as Michael came out of the closet. They embraced one more moment, and then they went out of the apartment and down the stairs to the car. He pulled out into the street and began making his well-practiced drive to the old airfield. It was only seven minutes away, and this part of their journey, although risky to some degree, should go smoothly.

And it did for one small, but very significant moment. Carter cried as they left the house. She couldn't hold back the emotion of this major event, even if it was four thirty a.m. and they had to move quickly as if their lives depended on moving quickly. She began to wonder what would happen to the many friends they would now leave behind. Would they even survive? She wondered if she and Michael would ever see their beautiful homeland of South Africa again and all its glory. It was hard to leave, but now they must choose between living and dying. They must go on living. She wondered if the future was going to allow them to do the things they wanted—but first they must escape the impending tragedy around them and live somewhere else to see that future.

Michael drove the black BMW 353i quickly but carefully through the dark streets that were lighted with the orange glow of the high-pressure sodium street lamps. He saw a few blacks on their way to work, which was normal at this hour and in this neighborhood; but some seemed in a special hurry or with some urgency to get where they were going. No one walking noticed the car, and that made Michael at least somewhat more confident. He thought, *Why wasn't the alarm sounded to keep their own people out of harm's way?* But since there were tribal agendas involved as well as political ones, he concluded that what was to begin that day according to the alarm and the radio was probably unknown to most of the black majority of South Africa.

Finally he came to the sharp right turn on the road that led to the airfield. It was an airfield in name only. Usage was limited to daytime, and the grass runway was only cut once each week by two blacks on riding mowers. The runway, as it was, was marked by pylons along each side, and at both ends stood a row of three hangers. In the center of the field and on one side stood the tin-sided, rusty office building and two-story lookout tower. The tower had white wood siding that was peeling badly, and, in the back, one could find a few boards that were coming loose from the interior studs. It had not been painted in over fifteen years.

The airfield was used now only for a few private planes and by a group of WWII airplane enthusiasts who met for some flying and much drinking every other Sunday. The flying was weather permitting of course, but the meeting and drinking went exactly as scheduled.

There was a night watchman, since the private planes kept there by several local companies, and several very wealthy whites were worth some money. He slept in the back of the office in a small room with his TV, radio, dresser, bed, and the ever-present bottle of Glenfiddich whiskey supplied by one of the wealthy plane owners who took his mistress on flights to Phalabora every other weekend. The whiskey was the payoff for silence if the plane-owner's wife called and inquired about her husband and whom he had with him that weekend. The whiskey was good, plentiful, and lasted for each two-week stint, and the night watchman never failed to provide the right answer to the wife of the plane-owner. The whiskey also made for a good night's sleep after long days of prowling around the airfield, doing some small chores as needed, and watching the most boring TV programs in the world.

This particular night the watchman, Jake Cuttler by name and an English midlander by birth with small height, small feet, broad shoulders, and a small, round face with two cheek dimples, had watched the soccer match of Manchester United against Hull by satellite. He rooted for Manchester United all the way and was overjoyed when they won with a goal in the last two minutes, 4-3. He turned that off at one a.m. and listened to the local radio as he continued to taste and appreciate the fine whiskey supplied to him every two weeks by the fine gentleman from Sandton. How easy it was to notice when the wife called or dropped by and to tell the right story. And there was usually a quite right tip at Christmas! He had fallen into a very peaceful slumber and was deep into it now at five a.m. He hadn't heard the car pull up or the few people now making their way around the perimeter of the airfield.

Michael put out the headlights as they came around the turn. He put the car in neutral and cut the engine off as it went down the old rutted, red dirt road, which dropped down the embankment from the highway. They stopped about ten yards from the back of one of the three grouped, weather-worn hangers.

"Okay, let's go," he whispered to Carter.

They both opened their doors quietly and got out of the car. Each grabbed two duffle bags and ran low to the ground toward the dark building. Michael found the combination lock on the main hanger door and moved the dial in his sweaty fingers. Carter held the small pocket light on the lock with one hand and shielded the light with her other hand. Michael and Carter were so close in the stillness that they could hear each other breathing. Carter maintained a vigil over the field while Michael got the lock open with a slightly perceptible click in the early morning stillness surrounding them. Slowly he pushed open first one door and the other as Carter ran inside to get the lift-jack truck to pull the helicopter outside.

She found the truck at the back of the very dark hanger in the corner by the maintenance toolbox. It was about eight feet wide, with a large pull bar on the front, two large rubber wheels mounted on either side of the frame, and a locking pin at the rear. She grabbed hold of the pull bar, moved it around to the front of the hanger, and pushed it up close to the helicopter. Michael finished stowing the bags in the plane and came around to help her. He moved under the front of the helicopter as Carter positioned the lift-jack in front to lower it and capture the locking pin into the clasp on the helicopter's lower carriage. She lifted the front of the truck, which lowered the opposite end, and Michael put the pin in place on the carriage clasp. He crawled out from under the helicopter and moved to the pull bar with Carter. With a strong push, the truck's front went down, and the helicopter front moved up and now could be moved by the lift-jack with its wheels on the rear of the undercarriage.

They looked at each other for a moment and began to move the helicopter out to the area in front of the old hanger. As Michael was pulling on the truck, he kept thinking about how many times they had practiced up to this point. Ten? Twenty? Now it was for real, and that was all that mattered.

Carter got into the helicopter and began the preflight checks. Michael went to the front and crawled back under it and unfastened the clasp and locking pin. Now he moved back to the lift-jack and moved it out of the way. Normally, it would be returned to the front area of the hanger, but tonight there would be no time. He completed this as the whine of the engine startled the birds on the other side of the runway, and the pulsating throb of the propellers shook the early morning quiet away.

Carter would do the flying, and Michael would navigate and act as spotter for any trouble. In making their escape plan two years ago, it was decided that Carter would be best at the controls, and Michael would be free to handle the automatic rifle in the event someone would try to stop them. The cost of Carter's training and joining the three-couple flying club that owned the helicopter was very expensive, but they had managed with a loan from Carter's father. Suddenly, Michael wondered what they would have done if one of the other couples had made a similar escape plan and arrived before they did. In any event, it didn't matter now.

With one final, quick look around, he said with a sigh and emphasis, "Now!"

Carter still didn't say anything. She was concentrating on everything she had been taught, practiced, and made second nature to her—almost like sex. She knew exactly what to do, and, with a slight twist of the lift handle, the small helicopter came off the ground. She increased the lift angle and directed the plane toward the grass-covered runway and checked the wind sock in the early morning light that was just now bringing the darkness to an end and the shadows of the old airport buildings into clarity around them.

This was the second major point of potential trouble Michael and Carter had identified in their plan. They knew about the night watchman and his drinking habits, and they had counted on that for the few moments needed to get the plane out of the hanger. What they were really worried about was the engine starting—would it arouse the watchman or anyone else?

As the machine lifted off and began the short trip to the runway, the lights came on in the shed. Carter saw it from the corner of her eye, but she kept on moving the helo. She turned it into the wind, increased the rotor speed and angle, and applied the lift, and it rose like a swift racing dove into the dawn sky, which now glowed quite bright in the east.

They looked back on the field and could see the watchman come out of the old tower and begin running after them. Michael watched for a minute and turned away as he saw the man fall to the ground. Michael didn't hear the shot of the rifle over the noise of the helo.

Unknown to Michael and Carter during their arrival at the hangers, a lone individual had watched everything through the latest USA-developed infrared sniper scope. He could have easily picked them both off, making them perhaps among the first casualties of the downfall, but he didn't fire a single shot at them. He was their unknown benefactor at this moment and had fired the shot that had brought down the night watchman; and Mr. Jake Cuttler now had the distinction of being among the first, but certainly not the only casualty of that infamous day. John Wesley Zooma got up from the ground on the runway side of the airport. He had hidden there from the moment his unit commander had called after midnight to let him know of the action to take place that day and where. He knew of Michael and Carter's plan to escape. He had given Michael the radio and the frequency at much risk to himself. His friendship for them knew no color boundary, and he owed them much. But now that debt was paid. All accounts were square with his only white friends. He dusted off his new fatigues and boots and quickly began the two-mile jog to his unit, which was now beginning to form up for the action planned for them.

CHAPTER 35

1 April 2001

Gilbert Parker was dreaming of being in a room full of strangers who all seemed to be talking at once. As his eyes went from person to person, he recognized none of them. Quite suddenly, they all stopped talking at once and looked toward a radio that was now making a terrible beeping sound. Parker walked through the crowded room and tried to fiddle with it and get it back on the station, But his attempts at turning all the dials were futile. The incessant tone continued.

"Damn it!" Parker shouted. "Will somebody fix this before we all go insane?"

No one in his dream moved. The others seemed transfixed and motionless, as if their lives were leaving them the longer the tone continued.

Parker awoke. His eyes quickly fixed themselves on the window and the growing daylight outside. He could feel the noise of the beeping go through him to the back of his head. His hands shot to his ears because the tone would not go away. He sat up in bed and tried to decide in an instant if he was going mad.

In a flash of recognition, similar to that of one being awakened in the night by a ringing phone, he knew that the beeping tone was coming from his radio alarm down the hall. The special radio had been installed in a closet by his son-in-law, Michael Stephens. Now it was beeping loudly.

Parker threw back the covers and raced down the hall, opened the closet, reached up to the special radio alarm, and turned it off. He stood there in his shorts and he wondered if the alarm was real. Did any of his apartment neighbors hear it? How long had it been beeping? Should he call Michael and Carter to tell them?

As his mind quickly formed each new question, the answers came just as quickly. Fortunately, the answers had reason and logic rather than emotion. He put his ear to the door and listened intently for any noises in the hall. None; no one else seemed stirring on his floor.

Parker walked backed to the bedroom and checked his watch on the nightstand beside the bed. It was 4:45 a.m. He thought again about calling his daughter, and he picked up the phone. The dial tone reassured him. *At least the phones are still working,* he thought. *But,* he wondered for another second, *why do I even think they might not?*

He sat down on the bed with the phone in his shaking hand and tried to think what he should do. He remembered that a phone call wasn't in the plan. He knew Michael well enough that the phone wouldn't be answered if he did call. Parker put the handset back.

He suddenly realized that he must act quickly. The plan that Parker, Michael, and Carter had developed over several evenings and nights among the three of them called for quick and deliberate actions. There was some flexibility, but of utmost importance was speed of action. If anything was to be on their side in their escape, it must be speed and quickness. They must react and get away before the uprising of the blacks became so widespread that their chances would be severely diminished.

Parker went into the bathroom and turned on the light over the sink. He stood at the toilet and thought of what he would do and the order in which he would do it. He washed his face and hands and decided on a quick shave. It was a part of him each morning, and he needed it to feel like he was truly awake and ready for each day. He lathered and, with practiced strokes, removed the stubble from the previous day and night. He washed his face, dried himself with the hand towel, and put on some of his favorite aftershave. The tingling sensation and the smell brought with him a smile of confidence. He now felt ready for whatever.

Parker took several more minutes to brush his teeth and hair. He prided himself on his appearance, and, today, no matter what was going on in the world outside his door, he would face it as he always had—at least looking good and well-shaven.

He moved back to the bedroom closet, dressed in his underwear, and pulled on a pair of khaki pants and a long-sleeved shirt. He rolled the sleeves up to the elbows for now. He put on his jogging shoes and pulled a partially packed, dark-blue sea bag from the top shelf of his closet. He removed it and was thinking of the risks they all might face. *Would he get out to sea? Would Carter make it to the rendezvous as planned? Would they get caught before or after that? Would they be taken prisoner? Would they be killed? They must have some luck on their side. Bad luck just would not do.*

Parker took the sea bag into the living room, where he packed his light khaki windbreaker, his tennis sneakers, and his lucky lap blanket. It was made of cashmere wool from Scotland and designed in the Dress Stewart plaid. He had won it in a crap game on a British destroyer in WWII while on patrol in the South Atlantic. The next day, his destroyer had been torpedoed, and he survived, along with the blanket. For some reason he could never explain to anyone—or even to himself—when the alarm sounded to abandon ship after being torpedoed, he grabbed the blanket and his life preserver and ran on deck. He jumped overboard with it tied around his waist. It dragged him as he tried to swim away from the sinking ship and the undertow. Somehow, he came up with a well of strength and found a raft. He drifted alone and used the blanket to keep warm and soak up rainwater to drink. Two days later, he was picked up by an American destroyer on patrol. He decided to keep the blanket with him wherever he went.

He went into the kitchen and took several tins of crackers, canned meat, fruit, and a large canteen of water from the pantry and put them in the bag. From the freezer, he produced a foil-wrapped package that contained over one hundred thousand dollars in travelers checks. He stuffed this into the back of his underwear after removing the aluminum foil and rewrapping the checks in a plastic sandwich bag. He now began to feel confident that this would all work out . . . well, somehow.

With a check of everything around the apartment, Parker removed a set of keys from a nail hanger by the window over the sink and shoved them in his pants pocket. *Only one item left.* He took the bag into the living room again and pulled a small .45-caliber revolver from a box under the sofa. He loaded it with shells, put the box with the rest of the shells, in the bag, and gave his apartment one last look. He felt some remorse at leaving this place he had lived since the death of Jeannette. After she died, he could no longer live in the house they had built and raised Carter in. It was too painful—too many memories. He moved to this apartment in a very secure and lovely area of Durban and carried on finding his new life without her.

Parker went to the door and unbolted it. He opened it carefully and looked out through the crack to see if anyone was there. All clear—there was no one. Now, he picked up the sea bag on the floor, turned out the lights, stepped outside, and closed and locked the door carefully behind him. *Why,* he thought, *am I doing this? Will I ever get back?*

As he approached the exit to the stairwell, he heard a ding from the elevator bell behind him, meaning it was going to stop at his floor. *Someone was on the elevator!*

Parker moved to the stairwell door and opened it quickly. He closed it just as the elevator door opened. He peeked through the door crack and saw a black with an automatic machine pistol get off and look around the hall. The black man went down the hall to apartment number four and knocked. This was the apartment of Mr. Eberhard, a tall European who seemed to always be traveling. Parker decided he had seen enough for now; it was time for him to get going. He tiptoed down the first two flights and took the next eight flights two steps at a time.

Parker reached the bottom from his apartment on the eleventh floor in a couple of minutes—much easier going down than going up. He opened the door to the basement parking garage and looked out the crack to see if anyone was there—empty. He opened the door all the way and walked quickly to the parking lot to his BMW. He unlocked the trunk and put in the sea bag, but he first removed

Downfall and Freedom

the .45 and put it in the pocket of his jacket. He closed the trunk with a small click and moved around to the driver's door, opened it, and got in. Now he felt comfortable again, with the familiar smell of the leather interior and the seat fitting his large body exactly. He put in the key and turned it.

He was supposed to open the door to the street before he started the car, but he wasn't going to take the chance this time. *To hell with the old ladies on the first floor.* They'd almost died when a very old man with Alzheimer's pulled into the garage one night and sat in it with the car running until asphyxiation almost killed him. He'd just forgotten to turn the car off. Parker thought how he felt at hearing the news of the old man, but he chuckled to himself about the two old ladies on the first floor who'd also nearly died from the fumes. They were always complaining about something or someone in the building, but now, they would have to deal with whatever would come.

The BMW engine had a very nice, reassuring sound. He needed that now; he was beginning to feel scared. He had a short drive to the harbor, but what would he find outside the door of the apartment building, in the streets? Had an attack started? Was the alarm for real? He fought the anxieties now.

Parker hit the remote control, and the big, overhead steel door from the garage to the street began to roll up. He put the car in gear, pushed down on the gas, and moved out of his parking space into the garage. Just at that moment, the door to the stairwell opened and the black man who had been up on his floor began to come into the garage. Parker saw him in the rearview mirror and increased his speed. As he left the building, the last thing he saw was the black man running toward him, yelling something. But Parker was not going back or waiting around to find out—not this time.

CHAPTER 36

1 April 2001

The streets of Durban were still lit by the streetlights with the orange glow and the early morning dawn. Parker noticed that they seem deserted compared to a more normal weekday morning, with blacks walking along the sidewalks, on their way to work. He then realized this was Sunday, and there would not be as many people out. He came to a corner at the bottom of the hill and could see the harbor up ahead. As he came to a stop, a black woman on the curb pointed to him and shouted out to a black man up the street. Parker couldn't hear what she said, but he saw the man begin running toward the car. He put the BMW in gear again and sped on to the next intersection. Again, his rearview mirror provided a view of someone yelling at him and pointing to his car. He was beginning to feel scared. Something must have started to cause these otherwise normally calm blacks to yell and come after him. He made an instant decision to make no more full stops at intersections. He wanted to get to the boat—and to safety.

Luckily, there were no more incidents on the way to the harbor. Parker drove the car into his assigned space and shut off the engine. He got out and walked around to the trunk and opened it, all the time looking around for anyone. He was alone in the parking lot, but he noticed a few other cars belonging to friends who would not normally be there this time of morning. He closed the trunk after removing the sea bag and locked the car. He moved down to the dock, always looking around behind him. He saw a couple of black men a few blocks away, toward the restaurants across the truck parking lot, but they didn't seem to notice him. Finally, he arrived at the motorboat and threw the bag on board, near the rear hatch.

The boat was fiberglass and very sleek with a main mast with jib, and a two-hundred-horsepower Chrysler engine. The boat was always in great shape. It cost very little to hire several blacks to keep it scrubbed and the engine, sails, and rigging in good repair.

Parker moved the hatchway open and went down to check the engine and compartments. Nothing seemed out of order. *Good.* He took the revolver out of the bag and stowed the food in the pantry by the small stove. Now it was time to leave and get out to sea for the planned rendezvous with Carter and Michael.

On deck, he started the engine and could feel and hear the sound beneath him. He waited for the gauges to read in normal, and he went forward to release the bow line. It came off easily, and he circled it on the deck.

Now he walked to the stern, but, out of the corner of his right eye, he could see a group of blacks, each one carrying something, moving across the truck parking lot toward the boat harbor. He didn't want to find out what they had—he had to get out of here, *now!*

The stern line would not come loose from the shore cleat. Parker stepped across the small chasm between the boat and the dock and worked to free the line. It was in a terrible knot. The blacks that had worked on the boat last week must have not known how to tie it. He looked over his shoulder and saw the group still coming, but they hadn't seen him yet. The knot still wouldn't free itself. He had no time to spend with it now. He jumped back aboard and went down into the cabin and pulled open the drawer that had the cooking knives and pulled out one for a fish-skinning. When he came back on deck, he saw that the group was now moving his way toward the head of the dock. He reached down for the rope and worked to cut it through. Finally, it dropped away to the deck.

Parker stepped over to the controls, moved the throttle ahead, and turned the wheel to move the boat away from the dock. He had a straight shot out of the harbor once he put the boat in position, but he would have his back to the dock and had to concentrate with all his effort to get through the opening between all the moored boats. He heard a yell. "Hey, man, what are you doing?"

Parker turned around and saw the group now running after him.

"Just going fishing for the day!" Parker yelled back.

"Hey, man, stop that boat now!" the lead black yelled. He was wearing fatigues and carrying a rifle slung from his left arm.

Parker ignored this last command and put the throttle full forward. *To hell with the wakes on the other moored boats.* The boat moved forward more swiftly, but the lead black was keeping up, yet still about fifty yards behind Parker. Parker looked around again and saw the black drop to knee-firing position as the others behind him ran to catch up. Parker dove into the cabin as the gun fired; he heard the bullet zoom past overhead. *At least the bastard is a poor shot,* he thought. Another round hit the wheel, and pieces of wood splintered at him while he crouched. He had to take a chance now and make sure the boat was still headed out of the harbor through the breakwater. He grabbed for the revolver in the holster by the gangway and fired it in the general direction of the dock, not really aiming at any of the group. The shot went over their heads, but they dropped to the ground and covered themselves. Several moved behind mooring piers for cover. Parker fired again and looked up over the hatchway to the bow and saw the boat was almost at the breakwater opening. *Almost free!*

As the boat moved out into the open water, he could feel the swells of the Indian Ocean now, and he kept heading directly away from shore. The group of blacks were now back on their feet and firing, but the shots were falling short. One of them, a smaller man, had left the group and was running toward the concrete breakwater where it met the shore. He was very fast for such a small person. Parker tried to judge if the runner would make it to the end and still find him in range. He decided it would be close, and so he took a chance and fired at the runner. The shot was so obviously short, but the runner paused for a second, and that bought Parker a little more time. Parker fired again, but this time the runner knew he was safe and just kept going.

Parker put the boat hard over to port. This would not take him further away from shore, but would move him much faster away from the south end of the breakwater where the runner was moving. The boat moved smartly in the water. Parker hit the automatic switch and locked the wheel in place while he moved around the starboard side of the hatchway and up the deck, crouching low.

The runner made it to the end of the breakwater and started firing the machine pistol. A couple of bullets hit the rear gunwale, and splinters of fiberglass and wood flew again. Parker hid behind the main mast and waited. *This is too close. What is happening?* He looked around carefully after the firing stopped and saw the black shaking his fist at Parker.

Now it was time to get away from shore and on course. Parker crouched low again and made his way back to the cockpit. He released the autopilot control and turned the wheel to the right; the boat now moved to starboard and out to sea. After about a half-hour, he could barely see the shore, and he turned north to move up to the rendezvous beach. He upped the throttle and increased speed. The wind was going to be great today, but he needed to take a quick pee as he started north up the Natal coast to the rendezvous point, Tinley Manor Beach.

He put the wheel in the locked position and went downstairs to make a badly needed cup of tea. He poured the water in the kettle and lit the gas stove. He was so confused now. It all seemed so natural earlier—leaving the apartment after the alarm; the drive out of the garage; making his way through the streets to the harbor . . . The rope was unusual, and the lack of blacks very noticeable. The ones that were out were militant. He shuddered. God he needed that damn tea. Now he wondered if Carter and Michael would make it. Their journey was much longer, over four hundred kilometers, and very treacherous. He thought, *More time for reactions of the blacks and more places for trouble to appear. God, how had all this happened? Life had been so good here. All he missed was Jeanette, and he was finally getting over her loss.* He folded his arms around himself and tried to keep himself from shaking.

Finally, the tea kettle began its light whistle, and he took it, poured some water in the cup, and added the tea bag. Carefully he dipped it in the hot water and saw the reddish brown of the calming liquid develop in the cup. When he thought it was right—and he had been doing this for almost sixty years—he took the spoon and placed the bag in it and gave a small jerk with the string and squeezed the bag with the string. He picked up the cup and held it with both hands. He needed to feel its warmth. He was scared, and he knew it. He blew over the top of the cup and took his first sip. He felt the liquid slightly scald his lips and tongue. The smell was wonderful, and he breathed it in and smiled. He took another sip and began to feel calmer. A lot had to be done, and it had been close the last time but the confidence was returning. He had tough times before and had always made it. And he would make it this time he thought. *God, I hope Carter and Michael are okay. Did they get to the helo and get away, or was the airport already secured by the ALFM? Had they had trouble during the flight? Where are they now? What is the weather like? No time to check—only time to run for our lives. Who gives a damn about the weather anyway now. It will be whatever it will be. What is important is to live!*

Parker grabbed a couple of biscuits from the package in the cupboard and went back up the stairs to the deck, taking his tea with him. When he got there, he saw that he was moving along nicely, but it was time to do some sailing instead of running the motor any longer. He went forward, unlashed the main mast, and returned to the wheel cockpit. He turned on the special winch and the main sail went up the mast and into position. The wind direction and speed indicator were reading on the gauges in the cockpit, and now he could adjust the wheel and mast to catch the offshore breeze and continue to move northward along the Natal coast, toward the planned beach rendezvous. With the main sail now set, he pulled the throttle back and turned off the engine. The silence now made him feel even calmer. The wind passing the sail and the ocean slipping underneath the sleek boat was all he could hear. The silence of sailing was one of his greatest joys, and the moments on this boat were the times he treasured. If only this boat could save them. It was a very long journey ahead to freedom.

He could hear a plane coming now in the distance, and now he could see it. It was a small one with one engine, painted white with green stripes down the length. He could make out the marking in black letters on the wings and the tail, GHZ-SA, and there were two people inside. The plane flew over him, turned, and came at the boat very low. He stood there in the cockpit and put his hand on the revolver, just in case. What were they looking for? Why were they out here? Who were they?

The plane flew about a mile away and turned and came back for another look at Parker and the boat. The pilot was talking on the radio this pass. Parker knew he had more trouble, but this plane was not it. Trouble would come from whoever was in charge on the other end of that radio conversation. He did notice this time that the pilot was white, or at least light in skin, but the passenger with the pilot was black.

After this last pass, the plane continued north up the coast as far as Parker could see it. With it gone, he decided it was time to hit the head again and eat a sandwich. After checking the bearing, he locked the wheel in place again and went downstairs. In all the excitement of the last hour, he hadn't realized the pressure building again until now, and a smile came to him with the relief. He washed his hands, moved back into the galley, and found the bread he had brought. He pulled some cheese from the refrigerator and made a quick, but very tasty cheese sandwich. *Just what I need,* he thought, *some great carbohydrates and some solid protein.* He made another cup of tea and now felt very refreshed.

Parker went back up to the cockpit and made a quick inspection of the boat. There were a few bullet holes now and some splintered wood here and there, but no major damage on deck. He paused to reload the revolver, and he went back down into the cockpit, opened the door behind the stairs, and checked the bilge area. It looked okay. The pumps were working, and no water was coming in. He closed the door, moved to the center area, and removed the hatch covering the engine. It too looked okay, but he smelled oil, and there was a splatter of it on the port-side inner hull. *What is this all about?* he thought. He moved closer, and it looked like a leak in the seal around the pump. *Great. Well, no time to fix it now. It will just have to wait until we get Carter and Michael on board and try to repair it then, when there is more time and someone else to help handle the boat.*

He replaced the hatch cover and went back up the stairs to the shell cockpit area. The sun was beginning to move up the sky now, and the ocean was quiet so far, with only small, two-to-four-foot swells. The boat took these in full stride. So far, the wind was also in his favor, but he could see some clouds forming to the southeast behind him. This meant rain later in the afternoon where he was now, but, of course, he would not be here. He would be out to sea and away from any close shore storm. He checked his watch and decided to turn on the radio. Only one channel worked.

"This is the Natal Provisional Commission. We are your friends and neighbors. We have taken control and seek your assistance. Call us on 737-5989 and let us know where we can find your white friends, workers, bosses, and those you know. We want them for questions. If they resist, however, we call for no survivors. It is our time now. This is our country, and we claim it and all it has for us, the natives of Africa. The ALFM is your friend and supporter. We will take care of you. Go to your jobs tomorrow. Stay home today. Call us. Help us. You will be saved if you save us. We are all on the same side. Do not be afraid. Call us. Help us. Help your neighbor . . ."

Parker turned it off. *No survivors, eh? Well, this old bird is going to survive, one way or another. Fuck them.* He looked around behind him at the sky and saw another plane coming at him from the south. This one was had two engines and was moving very fast!

CHAPTER 37

1 April 2001

The plane was now almost over Parker. It had dropped in altitude since it first saw him and was now only two hundred feet above the ocean and the ship. Parker ducked into the wheel well and watched it fly over. He stood up. The plane was coming straight along the coast and headed north. He made out the markings on the wing, SA-BFLN, but that didn't really mean anything to him.

He kept watching the north, but the plane didn't return. He checked the compass reading and the radio-direction finder. He knew he was getting close to the rendezvous point. He turned the wheel to the left and brought the boat to head in a northwest direction. He didn't hear the new plane coming up behind him as he made this maneuver.

The new plane was a single-engine, small, training plane used by the South African Defense Force for training spotter pilots. It was a fixed-wing aircraft with the wing overhead of the fuselage. And now it was coming directly at the boat from the south.

Parker jumped when he heard the engine. It was now almost on top of him, and it too was very low. He looked up and saw a glint coming out of the window—a rifle barrel! He dropped down just as a bullet hit the back railing behind him. A splinter caught him in the cheek, and it started to bleed. With another shot, the bullet went into the forward cockpit, far off the mark from his location. The plane kept on.

Parker went below and got the .30-30. It wasn't much defense, but it might help. He wiped his left cheek with a wet towel from the sink and went back up on deck, crouching low in the cockpit. He could see the plane turning and coming back toward him. He decided they would be looking for him in the rear cockpit, so he moved low and fast to the rear of the main mast and crouched behind the lower rigging in the shadow. The boat was now moving swiftly toward shore. He could just make out the top of the tree line and the lower hills and rocks of the upper Natal coast above Durban.

The plane was between him and the shore. *Damn.* But then he realized that this put the sun behind him and in the eyes anyone who was trying to find him from the plane. He watched carefully and moved the rifle to his shoulder. *Just like tracking a fast bird,* he thought. He led the plane and squeezed off a round, just at his target came almost even with the bow. He saw its left window shatter. He got off another shot before their own rifleman found him in the shadows of the mast and the rigging. A bullet hit near his foot, but missed him. Parker turned and fired once more as the plane had now passed, but this time he hit only the rear wing tip.

He watched and saw the plane glide slowly around to the left, making another circle to come back to him. But what he didn't know was that his first shot had found the pilot's neck after it had crashed through the window. The marksman sitting on the right side had been leaning over the dying pilot to fire his shots. The inexperienced marksman now was trying to fly the plane, but he had no idea what he was doing. As it made the circle, the plane's speed and altitude dropped. The marksman saw it dropping lower, and he hit the throttle. This only caused the plane to go into a stall. It was all over in twenty seconds. The plane hit the water and broke apart.

Parker watched all this from the mast area. He couldn't believe his eyes! *What a shot! What luck!* And this was part of the luck he thought they would need this day. What if the marksman had had it?

He ran back to the cockpit and began to lower the mainsail. He turned on the engine again and heard the small whine from the oil pump below. Damn, again. It had to make it. He couldn't get in as close to shore as he needed to without the motor working. He went below, put some more oil in the system, and looked at the seal again. It was leaking a little, but not badly—yet.

Parker went back up on deck. He could see the lower point of the rocky pinnacle. He knew he was only a mile from the rendezvous point, Tinley Manor Beach. He maneuvered the boat into a course along the shoreline and dropped the jib sail. Now he was fully on the motor. He wanted to stay about four hundred yards offshore at this point, and he would anchor directly off the beach. As he approached from the south, he could now see the beach come up ahead. He put the screws in idle and went forward, carrying the rifle, and threw the anchor overboard. It caught quickly and the line went taught.

He went to the stern and threw over the bright yellow inflatable boat. Parker went over the stern, took the small motor from the rear storage, and slipped it onto the stern of the smaller boat. He put the motor clamps in place and set the choke. With one pull, the little motor came to life with a very loud roar. *My god,* he thought, *I hadn't ever thought this would be a problem, but the little engine was definitely loud.* He decided to shut it off, and he climbed the ladder back into the sailboat.

Now all he could do was wait.

"Not a bad morning, so far," he said to no one listening. "One for the good guys!" he yelled. He thought his old navy captain would be very proud of him: *Fought off the attackers at the breakwater and shot down a plane! Not bad for an old man!* He was proud of himself, and rightly so.

Parker went below after making a check of the beach area. No one was around. He fixed himself another cup of tea after another quick visit to the head. *Definitely a weaker bladder as I've gotten older. But I still feel good, and this is a day for life.* He looked at his watch. They should be here soon if they haven't had any trouble. *God, I hope they haven't,* he thought.

Parker went back up top and pulled the binoculars from the case hanging by the wheel bracket. He looked at the road that went from the beach up to the hill and still could see no one or any activity. He looked out to sea and then up and down the coast, and all was clear. It was time to wait and stay alert.

193

CHAPTER 38
1 April 2001

Unit 8 of Mdelthe's command received the new mortars; they had already received instructions in their use. At 3:00 a.m., the unit was ready when the radio alarm sounded in their commander's house. They put everything into two cars and began the drive down Route 2 from Tugela to Durban. Their objective was the large Shell Oil refinery by the airport and then the airport tower itself.

Within forty-five minutes they could see the lights of the refinery. They pulled their cars off the left side of Route 2 at the intersection and set up. They did not have to wait long.

At the exact instant of 4:00 a.m., the unit commander gave the word to fire. The first shell landed short and burst in a field outside of the perimeter of the large tank farm by the refinery. These tanks, which held natural gas, gasoline, jet fuel, and other refinery products, were surrounded by a very high fence, almost twenty meters tall. The tanks were constructed of double thickness steel in order to be bulletproof—or at least the design engineers thought so. But they would not be mortar-proof.

The unit's mission was only to destroy the two tanks closest to Route 2 and the intersection. They would need the rest of the fuel stored there for their own use later, but they needed to start this reclamation of their freedom with a dramatic moment.

The second mortar found its mark. The tank of jet fuel burst into flames with a huge explosion and fireball that lit up the early morning sky as if it was already daylight. The third mortar missed, but the fourth found its mark on the tank to the left of the now-burning fuel. This one was filled with diesel fuel, which also made a huge fireball in the sky, but kept burning more slowly and with very black smoke curling upward.

The unit commander gave the instructions to pack up and get back in the cars. They drove off toward the airport entrance just down the highway as they heard the sirens of the fire trucks racing from Durban to tackle the burning tanks.

When the unit reached the main entrance to the airport, they drove to the control tower located at the north end of the field and terminal. The commander and his men exited from the two cars and quickly fired on the night guards, killing both immediately. The lead men were already at the door to the stairway, and they shot off the locks and opened the doors. They went up the steps two at a time and burst in on the controllers on duty; one was white and the other black.

The white man held up his hands, but he was shot by the unit sergeant, who pointed his weapon at the black man.

"Man, are you with us or not? One answer only," yelled the sergeant.

"Don't shoot me, man, I'm with you. I'm Zulu. What can I do to help?"

"Stay there. This man will stay with you. We are going to set up a guard for this control tower. Don't let anyone land unless they give the code word: *Tiger*. Do you have anything on radar?" the unit commander asked.

"No, it is all clear for a twenty-mile radius," the black tower controller responded.

"Good, we are going downstairs. Stay here."

The unit commander left the tower and, with five of his men, ran back downstairs and over to the adjacent building where the main radar controllers kept track of aircraft in a hundred-kilometer radius of Durban and controlled their landings and takeoffs. This was secured in a minute.

The tower controller saw two other cars head across the tarmac for the field firefighting station and watched as it was secured by the well-armed and well-trained Zulus.

Finally, he saw two more cars head for the local police-security-forces station. He saw the smoke and heard the grenades go off and knew now that the Durban airport was fully under the control of a local unit commander, whose name he still did not know. It would never matter.

* * *

At the same time as the unit began its mortar attack on the Shell Oil tank farm, five other cars filled with men pulled up at the two radio and TV stations in Durban. They entered with only a token resistance, and two persons were killed. Now they had control of this communications center.

Other units took over the main power-switching station and the telephone central control located south of Durban. Another unit took positions outside the main police station and delivered three direct hits with rockets, which destroyed the building in a matter of seconds. The Provisional Commission Government of Natal was now in command of Durban and could follow up the rest of the day in the city before moving along the upper coast to Tugela, the headquarters.

* * *

In the western Transvall areas, the units moved to take control of the gold mines. It was easier than many thought might be possible.

A unit moved to the Anglo Deep Gold Mine near Ellansrand and took position near the dormitories for the bachelor workers. From this vantage point, they could see the mine-security-control office directly up the hill behind some trees. At 4:00 a.m., they moved forward and hid easily in the supervisors' parking lot. The car sheds gave them more than necessary cover. When they were all ready, the unit commander gave the signal, and they rushed the security office. There were no white supervisors on duty, and two of the four workers in the office were part of another unit. Although they were at work and did not get the radio signal for the attack, they knew instantly what was happening and helped to subdue the others without a fight or alarm raised.

Two of the unit members were skilled in the program that maintained the security and personnel control throughout the mine. They changed the coding and created new electronic passes for only those that were part of various units. The units could now move to secure the other main areas, especially the main hoist controls.

There are four main shafts at this mine. Two are used exclusively for bringing the ore to the surface from levels as deep as three miles. The other two shafts could also be used for ore as needed, but were primarily used for miners traveling to the various levels for work and maintenance and for delivering machinery as needed. The platforms in the shafts had three levels and traveled at over sixty meters per second.

Security in this mine was controlled electronically by means of bar-code readers. Each person was given their own special badge and bar code. The main computer system would only let someone into certain areas if their bar code had been accepted for that area; otherwise, they were locked out. The computer also kept track of each person and where they were in a particular area of the mine, in case of emergencies or disasters.

The unit commander, now satisfied that his unit and that of his associate had full command of the mine, waited for the siren alarm for the current shift of workers to stop. He knew it would take some fifteen minutes for them to form up for the lifts that would bring them back to the surface. He waited twenty. With a look of supreme satisfaction to those in the security center watching him, he took the microphone from its wall mount in the security office and announced to all in the mine area: "Workers and supervisors of Anglo Deep Level Gold Mine, this is the brigade unit commander of the west Transvall area of the African National Party. I am pleased to tell you that we have control of our mine. We do not want any panic. No one has been hurt so far. We are in full control of the security and shafts. I want you now to proceed as you normally do to your exit-preparation stations and form up, just as you would for the end of the shift. The lifts will operate on same exit schedules. Come and join us in our freedom!"

As soon as the announcement was made, several of the white supervisors on the two lowest levels tried to call their own supervisors and the security office. They reached the security office, but the codes they used to try the telephones would not work. They did not panic.

On another level, three of the more militant workers, who were already waiting in the first holding area immediately at the lift elevator doors, turned and grabbed the white supervisors behind them and threw them to the floor. There was a general panic, and, within a minute, two of the three supervisors were dead from being stomped to death. The remaining one had his right arm and left leg broken, along with some ribs. The crowd calmed down and moved away. The instigators had broad smiles on their faces and were congratulating each other and those around them. Others shrunk away and did not want to see the murders. As the militant group moved forward to get on the lifts, several workers in the rear of the holding area now moved forward and tried to help the remaining, badly hurt supervisor.

The entire spectacle was witnessed by the unit commander in the mine security center via the cameras. He was not disturbed, and he thought that the actions would help in the short term to maintain order as the groups began to arrive at the surface.

"Post the guards at the lifts and get the men either to go to their regular changing stations or go directly home. We don't need any volunteers," the unit commander said over his walkie-talkies to his various sub-units.

As the mine lifts arrived at the surface with their loads—not of gold ore, but of human assets that made the mining possible—the guards directed them to the changing stations and told them all to go home and not to cause any further violence. Order was to be established and maintained. Freedoms for all were promised again, and better wages and working conditions were the words on the leaflets posted in the locker rooms.

The unit commander had watched the main road for the new shift of workers. They would be arriving in the next half hour on the many buses from the local townships surrounding the mines in the west Transvaal area. Another unit commander had secured the main gate and the other two gates to the mine, covering for all entrances and exits. The buses coming for the day shift were stopped at the gate and ordered back to the townships and to return as quickly as possible to pick up the workers now arriving at the surface and changing back into their street clothes. The bus drivers were conditioned to taking orders, and so they turned around and began their journeys in the early morning light back to the individual townships.

The unit commander and his assistants in the security center watched it all. They now controlled the flow of men to the surface and maintained their movement out of the mine once they were on the surface, just as it would have been for a regular shift change in this complex operation. Order was essential. But there would be no day shift or night shift for this first day. The world must learn quickly that the AFLP had control of the main gold resources, and only they would dictate now how much would be mined and exported. The world would listen to this KwaZulu economic control.

CHAPTER 39
1 April 2001

Carter was looking around at the horizon to the left. She saw the glint from the sun hit something in the air. *Another plane? It had to be.*

"Michael, look to the right of the smaller peak to the left of the mountain at ten o'clock. Do you see it?"

"No. Yes! Now I do. It's another plane. How far are we from the river?" he inquired over the headset.

"We are about ten miles yet. I think we should get low and get out of this sunlight. The sun is still in front of us, so I don't know if the other plane has seen us. What do you think?" she asked as she began to look for a lower pathway above the trees.

"I think we have to assume it's seen us. Let's get down fast and make for the river. We'll just have to chance being seen from someone on the ground."

Carter lowered the control elevator, and they moved down toward the tree line. The ground was flat now, as they had come through the mountains easily a couple of hours ago. This was the most dangerous part of the journey, because they were now in Natal and firmly in KwaZulu territory. They knew the blacks on the ground had automatic weapons, and probably even a surface-to-air missile or two. At this close range, they really had no escape from a rocket.

Carter flew the helicopter down and over the center of the Tugela River. The trees were high on either side, and they blocked a direct view of the river from the sugarcane fields. The sound of the helicopter at this speed would not raise attention until it was almost on top of someone—or until it was past. But this was the very heart of the KwaZulu Nation.

Michael looked up for the other plane.

"Carter, I can't see anything above us. I wonder if it saw us."

"I don't know. But I feel more comfortable down here than I did higher," Carter replied.

"Look out!" Michael yelled over the headset. "There are some people along the bank at the next bend, and they must see us."

Carter did not reply; she concentrated on the control and stabilizer sticks. She increased power, and now the speed of the helicopter increased. It was very difficult to fly this low along the center of the winding river and keep up with all the changes. She saw the group, but she kept her eyes on the course between the banks of the river.

They flew by the group on the bank with a rush. The group of Zulus was mostly women, but there were two soldiers guarding them, and one had a new mobile phone. He hit the speed-dial button and called his headquarters.

"Richard, this is Mdelthe on the river with the washer women. A helo has just passed—low, very fast, and SA markings. Do we have anything like that around?"

"I'll check and call you back. Stay where you are," replied Richard Grossta, the chief communications officer in Richards Bay, the headquarters for the KwaZulu forces in Natal.

Grossta turned to his superior, James Mbela, and said over the din of the headquarters, "James, Mdelthe on the river near Kranskop just saw a helicopter with SA markings flying low and fast. Do we have any forces in a helicopter there?"

"No. Get someone with a launcher down to the Tugela at Newark to spot and put it down. It must be government forces, or, in any event, someone we don't know. Treat them as the enemy."

"Right away, sir," Grossta replied. He immediately called back to Mdelthe.

"Mdelthe, thanks for the warning. Headquarters out."

"Mikooma, Mikooma, come in. This is HQ," Grossta said into the microphone of the communications gear.

"HQ, this is Mikooma. What do you want?"

"Mikooma, get a launcher now and get to the river at Newark. Rush it! There is a SA helicopter flying along the Tugela now headed your way. It is not one of our forces. You are authorized by Mbela to bring it down! Hurry! It is fast and was seen up river about twenty miles!"

"Okay, HQ, I have it! We are on our way now," Mikooma almost yelled into his radio microphone as the jeep began to lurch forward.

Mikooma was a KwaZulu and had been fully trained in the use of US Army SAMs. His instructor had been an Afro American, formerly with the US Army for over twenty years, who now made better than a very good living being paid by a security service out of Germany for teaching the uses of various field weapons to black nationalists throughout Africa. But the teacher was not in South Africa this day; he'd left four days ago to Mauritius and safety.

The jeep driver headed quickly down Route N2 toward the Tugela River crossing from Amatkulu. It would be close, but they owned the road this day. There were no trucks or other vehicles on the wide, four-lane, divided highway. Mikooma decided not to take the small road directly to Newark, but stay on the main N2 highway, since it was faster and gave them a better chance of getting there before the helicopter. He knew that the river made two very sharp bends at Newark before opening up for the remaining three kilometers to the Indian Ocean.

At headquarters, Mbela made a check with the radioman, Grossta, about the progress of the launcher unit to the river. Grossta reported correctly that Mikooma was on the way at top speed. Mbela returned to other considerations and did not think what might happen if Mikooma would miss.

Carter had the throttle at 75 percent now and was moving along at over two hundred kilometers per hour. She and Michael were only a hundred meters above the river and staying very close to the center.

"Michael, what is up ahead? Can you read anything from the map about the river course?" she asked over the headset intercom.

"Carter, it looks like we should be close to Newark. There is a sharp bend to the left and then to the right before it straightens out to the ocean. I think you will have to drop speed some to make the turns. Do you remember this from our car trip here two years ago?" he asked back.

"Frankly, no, I don't! And it is too late now to give a damn," she shot back, the strain of the flight now beginning to show. She fought the early exhaustion and middle-flight boredom with some coffee, but now the effort of keeping the helicopter on this wandering and very low course was taking its toll quickly on her.

"Okay, I understand. I'll keep looking ahead and to the sides for any problems."

Michael watched the trees and banks move past quickly. The trees were a blur of green, unless one took focus on one point up ahead and watched it pass. Michael saw several persons along the shore, but only scattered ones taking early morning baths or fishing. He did not see any group as they had earlier.

Carter spotted the town up ahead. The small Natal city of Newark was filled with small houses and a very small downtown with the usual mixture of stores that catered primarily to the sugarcane industry and the blacks in the area. Newark had once been a popular city for outings along the river, but now that the N2 highway passed it by to the east of the village, it had grown stagnant over the years.

Michael saw the first turn—a very sharp ninety-degree left turn.

"Carter, back off! We will have too much side slip and go into the trees."

Carter pushed forward on the throttle, and the speed dropped as she maneuvered the helicopter to a sharp banking position and went into the turn. Almost immediately, she saw the turn to the right. It was almost identical to the one they had just come through, although not quite as sharp. She moved the controls and banked now for this turn at the same speed.

As they came out of it, Michael and Carter could see the blue azure of the Indian Ocean up ahead—but they had to get across one more bridge before they could reach that space and freedom.

Michael could see a jeep coming down the road from the north and stopping. Several blacks in uniforms were getting out, and he spotted one of them with a long, pipe-like device. A SAM!

"Carter, they have a SAM up ahead. There—on the bridge."

"I see them," Carter replied. The adrenalin now flowed to the max. She realized that, although their original plan called for them to follow the river all the way to the ocean before turning south to Tinley Manor Beach and the rendezvous with her father, this development required a change in the plan. She pulled back on the throttle for more speed and went up in altitude and to the right, heading south along the N2 highway. She began zigzagging and didn't look back.

Mikooma was in the jeep with the driver and the launcher specialist, Akkumba. They heard the helicopter before they saw it coming through the turn from Newark.

"Stop the jeep! We won't make the bridge before the helo gets there," Mikooma yelled to the driver.

The driver swerved over to the shoulder of the highway, wasting precious seconds. Finally, he brought the jeep to a complete stop, and Mikooma and Akkumba jumped out and ran to the center of the highway with the launcher. Although Akkumba had practiced the launch several times, it was always against a very stationary target with some time for setup. Nevertheless, his adrenalin was also pumping to the max, and he and Mikooma worked quickly and efficiently in putting the launcher together and getting the missile loaded into the firing tube. He sighted on the helo, but, instead of still flying at a ninety-degree track to them and above the river channel, the helo was now disappearing quickly away from them, south along the N2 highway. He sighted and got a lock-on with the heat sensor and pulled the trigger. The missile shot away toward the helo.

"Carter, it's coming," Michael said into the intercom. He had been watching out the mirror and saw the men set up in the disappearing roadway and fire.

"Michael, hold on. This will be close."

Carter now turned the helo directly east and flew it directly toward the sun.

"It's following us, Carter."

Carter kept moving higher in the sky, still on course toward the center of the rising sun, and the SAM followed, coming faster toward them.

Suddenly, Carter dove the helicopter down to the ocean. She didn't have much altitude to do this maneuver, but it was their only chance.

It worked. The missile's heat sensor now targeted the sun and its bright energy flowing ninety-three million miles to the Natal Coast. The SAM kept right on climbing in altitude until it would finally run out of fuel, drop like a bomb to the ocean, and explode. But that would be far out to sea.

Michael took their bearing and they were off the coastline from Darnall. Their destination and rendezvous point with Carter's father, Gilbert Parker, and his boat was only ten klicks down the coast at a small resort area known as Tinley Manor Beach.

Tinley Manor Beach was a semicircle of sand, only fifteen meters in width; but the semicircle stretched about five hundred meters from one end to the other. It was very popular for picnics, sunning, swimming, and a day at the beach with a lover or family. A dirt, single-lane road led from the grassy area behind the sandy area directly west to the old coast road, some two kilometers away. The road ran along the northern small ridge that led west from the ocean. The entire area was similar to a bowl broken in half, the broken edge being the beach and the sea. As one drove down the road coming toward the beach, the entire vista of the open bowl opened up for the visitor, and the entire area was visible. The dark blue cast of the Indian Ocean, broken by the small bright, sandy strip of beach, with the green grassy area, all in an almost perfect half-circle, gave one an incredible picture in contrasts and peacefulness.

The south end of the beach ended in a ridge that formed the southern end of the arc. On top of the ridge was a promontory, right at the edge of the sea. It was fifteen meters above the sea level and was used by bird watchers and by families for picnics. It gave everyone an excellent view the entire area. This was the destination for Michael and Carter in the helicopter. It was a perfect landing site, and, although they would have to climb down from the promontory, it afforded them more protection than just landing directly on the grassy area.

Carter saw the beach, the grassy area, and the promontory up ahead. She moved further out to sea, since the wind was still onshore blowing out to the warmer ocean.

"Michael, I see Dad, down there on the beach with the boat. Let's get ready. I don't think we will have much time," Carter said.

"Okay, I'm ready."

Michael picked up the machine pistol and had it ready, just in case. He could see Parker clearly standing some fifteen meters from the base of the promontory where the ridge joined the beach and the sea, his inflatable boat on the sandy area.

He was watching them come in toward him. He turned and surveyed the grassy area and made out a glint from the road. A car was coming but was still back near the main highway.

Carter concentrated on the approach to the landing area. The winds were tricky as she got closer to the ridge, and she had to back off and try again.

"Carter, you've got to get us down this time! There is a car or jeep on the road coming toward the beach."

"I know, I know! Shut up and concentrate on getting ready to cover us when I get us down."

The helicopter behaved better on this second try. The winds seemed to stay constant and in the same direction for a moment. Carter brought the helicopter directly in and down in one movement. *Boom!* It was a hard landing, but they were down and in one piece.

Michael jumped from the helicopter and waved to Parker while Carter shut down the engine. As a last-minute action, she pulled the throttle stick from its mounting and threw it into the sea as she jumped down to the ground. Michael had already unloaded the four bags and was moving toward the edge of the promontory level. Carter followed him and took two of them.

At the edge, they found the small trail that went to the grassy area and beach and began to scramble down. Michael fell and rolled several meters.

Parker rushed up to him as Carter followed, sliding the rest of the way.

"Michael, are you okay?" Parker asked, arriving at Michael's side.

"No, Gilbert, I have done something to my left ankle. I think I just sprained it. Here, take the pistol and the bags. Cover us. Carter, help me up so I can hold onto you to get to the boat!" Michael yelled to them.

He turned and saw that the vehicle was a jeep, only about a kilometer away from the beach. Carter ran to the boat and threw her two bags in. She went back to get Michael and help him up.

"Damn, it hurts, Carter!" Michael screamed.

"I know. Hang on; let's get to the boat, or there won't be any hurt at all soon. That jeep is coming fast!"

They moved like two people in a three-legged race the remaining fifteen meters to the small boat. Parker was watching the moving jeep, the machine pistol pointed and ready. Michael fell into the boat, and Carter moved behind it to push it back in the water. Parker covered them and continued to watch the grassy area and the closing jeep.

"Dad, get in!" Carter yelled over the ocean surf to her father.

Parker turned, threw the pistol into the boat, and jumped in headfirst. Michael picked up the pistol before Parker landed and was already pointing it back at the jeep that was almost at the parking area by the beach and grass. He could see the four soldiers beginning to hoist their weapons to their shoulders. Michael was unsure whether to fire on them or not. He really didn't want to kill anyone, but in a few seconds more, as the lead soldier raised his rifle up, Michael realized in a flash that they were going to be fired upon. He shot in the general direction of the soldiers and the jeep, but somewhat above their heads. The soldiers either hit the ground or jumped back behind the jeep.

Carter was pulling on the oars with the help of Parker. The small boat was moving away from the shore and had passed through the first few swells. Parker started the small gas engine, and, luckily, it came alive on the first pull. The engine noise could easily be heard all throughout the Tinley Manor Beach over the surf on this very quiet morning. The boat began to gather speed, but it was still within range of the soldiers at the jeep.

Michael fired another burst. The lead soldier now stood up and shot back. He sensed that Michael was not trying to hit him, as there were no marks from the bullets around him. He took aim at the person in the rear of the small boat, holding onto the engine-rudder guide. He squeezed off three shots before he ducked the returning fire and hit the sand in a prone position.

The soldier's first shots were short, but another burst hit Parker in the upper right arm—luckily it was just a graze.

"Carter, I've been hit!" he yelled over the roar of the engine, grabbing his arm.

"Dad, get down! Michael, do something!" she yelled back.

Michael now aimed the pistol and fired directly at the exposed, prone soldier. He could see the marks of the bullets hitting the sand and tracked them quickly to him. Michael saw the burst continue with two hits, one in his left shoulder and one in his back. Michael kept firing and aimed the pistol at the jeep. The three soldiers there started firing back as they crouched around the back of their vehicle for cover. Michael tried for the radio and engine area and was rewarded by seeing water and oil begin to leak from the front of the jeep.

Carter moved to the rear of the boat and pulled her father to the middle. She grabbed hold of the tiller and steered them directly now for the large boat, still a hundred meters away. The firing from the group at the jeep was sporadic, but they were now just out of range. Carter and Michael ducked the shots and hoped none would hit the boat, let alone them anymore. Parker was struggling with his arm, but the shot had not hit any artery; it was only a graze on the bicep. He pulled out his handkerchief and used it to tie a bandage around the wound for now. He knew he was not really hurt badly, but they still had a long voyage ahead. Once on the boat and moving again, the medical kit would suffice.

The gunfight continued, but now the distance was too much for either side. The group at the jeep moved closer to the water, shooting all the while. Michael returned the fire, but not as much. He needed to conserve their ammunition.

"Michael, get ready. We'll be at the boat in a minute. Take care of tying us up, and then help Dad onto the boat. I'll get the bags and get them on deck. After that, I'll go get the engine started and get us out of here. Why don't you stow the things and see what we can do to help Dad. We need to look at that wound."

"Okay, Carter. Slower now; we are almost there," Michael said as he leaned over the starboard side to grasp the rear lower-deck railing.

Carter guided the small boat directly up to the rear lower deck. Michael tossed the line over and pulled hard until they were snug against it. Carter used the tiller to bring the stern of their little shore boat around, and now they were alongside. Carter shut off the engine, and the quiet suddenly overwhelmed them.

Carter reached for the sea bags in the center of the boat next to her father and threw them up on the stern of the motor sailboat.

"Dad, take it easy. Can you hang on while we get out of here and get going? We don't have time to get to your wound now. I don't know what they might throw at us next," Carter said.

"Carter, I think I'll be okay. Let's just get going."

With that, Carter climbed up the ladder, picked up the bags, and carried them up to the wheel-well area. She started the engine and heard the familiar, deep-throated pulse begin and grow stronger. She activated the anchor release and winch to get it up. She felt it come loose from the seabed, and the boat began to move forward. She turned the wheel and took her bearing for ninety degrees due east.

Michael reached down for Parker.

"Parker, come on. Let's get up there. Grab my shoulders and put your left arm around my waist. Can you get up the ladder?" Michael asked.

"Yes, keep holding onto me, Michael, and I'll get there. Let's go."

They moved from the small boat to the lower rear deck and climbed out on their stomachs. The engine had started, and they knew they would be moving soon.

The climb up the ladder was difficult. Parker had to hold on tight to Michael to keep his balance as the boat moved with the sea swells. Parker grabbed hold of the railing with his left hand and pulled himself over.

"Michael, I'm on deck. God, for such a small wound, this hurts!"

"Okay, Parker, I'll be there in a minute. I've got to take care of the boat here."

Michael went back down the ladder, pulled the smaller boat up on to the lower deck, and secured it to the cleats. Finally, he grabbed the pistol and the remaining ammunition bag and climbed up over the railing to the main deck. He looked at Carter by the wheel well and saw she seemed to have things under control. He could feel the swells beneath his feet and sensed the movement forward.

Parker was lying by the rear cabin steps, still holding the bandage on his arm. He was feeling the pain now, but he knew he hadn't lost much blood.

Michael yelled as they started down, "Carter, I'm going to take your dad below and look at this. Can you handle things for now?"

"Yes, but keep an ear peeled for me in case something happens here," she yelled back. Carter had the boat on full throttle now, and they were moving at eighteen knots directly to the east. She kept watch behind her, but the horizon was now empty. She couldn't even see the shoreline anymore.

Carter knew they would have to get the sails up very soon. She didn't want to use their fuel stores so much, but she was alone, and the main sail was too much for her just now. It would have to wait for Michael to come back up from looking at her father's wound.

Michael helped Parker sit down on the galley bench. He found a pair of scissors in the drawer and cut away the bloodied shirt sleeve. He pulled it away and could easily see the wound. It was in the upper, fleshy part of the bicep. It had made a puncture wound on one side and exited the other with an opening only a little larger. It would require some stitches, but hopefully that would be all for now.

"Parker, I think it will be okay. I'm going to get out the emergency kit and give you a local anesthetic so I can sew up the wound."

"Okay, Michael, but maybe I've lost more blood than it looks. I really feel weak all of a sudden."

Michael looked at his father-in-law and now could see the paleness in his face. He laid Parker down and covered him with a blanket. He found the emergency kit in the cupboard over the small stove. The kit was actually a small suitcase filled with many emergency items. It was required by the South African Navy and Coast Guard to take care of most emergencies on board a boat until help could be obtained. Michael located the small bottle of anesthetic and filled a needle with it. He moved back over to Parker, cleaned the wound areas on both sides with an antiseptic pad, and injected the it into Parker's arm.

"Parker, let me know if it feels any different. I'll fix the needle and thread to sew up the wounds. Do you want me to do it, or should I get Carter?" Michael asked.

"No, you do it. Carter was never much for sewing." They laughed together.

"Okay. Here, take this orange juice and drink it all. I'll get this needle fixed," Michael said.

Michael worked quickly and completed the stitches in a few minutes. Parker grimaced, but he could not actually feel the needle, except for the pressure.

"All done. Am I supposed to give you another medal for this one?" Michael asked Parker with a smile.

"No. This one does not count. Help me to the bunk, and I'll try and rest a bit. By the way, could you reach down under the lower cupboard and get that black sea bag? There is something in there I want while I lay here."

"Here it is," said Michael, and he gave Parker the sea bag.

"Thanks, Michael. I'll be okay for now. Get up top and get the main sail up. I'm sure Carter needs help by now."

Michael gave Parker a pat on his left shoulder and a big smile. *Damn,* he thought, *we might even make it.* He felt elation as he walked up the steps to the main deck. He had just sewn up two punctures after giving his father-in-law a shot. Wow, the things one can do when under this kind of pressure!

Parker opened the sea bag and found his lucky blanket. He pulled it close to his chest and closed his eyes. Exhaustion swept over him like a flood and he was asleep in a minute.

"Carter, I'm going to put up the main sail so we can cut the engine. As it goes up, pull the throttle back and back off the engine to let the wind take over. Also, we may need to change course some, as the wind is from the south. Let's use that for a faster course, and we will still be heading in our general direction."

"Okay, Michael. I'm ready."

He moved to the main mast and found everything already set. Parker had done a terrific job of lowering the mast earlier and keeping everything in a full readiness state. The sail went up easily, and Michael could feel the wind begin its push. He heard the sound of the engine drop, but their speed actually increased as the summer breeze from the south Indian Ocean became their savior and friend.

He moved now to unfurl the jib, and it too went into position quickly and easily.

"Carter, cut the engine off."

Now the pulsing of the engine was replaced by the quiet of the sailboat slipping through the dark-blue water. The wake behind them disappeared as the waves followed them, wiping their trail from South Africa as surely as an eraser on a blackboard.

Michael went back to the wheel well and put his arms around Carter.

"I love you, you know," he said.

"I know. I do too." And they embraced and kissed and held the wheel together.

CHAPTER 40

1 April 2001

The small aneurism on Gilbert Parker's aorta had been growing for over a month. He didn't know it was there. The events of this day and the stress had increased the size by threefold in eighteen hours. It was now the size of a small almond.

Parker awoke to nightfall. He had been asleep in the lower cabin, recovering from the flesh wounds to his arm. He wondered what time it was and turned over to look at the clock on the wall over the stowage locker by the cabin door—6:30 p.m. He could feel the seas rolling more under him. He got up very unsteadily and walked down the corridor to the head and relieved himself. When he came out, he felt the boat begin to rock even more. He also felt some pressure in his chest and decided to take some aspirin and an antacid tablet. He had been asleep for almost six hours, and he wondered how Carter and Michael were doing on deck. They should be well out of harm's way from the downfall by now and headed to freedom and safety once again. He slowly walked up the stairs and onto the deck at the wheel well. He found Carter and Michael there, watching the instruments and the sails. Parker could tell they were headed for a storm.

"Dad, how are you doing? Are you feeling better? Can you walk okay?" asked Carter as she saw him coming up the stairs.

"Yes, I feel better. I can walk okay, but still seem unsteady. The arm still hurts some, but the rest helped. And now I've gotten some indigestion. I took something for it. What is going on and where are we?"

"We are about two hundred and forty kilometers southeast of Madagascar now. We haven't been bothered by any planes or any other ships; all quiet except for the storm ahead. Carter and I have just been discussing whether to change course or not. The storm appears strong from what we see now, but I don't think we should change. What do you think?" Michael asked.

"Well, it doesn't look good. Very black to the north, but lighter to the south. What about changing our easterly course to more southeast and see if it continues going north and we can miss most of it?"

"Dad, I don't think we should change. If we go more southeast, then we will lose more time, and we don't have enough food and water for the extra three or four days it might take. I vote for continuing on and riding it out. We can lash things down before we get fully into it in about an hour, and it may even give us an extra boost to move further away from the coast. You know we are still very much within range of planes from Durban. I don't want to take any chances remaining near our beloved South Africa. We've gone, and let's get on with this," Carter said to the men standing next to her.

"Gilbert, I think I agree with Carter. Let's push on. Come with me if you feel up to it, and let's tie things down on deck."

"I'm with you then. Okay, Michael, what do you want me to do?" Parker asked.

"Come on, let's get the small boat taken care of, then we can go forward to lash the loose items," Michael said to Parker and began to move to the stern and over the side to take care of the small boat.

Parker moved with him, but when he started over the railing, his arm hurt suddenly so much that he cried out.

"Damn it! This arm is hurting now. And I feel this indigestion too, much stronger. Michael, I'm going below to just work in the cabin taking care of things. That way I won't have to move around so much."

Parker turned and went downstairs. He moved along the corridor to the galley and began putting all the dishes and the teapot away.

He decided to make himself and the kids another pot, and then he would stow it and the cups. While the water was coming to a boil, he moved into the main sleeping cabin and put the sea bags in the lower lockers. This put more of a strain on the arm and his chest, and he sat down on the bed for few minutes rest. He closed his eyes and suddenly fell asleep.

Parker awoke to the sound of the teapot screaming its pain. He got up quickly and felt a very sharp pain in his chest. *Damn indigestion! Why does one have to get old anyway?* he thought as he moved toward the galley. He took the kettle from the stove and turned off the gas. He put in the teabags and poured the water into the cups. After emptying the rest of the hot water into the sink, he rinsed the kettle in cold water, dried it, and put it away in the upper locker. He drank his own quickly and took the other two cups up the stairs, to Carter and Michael on deck.

"Carter, I've made some tea for you and Michael. It may be a while before we can make anymore, with what I see up ahead. Here, take this, and I'll take the wheel for a while. Michael, come get some tea!" he yelled.

"Coming! I'm almost done here," Michael responded from the bow area of the boat. He was working on the jib roller and power winch, securing the anchor line and beginning to put in a lifeline from the bow all the way to the stern. He moved toward them and took his cup. It tasted very good; he needed it.

Carter was standing in the well and now looked at the barometer. It had fallen more in the last half hour. *Not good,* she thought. Maybe she was wrong. Maybe they should have turned southeast for a while. They still could. *Why not?*

"I think we should turn southeast now. It looks pretty black up ahead, and the barometer has dropped a lot in the last half hour. And the wind has picked up," Carter said as she looked at the two men she loved most dearly.

"Michael, I think Carter is right. Let's go southeast for a while and try to miss most of this one," Parker said.

"Yes, let's do that," Michael agreed. Parker turned the wheel, and the boat heeled over more as the course change was made. Carter put the cup down on the railing and adjusted the mainsail line. The wind was now almost in their face. They knew the center of the storm was due east, but they could ride it out—they had made it in one worse than this two years earlier. The boat was now hitting the waves square on, and the rain started.

Michael took the wheel from Parker while Carter went below to get their rain slickers. She came back up on deck quickly, but the two men were already wet, as the storm had increased in just three minutes as they went through a squall line. Parker was holding onto the back wheel well railing with both hands. He took the jacket from his daughter and put it on. She came back to stand with him after she gave the other one to Michael.

"Carter, I love you, you know," Parker said as he looked at his daughter standing next to him. He could feel the pain in his chest more, and he grimaced, but Carter thought it was the only rain hitting him when she looked at his face. "I hope I have done well by you since your mother died ten years ago. I know you miss her as much as I."

"Dad, it is okay. I love you too," She said and gave him a big hug and a kiss on the cheek. She kept her arms around him and looked his squarely in the face. Now she could see some pain there in his eyes. She was immediately conscious of something wrong with him.

The rain was getting harder, and the wind was blowing very strongly. The boat was pitching now, each wave hitting the bow as Michael tried to keep the boat square with the oncoming storm. The waves were crashing over the deck, and water was running everywhere. It was getting slippery and hard to hold on.

A strong gust came, and the mast went the other direction. Michael turned and yelled to his father-in-law, "Gilbert! See if you can get forward on the port side and trim the jib. The motor is not on now. I think we'll lower the main sail and just use the jib and the motor."

"Okay, Michael!" Parker looked at his daughter, who was looking at him in a strange way, and he gave her a kiss on the cheek and released her from his arms. He went to the port side and pulled himself forward along the lifeline until he found the master line for the jib. Carter moved to starboard and into the wheel well with Michael and started the engine below. It came on easily, and she engaged the clutch. They looked at each other as the propeller in the stern began its hard job in the storm. She kept watching her father tugging at the line; it appeared to be stuck somehow.

Parker was having trouble now. The line had jammed in the small winch. The only way to clear it was to pull it free and loop it through a spare pulley to trim the jib. It was now fluttering wildly in the driving rain. He could hardly see, but this boat was his, and he knew every inch of her. A little storm would not stop him—if only the burning pain in his chest and arm would go away. He pulled with one stronger jerk, and the line came free. He was surprised and fell to the slippery deck. Carter saw him, and she moved to the port side of the wheel-well area. She was keeping a close watch on her father.

"Michael, something is wrong. Dad is down, and I see him struggling. I'm going up there to help."

As she started up the port side of the boat, a huge wave broke over the bow, and the onrushing water forced her to her knees to grab onto the lifeline on that side. She saw her father holding on, and she yelled, "Dad, stay there! I'm coming to get you!"

Parker grasped the jib line with both hands. The rain was making everything slick. The pain in his chest was increasing, and, all of a sudden, he knew it was not indigestion. He tried to get to his feet, but he fell back down on the slippery deck. He was losing the feeling in his legs. He turned to see Carter coming toward him slowly on her hands and knees, hanging onto the life line and the railing as the water continued to break over the bow and the sides.

The aneurism could no longer stand the strain of the increased blood pressure and the more viscous blood from the aspirin. As Parker watched his daughter come ever closer—now just five feet away—the aneurism popped, and blood immediately filled his chest cavity. His heart stopped almost immediately. His hands let go of the line, and the wave washed him over the side into the boiling, black sea. Gilbert Lloyd Duncan Parker was dead before his body hit the ocean.

Carter could see him look at her. She screamed as her father's hands dropped the line and his eyes closed and his faced grimaced in the final pain of the bursting aneurism and death. She held onto the railing and looked over the side to watch his body go below the surface in the waves. She began to sob heavily and yell out.

Michael had seen this out of the corner of his eyes, but he was trying to stay focused on keeping the bow square with the oncoming waves. He saw the sudden action of Parker dropping the line and going overboard, but there was nothing he could do. If he left the wheel, the boat would turn sideways into the water, and they would flounder at best and might capsize at the worst. He looked for his wife and saw her still holding on for her own life.

"Carter, can you hang on?" he yelled over the roar of the rain and wind.

She was sobbing so hard. She had seen her father die. She loved him so. She looked at Michael yelling to her and just moved her head up and down. She had to hold on—she had to live.

Michael turned the boat due south now. He knew the worst of the storm was behind them. The wind was slacking off, and the waves were smaller—they were still breaking over the sides, but not as much. He looked at Carter, still holding on up close to the main mast on the port side. *Oh, my God,* he thought, *to see her dad die like that and not be able to save him.* Neither one knew that, even if they had been able to catch Parker's body, the life in it was gone.

The seas grew calmer, and the wind turned back from the southwest. He turned off the engine and raised the mainsail again. He changed the course to northeast again headed for the open area of the Indian Ocean. They had ridden out the edge of Tropical Storm Evariste, which was now hitting the Madagascar mainland. Michael saw Carter still holding the lifeline, and put the wheel back on autopilot and locked it in place. Michael went forward to get his wife.

"Carter, I'm so sorry. I loved him too," Michael said to her as he came near, and sat down on the deck and held her in his arms.

"Michael, it was so awful. I was almost there to save him. He was barely holding on. Oh, God, please have mercy on him!" she yelled to the sky, that was now showing the night stars.

She cried some more, and Michael did too. They held each other and let out their hurt, sadness, and pain over losing someone they loved so dearly. They would never have escaped the downfall without him. Their plan depended on him. He had come through, and they were alive because of him. They would miss him.

"Come on. Let's get some tea while things are quieter now. We need it," Michael said to his wife. She was still staring at the stars in the sky.

Carter nodded her head, and they got up off the now-drying deck, walked back to the stairs, and went below. Carter went into the toilet while Michael took the teakettle from the lower locker where Parker had stowed it away some three very long hours ago. The water came to a boil. Michael poured the water in the cups and put in the teabags just as Carter emerged from the toilet. She had washed her face and arms and felt better with the salt spray and the salt from her tears now washed off. She went to the main sleeping cabin and pulled the sea bags from under the bed. Luckily, they were dry.

Carter stripped off all her clothes and put on dry panties, a T-shirt, and shorts. She began to feel better. She sat there for a moment and realized again that she had just lost her father and cried softly.

Michael came forward with the two cups and saw his wife sitting on the bed in the dry clothes, crying. He knew it would take time for them to get over all this, but at least they were alive. He wondered about the others left behind as he stood there and handed the cup to Carter.

Carter looked up at her husband and got off the bed. She took the cup from his outstretched hand and placed it on the table over the side lockers. She smiled and put her arms around him. They held each other tightly and kissed.

"Carter, I love you. We're alive and we'll make it. I know it now. I'm going to change and then change our course for Mauritius. It is too far to the Seychelles. I'll be back soon and then I'm going to change clothes. Why don't you take a shower and fix us something to eat. I'll take care of everything on deck. Okay, my love?" He kissed her again.

"Okay, but don't stay away too long. I am missing you already."

"I'll be back in about half an hour."

Michael finished his tea and went back on deck. He used the Global Positioning Device and, within minutes, he had their coordinates to within six feet either way. He put the map under the light by the wheel and pinpointed their location. Next he drew a line to the island of Mauritius and estimated they would be there in three days if the winds stayed favorable. Somehow, they would have to talk to the authorities there about safe refuge for a few days, as well as tell about the storm and the loss of Parker. *But those things happen at sea,* he thought. He could see the beginning of the new day's dawn on the horizon and began to feel very much alive. And, God, was he hungry! He changed course slightly to adjust for the wind and trimmed the mainsail and the jib. They were now running at over twenty knots and making good headway in even seas. The trade winds that had sent many sailing ships on this course to India and the East were now moving them to their new lives. With everything in order, he engaged the autopilot again, went below, and immediately to the head for a shower. He passed Carter in the galley and could smell sausages as he walked by and smiled at his wife. *What a terrific woman she is! God, I'm lucky,* he thought.

The shower felt better than it needed to. *I could stay in it forever,* he thought, *but the recycling system won't stand the excess.* He got out and put on dry underwear, shorts, and a new Nautica T-shirt that Carter had given him for his birthday last year. He went into the galley and found sausages, eggs, and some toast all waiting for him. They sat down and ate until they were stuffed. Toward the end of the meal, they looked at each other and saw the love in each other's eyes. They smiled, reached across the table, and held hands.

Finally, their gaze was broken, and they both got up.

"Carter, I'll clean up here. Why don't you go on deck and take care of the wheel for a while. Then, when I'm done here, you can come back down and get some rest. Okay?"

"Honey, that is fine with me. But don't take too long, I'm exhausted and need the rest badly." She gave him a full kiss and went up on deck. The sun was now over the horizon, and she checked everything and took the wheel off autopilot. Course, okay; barometer, rising nicely; wind locator and direction finder, okay. Radio, okay . . . *Radio?* She turned it on and was able to find the BBC almost immediately.

"Yesterday, elements of the AFLN in Natal and the Transvaal regions of South Africa overran government authorities and took over the power stations, airports, mines, telecom, radio, and television stations. The downfall of the Republic of South Africa appears to have started. Reports of looting, killing, rapes, and murders of whites in Johannesburg and all regions of Natal are beginning to come through. Mandela is under house arrest in Pretoria by unit commandos of the AFLN, who are very heavily armed with reportedly the latest in weapons. The financial markets were in disarray yesterday, and they will be closed today by agreement of the governors of all the exchanges around the world. As more information is received and confirmed, we will bring the news to you. Stay tuned."

Carter turned off the radio and trembled. If Michael's friend had not given them the special radio with the tuned frequency, they would still be in Johannesburg now and probably dead. She worried about the many who were still there and said a silent prayer for them. She heard Michael coming up the stairs, and she looked at him.

"Michael, I just heard on the BBC about the downfall. It sounds terrible. I'm so glad we are alive and got away, but I feel so badly about those we left behind. Do you think they will be all right?"

"Well, I don't know. I hope they will, but some won't. All we can do is pray for them. We are not fully safe yet; we still have ways to go, you know."

"Yes, I know, but I too feel okay now. I think God will see us through."

He pulled her to him and held her again. They would do this a lot the next few days.

"Go on below and get some rest. Come spell me in about six hours so I can get some sleep too," Michael said to his wife.

"I'm off. See you soon." Carter went below, collapsed onto the bed, and was soundly asleep in two minutes.

Michael checked everything again and turned on the radio. He listened to the same report and switched to another station. He found a station from Madagascar playing some classical music, and he thought about all the things they would need to do when they arrived in America. They had the money, but he had no job. He hoped they could get a visa in Mauritius as asylum-seekers; otherwise they might have to go to Australia or Singapore. But he knew they would make it. His parents had escaped Nazi Germany in 1932 and survived the war in France before they immigrated to South Africa in 1946. Now he and Carter were moving on, but they were alive. He kept coming back to that.

Carter came up the stairs with sandwiches and apples about noon. She had a big pitcher of lemonade. They sat in the wheel well and ate lunch and listened to music. They didn't want to hear any more news of their old homeland now.

After lunch, Michael went to the forward sleeping cabin and was asleep almost instantly. He hadn't realized until that instant that he had been awake for almost thirty hours.

The darkness was around him when he awoke. He got up and went to the toilet first and looked for Carter. He saw her still on deck.

"Carter, I'm going to make us some dinner and bring it up. Everything okay?"

"Yes, honey," she yelled down the stairs. "We are making good progress, according to the GPD. I just did a course correction, and the winds are steady."

"Okay, I'll be up in a little while."

Michael moved back to the galley and pulled two steaks from the freezer. He pan-fried them and made a salad to go with them. He pulled two Cokes from the fridge, put everything on a tray, and took it up the stairs. The night was on them now, and the sky was filled with some white, puffy, cotton-looking clouds that passed them by. They could see the lights of a couple of ships off the far port beam and knew they were close to the shipping lanes. Their running lights were on and the sails set.

They had enjoyed the steaks and salad, and, after the meal, Michael took the trays and plates back down to the galley and cleaned everything up. He kissed Carter as she passed by on her way to the toilet. When she came out, she went to her husband and put her arms around him.

"The autopilot is on, and everything is okay for a while. And I need you," she said as she pulled him close and put her lower belly next to his. She pulled him back toward the main sleeping cabin, taking off her T-shirt and shorts as she went. He followed her lead with a smile, watching and fully appreciating his wife as they went forward in the boat to the cabin. He pulled down his shorts and briefs all in one move and took off his T-shirt just before moving on the bed where his wife was laying, waiting for him. They made passionate, hungry, emotional love and gave each other the fullest.

Michael got up from the bed, dressed, and went back up on deck. The winds had shifted, but the autopilot had adjusted the mainsail, and they were still on course. He checked the GPD, recalculated their position on the map, and drew the new course. He unlocked the autopilot and took over the wheel. He could feel the boat under his command, and it felt good. They would be in Mauritius in another two days. He had left Carter sleeping on the bed. She needed it.

CHAPTER 41
1 April 2001

John Wesley Zooma's unit took off in their stolen truck as soon as he returned from the airport at which he had killed the night watchman. Their destination was the very upscale, white suburb of Sandton in Johannesburg. Their objective was to secure the Sandton Hotel and mall with two other units and move through three neighborhoods and take revenge. CNN and Reuters News Agency would report this in detail, since each had been alerted in advance by the Transvaal Provisional Commission.

The trucks arrived at the hotel together, and the units disembarked. They ran into the lobby with guns fully visible and took over the front desk and the security office behind it. Now they had control of the hotel and the mall, both in a matter of minutes, with no one killed or hurt.

They shut off the elevators after moving a member of the unit to each floor. From these positions, they could watch the entire interior of the hotel, which had a full atrium from the lobby to the top floor.

Zooma had maintained a position in the lobby and was now ordered to move to the mall for a full sweep. He went to the sixth floor, where there was a walkway over to the mall and the older Sandton Hotel, the lobby and security center of which was already under control of another commando unit.

Zooma went into the mall with ten others from his unit. They had been here many times to practice this exercise—now it was for real. The shops were all closed and dark, as it was early Sunday morning.

A bakery on the second level was open, and as soon as they entered, the white shop owner was killed by a quick burst of a machine pistol. The three blacks at the worktables and oven were told to go home, *now*. They rushed for the door. The unit commander raised his radio to advise the security center on what had happened and to let them out.

They rejoined the rest of the unit in the mall and continued the sweep. No others were found. The commander stationed each man until they would be relieved. Several of the members could not resist the temptation, and they shot out the windows of a jewelry shop on the first floor and a sporting goods shop on the third floor. Now they could have what they could never buy with their meager wages, like gold and diamond rings and especially the Chicago Bulls Starter jackets and sweat pants prized by everyone in their township.

In about an hour, the relief unit arrived, and the unit made its way to the front of the old hotel. Zooma felt ready for whatever was in store. His energy level was high, his adrenalin was flowing, and his hate was burning. Now it was time to show the whites what oppression felt like and what they had suffered for all these years. *Make them fear!*

The six units were very methodical. The streets in this section of Sandton were winding and wooded, the houses all had high fences, and many of these had barbed wire at the top. All were occupied by very upper-class whites who thought they were safe behind their big walls and security alarms, especially now that the election had given Mandela the presidency and the violence in Johannesburg was not as bad. The killings that had continued in KwaZulu Natal were not in their neighborhood. They really didn't care as long, as it wasn't next to them. They felt they were safe. They were not.

At the first house on the street, Zooma was given the order to take it with five men. He and the others jumped out of the truck, and the next five went to the house next door. Zooma and his small squad approached the front gate. They could see the contact wiring for the alarm and the electrification. The second person in the group pulled wire cutters from his belt and cut these. Immediately the alarm sounded and the lights came on in the yard. It was time to move.

Zooma opened the gate and motioned for the others to move in and get to the house. Already a light had gone on in an upstairs window. Three men rushed the door and shot off the locks and bolts. Other machine pistol shots could be heard at the same time in the neighborhood. The men rushed into the hallway and moved throughout the house quickly. No one on the first floor.

Zooma looked up the stairs and didn't see anything, but he knew the rich, white owner of this house was up there waiting. Zooma called out, "Mister, come out and come downstairs. You will not be hurt. We are from the Transvaal Provisional Commission and are here to protect you. The police force has fled. We are in control."

There was no answer—only the silence. Zooma was not scared. He knew what to do.

Zooma motioned to his assistant, Mbweli, to go outside and throw in a torch. Within two minutes, smoke was coming down the stairwell from the fire now burning in an upstairs bedroom. Zooma could hear movement coming toward him. He was ready. He fired his machine pistol through the smoke at the shadows. The unit members still with him fired also.

Three bodies tumbled down the stairs. They belonged to the owner, his wife, and a five-year-old girl. All were in their night clothes. The man was carrying a large shotgun that fell down the stairs before him. It had been fired twice, but to no avail.

Zooma and the others stopped firing and moved back outside and watched the house go up in flames. He felt very relieved. He had made his second kill of the day. It felt good. Time to move on.

Throughout out the rest of that long morning, Zooma, his small squad, and now the other six squads working the three streets in the neighborhood kept up the killing and destruction. By eleven o'clock a.m., the entire neighborhood was filled with smoke from the burning houses. Zooma had watched as Mbweli had raped the wife in the third house they entered. She was there alone and had fired at them from the front window, wounding one of them. When they entered, she moved back to the study and locked herself in, surely hoping the police would come to stop this madness in her street—a futile hope.

After shooting the door to the study off its hinges, they found her in a corner with a shotgun pointed at them. She pulled the trigger, and the blast hit Sponge in the right leg and knee. He went down in a pool of blood from the wound as Mbweli rushed the woman. He wrestled the shotgun from her hands and hit her on the head with the butt. She went down in a heap behind the desk. Mbweli grabbed the desk chair, threw it over to the side of the study, and opened his pants. The woman opened her eyes, saw him standing over her, and screamed. He hit her again with the butt of the gun, and she blacked out. He moved to his knees, pulled up her skirt, and pulled down her panties. It was over in two minutes. He got up and zipped up his pants, and looked at his buddies and Zooma watching him.

"Anybody else? She is ready. Come and get her."

One other member of the unit who had been tending to Sponge got up and raped the woman. Just as he was getting up from her, she began to come to. This member of the unit took the gun he had laid on the table and pointed it at her forehead. With one shot, it was all over. He looked at the limp shape on the floor and felt his rage burn. He wanted more. He needed more.

Zooma had watched all this from the other side of the room. He was not about to try to stop them. They deserved to take out their years of oppression; they deserved to let out their rage of all the years. But somehow, he suddenly felt sickened by the second rape and then the killing of this woman. He had a sudden vision of his mother and would not have wanted this to happen to her. He made a decision that there would be no more assaults like this by his men that morning.

"That is enough. No more raping white women we find. Do you all understand me?" he yelled to all his squad. Their heads bobbed in approval, and they moved back down the stairs to the first floor.

They left the house, carrying Sponge to the street, and called for help. A CNN crew was up the street filming the fires of the neighborhood and doing a live report for the world, as usual. Now all would see and know the downfall had truly begun. Zooma felt terrific. Freedom was near for his people and himself.

CHAPTER 42

30 March 2001

Friday night, Clarence van Dyke Jackson and Maria, made love as soon as he returned to the house from the office. Nina Carlton listened to the sounds coming to her from the bug in the bedroom, and finally turned it off. She couldn't really stand it as she was horny too.

Jackson and Maria went downtown to the Olde N'Awlins Cookery restaurant where he had reservations. They were met there by Jake Briscoe and his girlfriend, Carol. After dinner, they went up the street to Pat O'Briens and sang songs in the club room until one thirty a.m. when the couples stumbled out on to Saint Peter Street, hugged and kissed each other goodbye, and went to their homes. Jackson had talked with Briscoe in the men's room, and they had already decided to meet the next evening for a drink and dinner again. Briscoe liked Maria, and he saw the love in each other's eyes. He was happy for his friend.

When they both arrived at their homes, the ladies each went off to get ready for bed, and both the men checked in with the bodyguards.

"Lucas, this is Jake. What's goin' on?"

"Jake, we have watched you and stayed close, but not too close. God, man, do you have a loud singing voice! And you should watch those hurricanes in Pat's. They will catch up with you, you know. Well, the hitter is holed up in the Holiday Inn in Metairie by Causeway and I-10. Only Garzetti knows from that side. We told him so that your buddy would have protection. She got away earlier today, but we got lucky. Maryanne and Vincent are watching. She won't get away this time. You look okay for now. Have a good one, buddy. Talk at you tomorrow. Call us when you get up and get going, so we can be ready. Okay?" Lucas asked.

"No problem, man. Talk with you tomorrow. Thanks. See ya."

Jake felt much better now. At least his friends knew where the hitter was; and if they knew, then Jackson was safe. He went to bed exhausted. It had been a big Friday.

* * *

Carl Durnbacher ordered room service and stayed tight. He didn't want to take a chance on being seen. He knew from previous visits to New Orleans that the French Quarter was really one of the safest places to be at night, because the New Orleans Police had some three hundred plain clothes and three hundred uniformed police on duty there each night to protect the thousands of tourists and conventioneers. The city already was second this year in murders in the United States, and the publicity was not good. The city was spending over four million dollars of the new convention tax on continuing the promotion of New Orleans all around the world. He did not want to take that chance on someone seeing him.

Durnbacher's biggest problem was trying to get in touch with Nina Carlton. He knew that she was in the city, but when he checked the motor inn, he got nothing, except for a signal that the line to her old room was now bugged. He hung up quickly before the monitoring system deciphered his number at the Marriott. He called the answering service in Tampa and left a message. He knew this was secure, as it was really controlled and run by the family in Miami. He watched TV and then a movie. The phone rang.

"Yes," Durnbacher answered carefully.

"Hi, Nina here. I got the message. I will keep this short. Everything is ready. I'm planning on tomorrow, but I don't know where just yet. I think he will meet his friend Briscoe for dinner again somewhere in the Quarter. I would rather it be there, even with the police around. I'll know what to do. Why are you here? You are taking a big risk."

"I know, but I've decided I may need to be in on this personally. What else do you know?" asked Durnbacher.

"The local family has protection for Briscoe. He has paid for it, and I've been told he is off limits unless he accidently gets in the way. But I'm not to take him out—too many problems if that happens with my steady employer. Besides, you are not paying me for taking him out. Hope you understand, but that is the way it is. Remember, the local family here is actually stronger than the one in Miami. And they are close from many years of cooperation. Just remember 1963 and the Kennedy assassination. Anything else new?" Nina inquired. She really didn't like this direct involvement of Durnbacher on the scene. This had happened once before to her, and the deal went badly. She was getting bad vibes about this one too. The local family involved in protection of a friend, the local police protecting her target, and the CIA wandering around, looking for who knows. She had eluded everyone, but she just didn't feel good about all these developments.

Durnbacher sensed her caution over the phone. "Nina, don't be concerned about the family. They will stay out of this if it is clean. I've talked with Miami. Just do what you do best, and I'll not get involved, I just want to be close when it happens. You have to let me know where and when. This is too important. Do you understand me on this?" he asked her with a strong, domineering tone.

She backed off from a confrontation with him. She felt insulted by his demeaning manner, but she was too professional to let it show. Besides, this was useful information about her employer that may be beneficial in the future. She let him think he had the power and responded, "Yes, you are right. I am worried, but I am ready. They don't know where I am, and I have the bugs working on the target. Did you know that the Brazilian woman, Maria, is here now with him? She arrived this morning."

"No, I didn't know that. He is more stupid than I thought. Well, he has fallen in love I suppose with this woman, and I will admit she is very beautiful. I know her. And I knew he was getting involved deeply with her about a month ago. Is she staying with him? I would suppose so."

"Yes, she is at his house. They have been out since about eight p.m., but I expect them back soon. Is she a problem?" Nina inquired, very pleased with herself for turning the conversation from her feelings to this new information.

"No, and leave her alone too, unless she gets in the way. Keep focused on the target. All others are peripheral. Call me tomorrow when you make a move. I'll be here or on the mobile. Here is the number. Good night."

"Okay, good night." Nina Carlton played the conversation over in her mind again from all angles. *It must be really important to him for him to take the risk of coming into the US to make sure this job is done. Well, it will be.*

She went to bed and was awakened by the sensor alarm in Jackson's kitchen as he made a phone call. She listened only to his end of the conversation, since the bug on the phone was giving only static. *Damn, thunderstorm,* she thought. She turned down the volume on the recorder and went back to bed. *Tomorrow.*

* * *

The next day, Kelly Tegarro walked outside on the lower level of the New Orleans airport. The shade made everything feel cooler, but, after he got in the backseat of the car with Ferguson and Blackstone, they drove out into the sunlight, and he felt the warmth. It was bright, sunny, and warm, as usual, but the humidity in the Big Easy on this Saturday in March was low from the cold front that had come through the night before. The overnight information from the agency secure line indicated that some kind of trouble was brewing in South Africa. What next?

They drove downtown and parked next to the Hilton by the Riverwalk. Tegarro was brought up to speed on the latest with Carlton and Durnbacher. The CIA didn't know where either of them was in the city, but the local agents did know that Carlton was still in town. Where Durnbacher was hold up was a mystery that they probably could not solve for a while.

After Tegarro checked in, they walked over to Chartres Street in the Quarter and had lunch at K-Paul's. The wait in line was only an hour, but to Tegarro, it was worth it. Every sixty minutes, Ferguson would make a call on the mobile phone, but the reply each time was to be patient. No one knew where Carlton or Durnbacher were, but the search was on. They enjoyed the lunch—there was nothing else to do.

* * *

Jake Briscoe woke up about ten o'clock a.m. and reached out for Carol. She stirred pleasantly to his touch, and it was eleven before they got out of bed, sweaty and still feeling the rush, and took a shower together. While Carol continued to get dressed, Jake went downstairs and made some breakfast for them. He picked up the phone and dialed the number for Lucas. He got Vincent.

"Vincent, what are you doing on the line? Where is Lucas? What is happening?"

"Jake, take it easy. Lucas is right here. We are having lunch over at Chili's on Veterans. Big Ed Grayson is about a hundred feet from you, and you are covered, man. Don't sweat it. She hasn't moved yet. But stay in close touch. Are you going to see Jackson today?" Vincent asked.

"Yeah, I've got some work to do at the office and a few errands to run after Carol goes go home. I'm going to meet Jackson for dinner again tonight, probably back down in the Quarter, but I don't know where yet. I'll let you know."

"Okay, man, but stay in real close touch today. Word from my boss is that the hitter's employer is here in town too. We don't know him, but we are guessing that he may try to be close when the hitter decides to do her action thing. Word also is that you are not a target, but we will stay close anyhow."

Jake felt reassured by this, but also felt alarmed by the confirmation that his good friend, Van Dyke Jackson, was definitely the target. He put all his senses on guard now. He was awake and felt great, and it was a beautiful day outside.

"Okay, see someone at the office in about an hour. Take care. Thanks," Jake said and hung up the phone just as Carol walked into the kitchen. He gave her a big smile and kiss, which she returned. They sat and ate and said goodbye for the next two days. Carol had to work the evening shift today and tomorrow at Ochsner Medical Center.

Jake left and saw the dark-red Camaro follow him to the office. He knew it was Big Ed. He felt very comfortable with this protection.

* * *

Durnbacher awoke this Saturday, March 31st, with a start. He was suddenly startled to find himself in a hotel room with sunlight streaming in. He sat upright and looked around and it came back to him where he was and why he was here. The window overlooking the river beckoned to him, and he got out of bed and walked over to it. From this room on the twenty-seventh floor, he could see the Mississippi River and the riverfront below for several miles. The sky above was a brilliant blue, almost the color of bright cobalt, and there were no clouds. The storm the night before had foretold a spring cold front with a high-pressure area now over Texas that brought a northwest wind and low humidity to the Crescent City. *Today will be a great day,* he thought.

Durnbacher walked over to the nightstand, picked up the remote control for the television, and turned it on to CNN news—nothing unusual so far this Saturday. He wondered when the KwaZulu customers of his were going to make their move, however. Other than that, it never crossed his mind anymore about what his part had been to bring about the deaths of so many people around the world for the past twenty years. He thought only that he was supplying products to those that needed them for their own use. Besides, they would obtain them somewhere from someone, so why not Carl Durnbacher? He had gotten very rich in this business. *Today, though,* he thought, *I will probably be a witness to his partner's death. It had to happen. Jackson knows too much, and it's obvious that he wants out, and no one deserts Durnbacher unless he wants them to.*

He showered and dressed and called for room service. He started to order breakfast, but realized he had slept for almost ten hours and it was now noon. Lunch was in order and it came in the usual twenty minutes. He ate and considered what to do this afternoon and evening. He really didn't want to just sit around this room any longer and wait for Nina's call. However, he knew part of her plan was to do the hit in the Quarter, so he didn't want to go too far away. He decided to visit Jackson Square and see a few sights as a tourist. This would keep him close perhaps, and he could stay in touch with Nina by his mobile phone.

He finished lunch and went downstairs and out to Canal Street. He walked to the corner and purchased a small camera and a hat in a souvenir shop. He began his tour of the French Quarter by walking down Decatur Street toward Jackson Square with all the other tourists this bright Saturday afternoon.

About three fifteen p.m., his phone rang while he was having beignets and coffee in the Cafe Du Monde.

"Yeah," was all he said.

"It's me," said the voice on the other end. Nina Carlton now had her plan in place, and it was time to notify her boss for this deal. "They are going to have a casual dinner at Louisiana Pizza Kitchen on Barracks Street, across from the old US Mint by the French Market about seven p.m. Do you know where this is?"

"Not really, but it must not be far away from here. I'm at the cafe now."

"Yes, it is just about four blocks farther down the street away from Canal from where you are. But I would not advise going there until later. However, if you want to see what the area is like, take in the flea market, and you can see the restaurant over at the corner. Call me about six forty-five p.m. and let me know where you are. But my plans are for the hit there during their dinner." Nina hung up.

Durnbacher listened to the call with his back to the central part of the cafe while he faced the floodwall of the Quarter. He turned and looked back at everyone in the café, busily eating their French doughnuts, talking, and drinking the strong coffee. His eyes traveled methodically from table to table; the fact that he had taken a call in this place, which was busy twenty-four hours a day didn't seem to matter to the current clientele. The use of mobile phones was a common sight almost everywhere in this day and age. He felt secure again.

Downfall and Freedom

After he finished, he walked out of the cafe and turned right toward the old French Market area. It was only two blocks away, and he stopped several times to look in the windows of the souvenir shops at the T-shirts, books, and candy. But he was really using the window as a mirror to see if anyone was following or watching him. No, all seemed clear. He continued his walk across the street to the food stalls with fresh fruit, seafood, and hanging garlic strands. In the next two covered areas and some open stalls, he could see the flea market. He moved with the crowd, always trying to keep some distance, but the weather had brought many to these weekend markets. He was jostled by three old ladies who kept pushing him to move faster. They wanted to get to a particular stall area with low-priced purses. He moved out of the way and let them pass.

He reached the end of the market and stopped to look at sunglasses from one vendor. He tried on several pairs and used this time to study the restaurant on the corner of other side of the street—Louisiana Pizza Kitchen. There were two doorways open to both streets, and tables outside in the French cafe style. The late-afternoon diners were enjoying the sun and the food. It was very open. He could see why Carlton had chosen this place, since the target was going there for dinner. The corner location was a short block from Esplanade Avenue and two blocks from Elysian Fields Boulevard, both exit roads to more streets, the freeway, and hiding areas in the old part of New Orleans. This area of the city was like several others where three major streets came together, fanning out from the river in different directions. It afforded several choices for getaway. *Good planning, Miss Carlton,* he thought. He admired her style even more.

Durnbacher walked around the old US Mint to Esplanade Avenue. This tree-shaded avenue became a rundown area outside of the Quarter, but here, close to the action, were several new music and dance clubs, and the street seemed like a giant greenhouse umbrella shading the city from the late March sun. The temperature was noticeably cooler, and with the lower humidity today, it seemed even more pleasant as he walked around the Mint, looking at the overall street situation. He saw his vantage point. He would stay on

Esplanade, where he could watch the restaurant on the corner but would be hidden in the shadows of the avenue. *Excellent!*

Durnbacher walked another two blocks on Esplanade and returned to Canal by going up the infamous Bourbon Street. It was much different in the daylight than its wild reputation at night. Once the mighty and almost mighty in jazz played here in the music clubs, of which there were still a few left. Mostly, though, the street was filled with t-shirt and souvenir shops. He paused to step into the Famous Door Bar, a very old jazz club, and smell the misty odors of the past come to him. He wanted to stay, but it was almost five now, and he wanted to get prepared for this evening back at the hotel. He went the remaining five blocks and entered the Marriott at the parking entrance. After getting to his room, he checked everything, and all was in order. The room had been cleaned, but his special travel case had not been touched.

Durnbacher took the small nine-millimeter pistol from its secret case and loaded it carefully. He showered again and put on his usual tan slacks and a favorite linen shirt from Peru. He looked very casual, and it gave him a place to put the pistol in his belt inside the loose-fitting shirt where it would not be seen or noticed. It was almost six o'clock. He sat by the window, watched the beginnings of dusk fall on the city, and waited for the call. He had patience. He had always had patience.

* * *

After making love in the morning with Maria, Clarence van Dyke Jackson went outside to his garden and made a call.

"Garzetti, this is Van. What is goin' on?"

"Van, you are okay. We have the house covered still at the alley and the street. I know where the hitter is, but she hasn't moved today. The family is watching her, but I'm not supposed to know that. The local CIA guys are trying to find out where she is, but they don't even know who to ask. What a bunch of amateurs! What are you plans, so we can track you?" Garzetti asked his friend. He wondered if Jackson should really go anywhere. It would be a lot easier on everyone if he would stay put—for today at least.

"We are going over to New Orleans Plaza Mall. Maria needs to do some shopping. And then we are going to meet Jake Briscoe at Louisiana Pizza for dinner about seven. He will come alone, as Carol has to work this afternoon, but I haven't called him yet to confirm this. But that is the plan, I think."

"Okay, no problems, it seems. But keep the phone on, and, if we call, get to secure cover quickly. You might not have much time. Got me?" Garzetti asked with some authority in his voice.

"I got you. We will be leaving here in about a half-hour. I'll stay in touch. Talk with you later. Bye. And thanks!"

"No problem, buddy, just stay loose. No confining locations. See you later."

Jackson called Briscoe on his mobile. It was the easiest way to find him.

"Yeah, this is Jake," answered the voice.

"Jake, where are you?"

"I'm at the office now. I've got some errands to do this afternoon. What's the plan, my friend?"

"How about dinner at Louisiana Pizza Kitchen down in the Quarter about seven? It will be really pleasant, not be too cool yet, and we can then decide what to do. Okay with you?"

"Yeah, that is okay by me. I'll see you there. Gotta go, man. Bye," Briscoe said in a rushed voice. He still didn't feel good about today; the vibes were bad. But Louisiana Pizza Kitchen was open, and it had the best non-Italian pizza in the city. He called Lucas and told him the plan. The hitter was still holed up and under watch. They would call him if she moved.

* * *

Tegarro, Ferguson, and Blackstone finished lunch and walked down Chartres to the Cathedral. Tegarro wanted to go inside, and the huge church gave a sense of inner calm to him. It was quiet, cool, and peaceful. He knelt in a pew and said a prayer for his deceased father and for his mother's health while the others waited outside. He was unsure of what to do next for his mission, but he just couldn't keep in one place. He walked back outside into the bright afternoon sunlight. The crowds of people were everywhere. Well, maybe a little dessert would help. The three CIA men went up St. Peter Street to the Cafe Du Monde.

Just as they were about to enter, Tegarro spied someone over by the back near the floodwall getting up and talking on a mobile phone with his back to the street. *Durnbacher!* Tegarro pulled at Ferguson's arm, and they continued walking to the front of the restaurant. Tegarro told Blackstone to go around the back, come in from the area by the floodwall, get a table for one, and read a paper. Durnbacher might recognize Tegarro from the plane from Frankfurt. Ferguson walked back up the street on the other side, and now they had the restaurant covered. Durnbacher wouldn't get away. Tegarro called the office and asked for a rush for three more agents. No luck—no one was available. They were on their own.

Kelly Tegarro had a decision to make—he felt sure that this encounter was lucky, or maybe an answer to a prayer a few minutes ago; but should he call the local police or not? He decided not to. Durnbacher wasn't wanted for arrest, as there was no specific warrant from anywhere outstanding. He was just wanted for a few questions, as his boss had politely put it one day. *Well, Kelly, old boy, keep your wits about you and keep him under watch. With a little more luck, you just might grab this guy today if he makes a wrong move.*

As he put the phone away, he saw Ferguson wipe his brow with a handkerchief. Tegarro ducked into a bookstore and moved to the back, where he could watch when Durnbacher passed by but would not be seen, since he was in the darkness of the store. He got a good look at Durnbacher, who stopped to look into the window. *Just like his picture*, Tegarro thought. *He is looking to see if anyone is following him, and we are, but he won't know it. There are three of us, and he is on foot.*

As Durnbacher moved away down the street, Tegarro went cautiously to the front of the store. He saw Ferguson on the other side of the street, acting like a local. Ferguson walked ahead of the

Downfall and Freedom

same position as Durnbacher on the other side and went into Central Grocery. From the side entrance near the floodwall, Blackstone emerged and followed Durnbacher directly.

Tegarro walked across the street and stayed there as Durnbacher made his way through the French Market and the flea market. All three continued this surveillance tactic for the next hour as Durnbacher made his travels in the lower Quarter. Ferguson was in the lobby of the Marriott when Durnbacher walked in and took the elevator to the twenty-seventh floor. *Gotcha!*

Blackstone took a position in the hotel security section so he could monitor the elevators and stairwells. Ferguson moved to the area, and Tegarro hovered by the back entrance, reading a paper. The wait was on.

* * *

Nina Carlton was ready to go. She would not be back here. As she left the back entrance and drove away onto the service road, she was trying to see if anyone was following her—but the early evening traffic was so heavy that so she could not tell. She got onto I-10 and headed east toward downtown. She got off at the Esplanade exit, drove all the way to the river, and parked the car on a street close to Elysian Fields Avenue. She had several routes planned for this escape, and this location afforded her many options. She rolled down the window and waited patiently. For her this was the hard part, but she had worked years perfecting her craft of killing, and she had gained full control over this attribute. She looked at the clock in the car: 7:10 p.m. She wondered where Durnbacher was, but she had given him all the information he needed. She waited a few minutes more.

* * *

Maryanne Delgado was the first to see her. She started her car and called the number at the same time. Traffic into the city was very bad at this time of night, especially on a Saturday evening when it seemed everyone was headed for downtown New Orleans. They were not sure where she was going, but they would know soon.

It was easy to follow her once they got on I-10. Delgado knew that Lucas was on the way, and Vincent was behind her about three car lengths. She called him, and he moved up and pulled directly behind Carlton's car as they took the I-10 directly toward the Central Business District. Maryanne got closer, and everyone exited at Esplanade. Maryanne and Vincent kept the line open as Carlton went straight across North Peter Street and parked between the railroad tracks and the wharf. Maryanne followed and parked her car next to an electric substation fence on the same street, just past Elysian Fields Boulevard. Vincent saw all of this and turned right onto North Peter Street and right again onto Barracks Street. He saw Jake, Jackson, and what he assumed must be Jackson's woman at the second table from the corner at Louisiana Pizza Kitchen. He continued across Decatur and turned back again toward Esplanade on Chartres. He lucked out and found a parking spot on Esplanade in front of the old US Mint and called Marty to let the boss know where they were and what was going on. Marty called Briscoe.

"Jake, this is Marty. Where are you?" Marty asked.

Jake got up from the table where he, Jackson, and Maria were seated. Jackson gave him a startled look as the phone rang, but tried to pretend for Maria's sake that he was not concerned—but he was. "Marty, we're at Louisiana Pizza Kitchen here at the French Market. What's the news?"

"She is close by, Jake—maybe two blocks away. Vincent is parking his car on Esplanade not far from you, and Maryanne is on Chartres. She will turn around and come back so she can see the hitter's car. Vincent will come over by the mint and stay close. This might be it. Stay loose. Bye."

Briscoe returned to the table. "Sorry about that, but business never seems to stop anymore." He gave Jackson a look that told him instantly to be on guard before sitting down. He pulled the napkin up over his lap, but reached down to his boot and pulled from its holster the .22 revolver he had brought with him and put it under his right leg. He didn't have a permit to carry it, but neither did criminals, and he wanted some protection tonight.

The pizzas came, and they all began to eat. Jake looked at his watch—7:45 p.m.

* * *

Carl Durnbacher left his room at 6:45 p.m. after receiving the call from Carlton. He walked down Royal Street toward the lower end of the French Quarter. He walked over the three blocks to Decatur Street and passed Jackson Square. *How aptly named,* he thought, but he wasn't really familiar with the hero it was named after. When he reached Decatur, he went left and milled with the late-afternoon crowds at the French Market, always keeping a watch to see if anyone was following him. He didn't see anyone. Finally he arrived at the very end of the French Market at Barracks Street and North Peter Street. Before going out into the evening light, he stopped short and stayed in the shadow of the market, but he could see clearly his partner, Jackson, another guy, and the woman, Maria, all sitting at a table on the street by a restaurant on the corner at French Market Place, across from his vantage point. They were drinking and laughing. He smiled and wondered how close Carlton would get. He knew she was the professional and would get the job done. He had supreme confidence in her. He wondered how long it would be, though, before she showed up. He decided not to move, as this position gave him a clear view of the restaurant and the approaches to the corner—except for someone coming from Decatur Street along Barracks Street. He waited and looked at his watch again. It was 7:45 p.m. Dusk was falling, and the evening breeze lent a refreshing coolness to the warm, spring day. He felt ready for any eventuality.

* * *

Marty decided to make one more quick call after he talked with Briscoe. He called Garzetti and got an instant answer.

"Yeah, this is Garzetti."

"This is Marty. We think the deal is on at Louisiana Pizza Kitchen in the Quarter. We followed the hitter, and she is nearby, but still in her car. Jake and Jackson are having dinner there with some woman. This is a favor, and I know it will be appreciated."

"Marty, it will definitely be remembered by those who will need to know. Thanks." Garzetti hung up and made a call to dispatch. He told them to get in touch with three undercover cops on Decatur and get them on the double, but not too noticeably, to Barracks and French Market Place. The call went out; one was close by, and the other two were further up the street a couple of blocks away. Dispatch also notified the Orleans Parish sheriff of possible trouble and asked for nearest black-and-white car to go and head for area. The nearest car was on Rampart Street, a full mile away.

* * *

Ferguson was the first to notice Durnbacher walk out of his room and get on the elevator. Ferguson was in the Marriott Hotel security office. He called Tegarro, who was waiting at the front door. Tegarro moved away to the center of the bar area and sat down where he could watch all the exits from the elevators. Blackstone was at the bell stand and ready to go in either direction.

Tegarro saw Durnbacher come out of the elevator area and walk out the front door, with Blackstone only a few steps behind. He went out the side entrance and walked down Bourbon Street, parallel to Durnbacher and Blackstone. Ferguson ran out of the hotel and down Canal to Chartes. Now they were all parallel to Blackstone and Durnbacher.

During the next half-hour, as Durnbacher made his way to what he thought was a very secure and unseen vantage point in the French Market, he was kept under constant surveillance by one of the three CIA agents who used a crisscross pattern to keep track of him, yet allow the suspect to not notice the changes. Tegarro kept a half-block distance from Durnbacher when he was in direct contact, in case Durnbacher might notice him. But when Durnbacher looked back, he didn't seem to see Kelly Tegarro walking toward him. Durnbacher never fully stopped, but slowed only when he started walking in the French Market with the evening crowd.

Ferguson called the team on the radio and told them Durnbacher had stopped at the end of the French Market and was waiting and looking around. Tegarro moved forward on the sidewalk across from the market along French Market Place and walked toward Barracks Street, where he saw the three people sitting at the table and recognized one of them as the other person in the satellite photo from Brazil. It was the black person who was in the meeting at Santa Rita with Durnbacher. Un-oh. *This may be it,* he thought and told everyone to stand pat. He waited and watched.

* * *

Vincent saw Carlton walking across the railroad tracks, headed for North Peter Street from her parked car, carrying a large purse. He told Maryanne to get on the move, and she got out of her car and also began the short walk toward the corner. As soon as Vincent knew Maryanne had Carlton in sight, he got out of the car and went around the other way to Decatur and quickly up Barracks Street toward the French Market. He could see Carlton turn the corner and begin to move with a faster, determined pace on the sidewalk by the old Mint toward the restaurant. He saw Maryanne come around the corner about six paces behind Carlton. He remembered the orders. Don't touch the hitter unless Jake is the target. The undercover cop was about half a block away, still on Decatur and headed for Barracks Street

Jake saw the woman coming down the sidewalk and saw her move forward a little more quickly. He moved the safety off his pistol with his thumb.

Carlton had Jackson clear in view from the corner. She moved quicker and reached in her large purse for the .357 Magnum. As she got to the corner, she pulled the gun and started to aim and fire at Jackson. But the other person at the table already had a gun out and was pointing it at her.

"Don't do it, or I'll kill you!" Jake yelled to Carlton. Her gaze was still fixed on the target. Jackson had turned now and was moving toward the door of the restaurant. Maria started to scream. Vincent began to run toward them. Tegarro saw the two people with the pistols and began to run toward them, pulling his own pistol from its shoulder holster. Carlton froze. She didn't know what to do—shoot the target or shoot the person with the gun pointed at her first.

The problem for everyone was solved quickly. Durnbacher moved out from the shadows, lifted his own pistol from his coat pocket and fired at Jackson, who was hit and went down. Jake turned his attention from Carlton—standing just ten feet from him—and ran toward Durnbacher, firing and yelling. Tegarro was almost at the table, lined up Durnbacher and fired. He saw Durnbacher go down on a sunglasses vendor table.

Carlton decided to turn and run. The target was down, even though she hadn't made the hit herself. As she spun around, she saw Maryanne standing on the sidewalk with a pistol pointed at her. Maryanne yelled, "I'm family. Don't shoot. Here, take my keys and let us know where your car is. Green Mustang by the electric substation. Go! I'll cover you." Nina Carlton gladly took the keys to another vehicle and ran.

The other CIA agents arrived and started to go after Carlton, but saw the guns now pointed their way by Vincent and Maryanne. They decided not to follow. Besides, they had nothing on the hitter anyway. That was for local police. Tegarro held up his badge and ID for Briscoe to see and yelled for him to drop the gun. Briscoe complied quickly and went to Jackson. Maria was already over him, crying loudly.

Carlton reached the car and sped off down Elysian Fields. She knew if she kept a speed of thirty-three miles per hour, she would make all the lights. When she arrived at the I-10 East entrance ramp, she entered and increased speed to leave New Orleans behind. She would not get paid for this time and effort. Her employer was dead, but she was alive. She drove all the way to Mobile, Alabama, and took a plane to Atlanta and home to Tampa. She would lose something in her reputation because she froze, but not many would know it. She would make it up to the families, both in Miami and

New Orleans. She was safe again. Before the flight, she called a contact number in New Orleans and gave them the location of the car in the Mobile airport parking lot.

Jake bent over his friend and saw the wound above his stomach. Jackson was still alive, but he knew he wouldn't even make the trip to the hospital. He could hear an ambulance coming, still far off.

"Jake, I'm sorry," Jackson said with a tight grimace. He looked at Maria. "Maria, I'm sorry. I hope you will forgive me. And may my God forgive me."

"Van, you will be all right. Just hold on," Maria said between her sobs.

"No, I know it will not be all right. But don't you worry; you and the boys will be taken care of. Is Carl dead?" he asked, now looking at Jake.

Jake looked over at the body across the street and saw Ferguson and Blackstone standing over it. They shook their heads. "He's dead, Van. No trouble to anyone anymore," Jake said to his friend.

"Good, it's over." Jackson smiled up at Maria again, and then he was gone. He had found the peace he had wanted for a long time.

The ambulance, the undercover police, and the sheriff's deputy all arrived at the same time—too late. The ambulance loaded the body of Jackson and took it, Maria, and Jake to Charity Hospital. But it was too late for Van.

Another ambulance arrived and took Durnbacher's body to the morgue. Tegarro and Blackstone rode with it and took pictures after they arrived for final identification. Tegarro called Peterson from the ambulance to give him a complete update.

The Sunday Time-Picayune carried the shooting on page one. Jackson was somewhat of a local, black hero, so this killing by some German and the gunfight at the French Market was news. There was no mention of Carlton.

The funeral on Tuesday, April 3, at the Metairie Park Cemetery, had over three thousand attendees. Even the governor came down from Baton Rouge for this one. This killing was hot political news, and it was a time to be seen. The information about Jackson's other business would never come out. The motorcade stretched for three miles as it made its way, with forty New Orleans police and ten Louisiana State Troopers as honor guards on their way east out of town on I-10. Burial would be in his home town of Wiggins, Mississippi, as he wanted it to be.

When they reached the Louisiana-Mississippi state line, one car belonging to the Louisiana State Troopers and ten belonging to the New Orleans Police continued as the Mississippi State Police took over for the rest of the two-hour journey to Wiggins. The mourners all continued. It would be a long afternoon.

Finally, about two fifteen p.m., they came to the small cemetery on the north side of Wiggins. It took another ten minutes for all to reassemble at the gravesite. Jackson's mother took all this in and was supported by her friends from the church. The coffin was placed over the grave, and the small service was over mercifully quickly. Everyone cried for the friend they had lost. The remains of Clarence van Dyke Jackson were laid to rest for all eternity.

CHAPTER 43
3 April 2001

John Wesley Zooma rode in the truck through the Alexandra township in Johannesburg. He was back in his old hometown. He knew the streets well, and he waved to the people he knew. It felt good to be back.

His commando unit had been told to withdraw from the Sandton area of Johannesburg, where they had caused violence and chaos as directed. Their work was done for now. Other units had relieved them of their duties after forty-eight hours of action.

Zooma walked to his home and was met by his mother. She had suspected what he was doing all these years, but she felt she could not stop him. After all, they were KwaZulu. He came into the house and held him tight to her. He was alive, and that was all she wanted for now. She took him by the hand as if he were still the ten-year-old boy she remembered and led him to the small kitchen. She began the work of a mother who loved her son—she fixed him some dinner, even though it was almost midnight.

He sat there at the small, wooden, battered table and watched his mother with awe. He had inherited her emotions, and luckily, the physical strength from his father. He now realized that all that he had been through the past forty hours was a giant catharsis for him. As the food was placed before him, his mother kissed him on the forehead and sat down.

"John, I am so happy to have you alive. I was so worried about you, and there were so many rumors about what was happening outside the township."

"Mama, I have done much that perhaps I'll be punished for some day. But I hope we will have our freedom. If we get a new Natal nation, I want to leave here and go to Durban and work. I want to be proud of my heritage and be a part of whatever comes to pass."

"Son, I know you will. I may stay here with all my friends, but after you get settled, maybe I'll come to stay with you there. I pray that God will forgive you and all the others for what they did. I can understand your feelings. I have had them too, for so many years. But let us pray now that the killing and violence is over."

He looked at his mother and began to cry. She got up from her chair and cradled his head in her arms next to her breasts and heart. He sobbed, and she held him more tightly to comfort him, and the feelings he had began to slowly ebb away.

Zooma got up from the table and gave his mother a kiss and a hug and went into his old bedroom. He looked around and saw the picture on the dresser of his three friends. As he held the picture and looked at it closer, he hoped they were alive.

The bed beckoned, and he laid down on it and closed his eyes. He had not been in this bed for five years, but it still felt the same. It was home.

He opened his eyes once more and thought about Michael. He wondered if he would ever hear from him again. Did they make it after they took off? What was their plan? Would he ever try to find out? *No,* he thought. *I have repaid my debt, but I now wish them well.*

Finally, he closed his eyes and began to pray.

"Dear God, please forgive me for what I have done to others. I hope that you will consider the good things and weigh them all. I trust your promise of forgiveness and put my full faith in you. I know not what tomorrow, or the day after, or the day after that will bring, but I do promise that I will no longer fight or kill. I will work for our independence and freedom, and, if it be your will, that will happen. Please bless my mother and all my friends. And please watch over my father in heaven with you. Thank you for watching over me and let us have peace."

John Wesley Zooma opened his eyes again and saw a faint light through the small window of his room. He felt a rush of feelings and a tingling all over. He felt a giant weight being taken from his body. He felt angry no more. He was tired and fell asleep immediately, as the dawn of the third day after the downfall of South Africa began. After all these years of anger and hurt and hate, he was finally at peace.

CHAPTER 44
7 April 2001

Nelson Mandela had been under house arrest from 4:00 a.m. of that first morning. The units of the palace security guard had given way to the commando units. The capital offices in Pretoria were under the control of the African Freedom Labor Party units. Communications were cut off, and the officers of the Republic of South Africa were kept under close house arrest.

Mandela had known of the impending downfall two days before it happened. He kept his knowledge totally secret. A loyalist to him in Pietermaritzburg had sent a message by fax to his private office from a small trading company office in Durban. Mandela was unsure what to do with the knowledge. Should he put the South African Defense Forces on alert? Should he take a sudden trip to Kenya or Zambia? Finally, after a very long night in his study without sleep, he made a fateful decision. It might cost him his life, but that was the calculated risk he would have to take for the greater good and progress of the new South Africa. He assumed that many would die, but from the short-term terror and loss of life and property, a different South Africa could emerge that would take a new place in the world of strongest nations.

During that night alone, he wrote in his journal that the decision not to send out an alert would allow:

> ... him to negotiate with Buthelezi for the secession of KwaZulu Natal as a separate state and nation without need for further

compromises within his own party or with the Afrikaaners. All would readily respond to his leadership in the new crisis to be expected.

. . . for the KwaZulu problem to be ended for the rest of the Republic of South Africa. Buthelezi would be responsible for making and keeping the promises that everyone had made, himself included, during the election campaign. Yes, South Africa would have to provide some financial support, but that would be much easier to obtain from the revalued assets of the country.

. . . the price of gold, silver, platinum, diamonds, and all the extremely rare metals, some found only in South Africa, to rise in value. This would increase the value of the rand, and the total financial assets of the country. He bet that the prices would not return to their previous values for many months or years—if they did at all.

. . . the whites that had held out on power from him—the ones that had refused to negotiate in his now famous private sessions—would bend easily to his call for accommodation, compromise, and peace with the KwaZulu and Buthelezi.

. . . world investment to keep on flowing in ever increasing amounts after the new peace would be negotiated.

. . . that he could keep more of the promises to his people with the new funds, asset valuation, ability to borrow from the World Bank, and the improved economy that would result in a few months after a short dip.

He looked up from the pages he had just written and out into his garden and thought, *Yes, this will happen. I hope I don't get killed by some crazy, young, Zulu that is bent on revenge for me.*

* * *

The phone rang in the office of Mangosuthu Buthelezi. He sat there while an aide answered it. He knew it would be Mandela calling him. He would make the great one wait.

Each day Mandela made the call twice to Buthelezi. He called with two of his cabinet members with him each time, along with the past President F.W. DeKlerk seated at the side of his desk. He wanted witnesses. And each time, for two days, he was rebuffed—but he never lost his temper.

Finally, on the third day, Buthelezi took the call.

"Buthelezi, I have prayed that you were all right and not hurt. I have heard so many unconfirmed rumors, and my calls have not gotten through to you. We were worried here that perhaps some renegades in the Zulus had killed you. Are you okay?" Mandela asked very softly.

"Yes, Nelson, I am fine. It has been most chaotic here, and I only found out last night you were calling," he lied.

"Good. Well, when can we meet to resolve this crisis? The KwaZulu guards are all around Pretoria, my house, and the houses of the rest of the government officers. I hope we can come to some agreement to end the madness before the downfall of the entire country takes place, and there is nothing left for anyone. Will you meet with me?"

"Yes, of course. Where and when? I will try to be accommodating," Buthelezi responded, now sincerely. He knew he and the KwaZulu would win at last.

"I will come to Durban if you can guarantee my safety. Could we meet in some very public place? How about the Gazebo Restaurant by the beach? We could be out in the open for all to see us from a distance. I think it would be good press for both of us, if you know what I am saying. Do you agree? How about tomorrow at noon?" Mandela offered.

"I accept your terms for the meeting. Please leave all the arrangements to me. Your safety and the safety of your traveling staff will be personally guaranteed. We really want no more suffering and chaos—but we will have demands. I hope you will come prepared to really negotiate with some power from the parliament and the rest of your cabinet."

"I will have the authority to come to agreement with you. Will you speak for all the KwaZulu? What assurances can you give me that, if we negotiate together in good faith and come to agreement, the destruction, killing, rapes, will end and control of the mines, power plants, telecommunications, airports, and ports will be returned?"

"You will have my assurances. I will speak on behalf of the great KwaZulu Nation as their president-elect. Chief Goodwill Zwelithini will guarantee the control of his people and the actions after our meeting, if we come to agreement," Buthelezi said without arrogance.

"Good. I will see you tomorrow at noon. Can you please stop the violence now, so that the people in the nation will become calmer in the next eighteen hours? It will help greatly. I know you understand this," Mandela asked.

"Yes, I will send out the order for a truce, unless fired upon. I will see you tomorrow at the restaurant. Goodbye." Buthelezi hung up the phone. Quite pleased with himself, he immediately gave the order to cease all hostilities to the generals. Within an hour, all the commando units of the AFLP had stopped their takeovers and violence against many of the remaining whites in Natal and the Transvaal. They remained in place and on full guard, but they began to stand down. Peace was coming slowly to the country.

* * *

The convoy was heavily armed as it escorted Mandela and DeKlerk on the way to the airport in Pretoria. The flight was not long, only one hour. Mandela and DeKlerk talked quietly in their seats, but not about the discussion that was to take place. That had already been done the previous evening. They were ready, and they knew what they could and could not do in the negotiation with Buthelezi.

The arrival at Durban was not full of the usual ceremony. The reporters, foreign television, and many KwaZulus were there for the plane's arrival at noon. Once again, Mandela and DeKlerk were whisked away in a waiting car and convoy escort to downtown Durban and the bay-front area. Mandela and DeKlerk could still see the smoke coming from the fires around the city and the Shell Oil refinery north of the airport. Mandela already knew the violence must stop. He knew how to do it, and he would.

Once they arrived at the restaurant, a very popular place along the bay front with tables inside and outside, they found Buthelezi waiting for them at the front door. Smiles and greetings were exchanged all around, but Mandela felt uncomfortable with all the armed KwaZulu guards around him. He prayed that no one among them had an itchy trigger finger and some long, pent-up desire to see him dead. He was too close now to achieve his dreams of his South Africa for that to happen. They walked to the special table at the edge of the outside patio.

"Nelson, please sit down. Let us try to resolve this unfortunate thing quickly," Buthelezi said as he motioned for Mandela and DeKlerk to sit. He continued to the guards around them, "Go. Leave us to talk. I want protection for us, but we want privacy," he commanded.

The guards moved a respectable distance away.

"Buthelezi, thank you for your guarantees. Mr. DeKlerk and I are ready to talk and find a resolution. Are you ready?" Mandela opened the most important discussion.

"Yes, Nelson, I am ready. The united and mighty KwaZulu are prepared to come to agreement with you, and the AFLP and its units will return the taken facilities as soon as we can reach agreement. May I detail our demands?"

"Yes, please do so. We are ready to listen," Mandela responded, and DeKlerk shook his head in agreement.

For the next thirty minutes, Buthelezi delivered his well-prepared speech of the KwaZulu history, the power they had, the arms they had, and the control of the country they had made in Natal and the Transvaal in just four days. Mandela withstood this diatribe as he had the many years of breaking rocks in prison. He knew he would have to endure this pain before the healing could begin. He listened dispassionately as Deklerk began to slowly fume inside with anger. Finally, Buthelezi was finished.

They talked for two hours. At the end, they all got up from the table, shook hands, and the deal was set. They gave orders for CNN and the World African News Service to set up a press conference immediately at the front entrance for all the local and foreign press. Buthelezi would make a statement after Mandela.

Everything was in place in half an hour. The entire world was watching. The president of the United States was now in the Oval Office with his closest aides listening, along with the rest of the waiting world. Was the downfall of South Africa over? Would freedom come?

Mandela began, "Ladies and gentlemen of South Africa and fellow world citizens, we have come through many dark nights. Once again, our wonderful country has been wrought with violence. It is time this is stopped. Mr. Buthelezi, Mr. DeKlerk, and I have now agreed on the following to bring an end to this chaos and start immediately on the reestablishment of order within our country. The following points have been agreed to by all parties. Mr. Buthelezi will speak to the KwaZulu Nation and the African Freedom Labor Party after I have concluded my remarks. Unfortunately, because of many things yet to be done, we will be unable to answer questions at this time. We solicit your understanding." Mandela then continued:

"Our agreement is thus:

"One, all hostilities by the AFLP and various commando units of the KwaZulu will cease immediately. Control of all establishments and companies will be returned by 7:00 p.m. today, four hours from now, to the previous owners and operators. The units will withdraw without further bloodshed or violence.

"Two: the government of South Africa has promised no reprisals against the commando units or AFLP.

"Three, the people of Natal will be allowed a free vote, to be witnessed by international representatives and the UN for certification, on the establishment of a new nation, to be called KwaZulu Natal, with its own government headquartered in Pietermaritzburg. It will be independent of the Republic of South Africa. If the vote is in favor of this, the new nation will be formed within thirty days from the certification of the election. This is in recognition of the long and proud history of the KwaZulu and Natal as their homeland. A new constitution will be established that will guarantee freedoms to all. The election will be held ten days from today.

"Four, the Republic of South Africa will provide a grant of 500 million rand to the new KwaZulu Natal Nation as a sign of good faith and support in the new government, if the people choose this in the election. The money will be used to build new roads, hospitals, schools, and manufacturing investment for new jobs.

"Five, a full amnesty will be granted to those KwaZulu and AFLP units in Transvaal if they return to their homes and turn in their arms within forty-eight hours. If they choose to relocate to the new nation, they will be given their arms back upon their move.

"I hope everyone in our nation joins me in our wishes and desires for a successful transition, should the vote prove positive. Let us have peace once again, and let us work with each other as neighbors for the betterment of our land and Africa. Together we will achieve a new role in the world order—a more important and highly respected role. Thank you."

After Mandela spoke to the crowd and the world reporters, he moved back from the microphones and turned and smiled to Buthelezi. Buthelezi returned Mandela's smile and moved directly in front of the cameras and microphones. This was his moment, finally. He would now attain the glory and power he had cherished and wanted so badly since the original trouble began in 1975.

"Fellow KwaZulu, South Africans, all Africans, and people of the world, I speak to you now, immediately after this meeting today with my most esteemed friends and political colleagues, Mr. Mandela and Mr. DeKlerk. We have come to agreement on the beginning of a transition for a new KwaZulu Natal, our own country; a new nation and place in the destiny of Africa and the world; a nation we can all be proud to call our own; a new nation and country that will take its place in the forefront of the leadership of Africa; a nation with its own independence and freedom, something that we KwaZulu have been fighting for for over four hundred years. Let our ancestors rejoice at what we have accomplished!"

The applause and cheers were deafening to the assembled. Buthelezi treasured the moments and waited patiently. He began again, "What we have achieved has not been without violence and bloodshed. Yet, what, to many, may have seemed unnecessary was very necessary to us. We have been repressed and held down for too many generations and years. Mr. Mandela promised us many things five years ago in the elections. We have waited patiently, but we could not wait any longer. Even though the chief and I tried desperately to calm our more aggressive brothers, in the end, we could not contain them. I do not condone what has happened, but it could not be stopped once underway. I ask now for all the KwaZulu units to relinquish control of captured property and operations back to their original managers. This is to be done in the timeframe detailed by Mr. Mandela and agreed to by the chief and myself. We order you to obey, as we have given our word that this would be done. In return, you are to be given full amnesty for your actions. However, I warn those of you who may be thinking of maintaining your control: don't do it. We will authorize other units under our direct control to take out and destroy any units and KwaZulu that do not come into compliance with this agreement and timetable. My warning will stand.

"And now I want to congratulate those of you who have risked your lives, as many of your fathers and grandfathers did before you, in the desire for an independent KwaZulu nation. We will achieve that goal finally, thanks to you and your courage.

"To those many who have been hurt and to the survivors of those killed, we offer you our condolences. We wish no more violence, but always make clear our resolve that we will have our independence now granted to us and to be confirmed by the elections. Let our message be clear now to all in the world: we are the KwaZulu Natal Republic. Our land is ours, and we will defend our borders and our sanctity. We urge the world leaders to recognize our new nation, and we welcome their ambassadors to Pietermaritzburg, our new capital. To welcome trade and investment; we will make Durban a free port, open to all traders, and we promise expansion of our port facilities and services. To our fellow KwaZulu, we offer a new land for you where you will be accepted freely and will be able to find jobs to earn a living for you and your family. Schools and hospitals will be built in this next year with the money to be provided from our neighbors to the north, the Republic of South Africa. We acknowledge your generosity and faith in our country. We shall live together in peace. This day is for you, my fellow KwaZulu! Rejoice and join us in celebration. Let us go now in peace and friendship to build our new country for us, our children, and our children's children. Thank you."

Again, the crowd erupted with a roar. The cameras saw Mandela and DeKlerk shake hands with Buthelezi and King Goodwill Zwelithini. They had the smiles of politicians who had said the right things but were still unsure of the outcome. Buthelezi was sure of what he had accomplished in his moment in history: a new nation. And Mandela was sure of what he had accomplished: freedom to a people that he could now count on as friends and supporters in his political struggle—and for a much greater position for the Republic of South Africa in the world.

* * *

World Africa News Service Johannesburg and Durban. "All elements of the commando units in Natal and the Transvaal regions of the Republic of South Africa have begun to recede from their control. The airports, electricity-generation stations, the telecommunications control centers, and the radio and TV stations are now back under regular control.

"Several units have given way at the mines in the east and west Transvaal, but it is reported that there is some fighting at one mine at Anglo-American Deep Gold Fields. Units of the SADF are moving into position, and they are being assisted by commando units of the KwaZulu from Johannesburg to reestablish control from the rebels.

"Information has been received from our reporter in Pretoria and Pietermaritzburg that the nations of Japan, Indonesia, Israel, Malaysia, Egypt, the UAE, Saudia Arabia, Bahrain, India, Oman, and Thailand have all recognized the new KwaZulu Natal Republic and are sending ambassadors with credentials to Buthelezi at this moment. The prime minister of England and the president of the United States have called for immediate meetings with their government cabinets to discuss the new developments.

"The price of gold has stabilized on the Chicago Metals Exchange and in New York at a new price of $476.40. Traders think the new government of KwaZulu Natal will be able to restore order and development within the country.

"Cleanup has begun in all the areas formerly under the control of the KwaZulu commando units. Mandela promised in a short speech after his return to Pretoria that new monies would be made available for restitution of damage, and a new investment law would be passed within days for foreign investment protection, if made within the next ninety days, to help rebuild the destroyed houses, factories, and infrastructure.

"It appears to this reporter that the downfall of South Africa will not happen. A new South Africa is appearing—a stronger one with greater assets and resolve. Another new nation, the KwaZulu Natal Republic, has been born and may become strong. The opening of Durban as a free port, similar to Hong Kong and Singapore, will make it a new haven for foreign investment and money centers for perhaps all of southern Africa. A new center of power and wealth is here. William Christopher reporting. Durban, KwaZulu Natal Republic."

EPILOGUE

Kelly Tegarro accompanied the body of Carl Durnbacher back to Dusseldorf. There were only five people at the funeral service, and only he and the priest were at the gravesite. Tegarro wondered why there wasn't even a representative of Interpol, MI5, or one of the other European government police agencies there to bid farewell forever to this man who caused the deaths of so many around the world.

As the priest walked away, Tegarro picked up some dirt and threw it onto the coffin down in the grave. He realized suddenly why there was no one else there—the death of Carl Durnbacher, while it did make a few headlines worldwide, was really only that of one evil man. The arms business was very much in operation around the world, with others like Durnbacher still hard at work, and the people in the many government agencies around the world who searched each hour of each day for others like Durnbacher were also at work. Why stop to honor the death of someone so evil? Tegarro walked back to the car, determined to find others in this business and bring them to their justice. He now understood what he would do for the rest of his life. He felt very pleased with this revelation, and he started to whistle as he left the final resting place of Carl Durnbacher.

* * *

Jake Briscoe and Maria Bonaventure rode back silently to New Orleans in the long limousine provided by the funeral home, each with their own thoughts. Jake and Carol had moved into Jackson's house for the three days following the murder to be with Maria. After the initial sleepless night, she seemed to be better and became somewhat resigned to her fate, in which she would return to Santa Rita and take up part of her old life. She didn't talk much those three days; she just contemplated all that had happened.

Three days after the funeral, Briscoe, Maria, and Jackson's longtime business partner, Winston Defontaine, all met at Jackson's lawyer's office for the reading of the will. The lawyer, a white, had known Jackson for twenty years and had helped him in many ways as Jackson and Defontaine expanded the business. The lawyer was well connected to the city government and had been on the city council for five years. It was during that period that ordinances were passed, providing set-aside contracts and specific awards to minority-owned businesses that worked with the city government.

Martin de LaFer spoke softly after they were all seated in the large conference room. "Ms. Bonaventure, Mr. Briscoe, and Mr. Defontaine, I am pleased you could all be at this very important meeting for the reading of Mr. Clarence van Dyke Jackson's last will and testament. I had the distinct pleasure of knowing and serving Mr. Jackson for over twenty years, and his sudden death has still shaken me. However, if you will bear with me, I will propose to read the will and answer any questions you may have. This last will and testament will be probated before Judge Gloria Beckwith this afternoon. I expect no problems with the will. It is dated two weeks ago, and is formally signed by four authenticated witnesses. I personally drew up this will at the request of Mr. Jackson last month."

Mr. de LaFer began, proceeding through normal language to implement the will and testify to its veracity. He continued, "To my dearest mother, I leave the sum of $500,000.00 to be placed in trust, and interest to be paid to her for the rest of her life. The trustee is to be my lawyer and friend, Martin de LaFer, III, Esquire, of New Orleans, Louisiana. The principal sum will not be reduced, and the trustee is personally responsible, and will place surety bond with the court, to maintain and grow the trust. A payment to the trustee of 2 percent of the principal at balance will be allowed for services rendered in this regard. At the death of my mother, the entire principal sum will be used to finance a new four-acre park for the children of Wiggins, Mississippi, and to be named after my mother and father.

"In regard to the 100 percent shares of the business, Dynamic Electrical and Construction Co. Inc., of New Orleans, Louisiana, 45 percent is to go to my longtime partner and friend, Winston Defontaine; 10 percent is to go to the love of my life, Maria Bonaventure; and the remaining 45 percent to the person who was loyal to me under many different circumstances and could always be trusted, Mr. Eugene 'Jake' Briscoe. This will guarantee the continuance of a minority-owned business and the competitive advantages that particular attribute brings to the long-term sustenance of the business."

There were more amounts bequeathed to his ex-wife and children of that marriage, but the rest seemed a blur—to Jake, especially. He had absolutely no idea what the business was worth or what his share represented. His mind anticipated, though, that he might suddenly be very wealthy.

When de LaFer was finished, he put down his reading glasses, looked at all of them, and asked for questions. Maria asked if she needed to be a resident of the United States in order to own her shares of the business. De LaFer replied that she did not, but since she was now a stockholder, she could apply for residency and a green card, and, with his assistance, she would have no problems. He had many contacts and friends in the New Orleans Immigration office and was a personal friend of the Brazilian Consulate General in New Orleans and Houston. He also advised her to move here and consider taking a relatively active part in the business, as that would guarantee the minority status and continuance of the government and private contracts the business currently held. Maria recognized what this meant. She could immediately move to the United States and start a new life. And with her accounting background, she could also take a hands-on role in the operation of the business. She smiled at everyone, and her radiance at the meaning of all this was contagious to the assembled group. They all realized that the death of their friend had brought them opportunities that would at least have the possibility of changing their own lives.

Jake and Maria left the office and walked down Poydras Street to the parking garage. They knew that the business was worth about $50 million, which gave Maria a new net worth on this bright, but very humid, spring morning in New Orleans of about $5 million and Jake just increased his net worth by almost $22 million. He drove Maria directly to the airport, as she wanted to go back to Santa Rita and make arrangements for her and her sons to return to New Orleans. Along the way, they talked about Jackson and their love for him—not because of the money he had left them, but because of what he had given to each of them as he lived: his loyalty, integrity, honesty, love, and devotion.

Jake walked Maria to the security entrance at the top of the concourse, and they embraced and kissed as friends saying good-bye.

"Maria, I don't know all the right words to say. Let me know if there is anything I can do while you are gone, and as soon as possible when you are coming back," Jake said quietly while holding her hands in his.

"Oh, Jake, this is all so new to me. I'll call as soon as some plans are made and, if you would, please assist with all of the arrangements with Mr. de LaFer. I want to come back as quickly as I can. This is going to be my new home."

"Take care, Maria." Jake gave her a kiss on the cheek with a last affectionate embrace.

Maria let go of him and walked through the security process area and down the ramp. She waved to Jake one more time, but he was no longer there. He was on his way to his own business and dinner later with Marty. They would celebrate the family's protection of Jake and their future success. It was a given.

The next day, Saturday, Jake drove back to Wiggins to visit Jackson's mother and the gravesite of his friend. He arrived at the cemetery in the early afternoon, and it was almost deserted. The light-brown, sandy soil over the grave had not settled yet, and many of the flowers were still laying on it. The tombstone was set, however, and Jake found himself all alone in this quiet place as a spring thunderstorm began to develop on the near western horizon. The wind began to rise, and it became darker. The air was heavier, and Jake felt like returning to the safety of his car, but he found himself rooted to the spot. He prayed silently for several minutes for the soul of his friend. He wondered why he had been chosen by Jackson for the business shares, and then he remembered all the times when Jackson asked Jake for favors and his trust. He always gave it without question.

The lightning was coming, and the first huge drops of rain were falling on Jake and the new grave and the dying flowers. He ran to the car and got inside, just as the full force of the storm burst on the cemetery and the little town of Wiggins. He finally let out all of the emotions he had been holding inside for the past seven days and cried very hard, resting his head down on the steering wheel. He felt the full loss of his friend. He let go with all his pent-up anguish, in the car, in private, and in this small-town cemetery in southern Mississippi, close to his own home. He pounded the steering wheel and dashboard with his fists in anger, and then he started crying again from the overwhelming sadness and hurt.

Jake began to get control over his emotions just as the storm began to lessen. Already the dirt on the grave was lower. Jake would return time and again to this spot to talk with his friend, but now he could let him go.

Jake decided to drive to Jackson's mother's house on the east side of town. As he pulled into the front driveway, he could see her standing in the doorway, smiling at him. He got out, and, as he walked up to the white frame house, she opened the door and gave him a glass of iced tea and a hug. He was always welcome here. There was no hate in this house any longer.

* * *

Six months after the downfall of South Africa and the birth of the new Republic of KwaZulu Natal, John Wesley Zooma and his mother moved to Durban, where he obtained a job in the public-works administration. He married a very beautiful KwaZulu woman from

Melmoth whom he met in graduate school a year later. His mother died the following spring from pneumonia.

Two years later, in 2003, he was appointed director of utilities in Durban. In the fall of that year, he and his wife made their first trip to America, but their attempts to find Michael and Carter were fruitless. He returned to his beloved country of KwaZulu Natal, now a full member of the international community of nations.

And at night, he would sit on his porch and watch the evening light on the Indian Ocean. He was never bothered by the dreams and nightmares many of his friends had of those dark days and nights during the downfall. He had obtained his freedom because of it. He knew he had been forgiven, and he was glad.

* * *

The Republic of South Africa became a haven for investment and development after the downfall. It was viewed by world bankers, manufacturers, and investors as even more secure. The mineral resources were still there and now worth very much more. And the government of free men of all colors begun in the spring of 1994 continued—not without a few tough moments, but now there seemed to be a common effort of all the people of South Africa to compromise and find ways to move their country forward. The mistakes of the many nations to the north were not made in South Africa. It became the new gateway to the rest of the southern cone and central Africa.

Mandela stayed in power for his entire term, presiding over the birth of KwaZulu Natal. He had promised he would not stay on for a second term, but, like many persons in other countries, his retirement was from visible participation in the government only. With hands forged in the rock mines of the prison, he maintained his iron grip over the various factions in the government that would bring about another downfall, if they could. Although not visible every day, he would maintain this control until he died.

* * *

Michael and Carter made love four times more before they made landfall in Mauritius harbor. God and lady luck were with them for the rest of the journey. They had many challenges to meet and a new life in America to begin. Asylum was granted without question by the local US embassy, and their visas were arranged. It was also easier, since Michael had a contact in the embassy, his good friend Craig Roberts, who verified that Michael would have a job with his parent company after their arrival.

The absence of Gilbert Parker was explained to the Mauritius Port Authorities the day after their arrival. The interview was over in ten minutes, and the death certificate was signed and notarized as "lost at sea." Michael and Carter arranged for a small memorial for Parker in one of the local Anglican churches the day before they boarded a British Airways 747 for London and New York.

Six weeks after their arrival in America, Carter did a home pregnancy test. It was positive. Inside her womb, a boy fetus was growing each day. It was conceived four hours after they had made love the first night on the boat, while Carter lay in the cabin sleeping and Michael was on deck looking at the stars and the sea and wondering about their new future. They named the boy, born on Christmas Day, David Gilbert Wesley Stephens.

Michael and Carter had found their new life. They had found the freedoms they wanted. They would never need to run away from oppression again.

The End

Manufactured by Amazon.ca
Bolton, ON